"If you don't put me down, I'll scream loud enough to wake the entire town."

"We are at war, madam," he snapped, not breaking stride. "A scream in the night is a frequent occurrence."

Her breath caught. At war! Dear God, could it be? Had she somehow tumbled into the very place she needed to be? "How goes the fighting? I have had no news in days." Not bad. She sounded like a cross between "Masterpiece Theatre" and *Poor Richard's Almanac*.

"Clever, madam. A simple request for information." She felt his chest rumble with laughter. "These are dangerous times. Spies come in many guises, some more memorable than others."

"You think I'm a spy?"

"I have yet to make that judgment, Mistress Dakota Wylie." They reached the horse. He swung her up onto the saddle, then took his position behind her. He grabbed the reins and they were off in a swirl of snow and leaves.

Twenty-four hours ago she'd been camped in the woods with a bunch of women and kids, wondering if she was doomed to spend the rest of her life with people who couldn't remember her name. They'd called her Utah, Nevada and Montana, and she supposed she should have been grateful they'd restricted themselves to states west of the Mississippi.

Now here she was galloping through the woods on a moonlit night with a man, who not only remembered her name, but was able to carry her in his arms without turning red in the face or gasping for air.

Too bad it would probably end with her in the town jail before sunrise.

"Bretton's characters are always real, and their conflicts believable." —*Chicago Sun-Times*

BARBARA BRETTON

Destiny's Child

MIRA BOOKS

MIRA

ISBN 1-55166-090-3

DESTINY'S CHILD

Copyright © 1995 by Barbara Bretton.

Printed in U.S.A.

For The Graduate,
best husband in this world or any other

Destiny's
Child

Prologue

Dakota Wylie had spent every summer of her youth in the back seat of her parents' van, wedged between her younger sister, Janis, who existed on mascara and diet soda, and her twin brothers, Conan and Tige, whose joint claim to fame was the ability to play "Disco Inferno" with their armpits.

Frederick and Ginny Wylie believed that the best education they could give their children was to be found at sixty miles per hour on Interstate 80 as they crisscrossed the country paying homage to every national monument and rest stop they encountered. Other kids went to Camp Winnemukluk and learned how to braid lanyards and smoke cigarettes without inhaling; Dakota learned the location of every Stuckey's between Princeton and the Grand Canyon.

Her father, a professor of physics, spent the dreary winter months with his desk littered with road maps and notebooks while he planned every step of the summer's journey. He approached the project with mathematical precision and an engineer's sense of efficiency. Getting there wasn't half the fun for Dr. Wylie; it was everything.

Her mother, a bona fide, card-carrying psychic, indulged her husband's love of ritual and technology but she despaired when she saw those careful traits rearing their heads in her children. Ginny knew life's greatest adventures were the ones that were unplanned, and of her four children only her oldest seemed to understand.

Which was how Dakota Wylie—unmarried, unemployed and overweight—found herself that fine late summer morning in the gondola of a hot-air balloon bound for the eighteenth century.

At least, that's where Dakota thought they were headed. It suddenly occurred to her that, considering the circumstances, she was taking a great deal on faith.

When you were about to challenge the laws of nature, you'd think there would be trumpets and fanfare, some kind of celestial send-off that acknowledged the enormity of what was about to happen.

It wasn't every day a woman went leaping through time. Except for Einstein, most rational human beings put time travel up there on a par with the existence of the Loch Ness Monster and the Easter Bunny. Fun to think about, but not bloody likely.

For weeks Ginny had told her something was on the horizon, an adventure more amazing than anything either woman could imagine, but Dakota had been so busy trying to figure out what Andrew McVie was all about that the signs had passed her right by until it was almost too late. Every time she'd seen Andrew she'd passed out at his feet, overwhelmed by the force field his presence generated.

It hadn't taken her long to realize he wasn't part of the twentieth century, and even less time to discover that he and Shannon Whitney, the woman he'd traveled across the centuries to find, had to go back through time to the place where they both now belonged.

Still, she hadn't figured they'd be taking her with them.

The basket shuddered as an air current buffeted it from the east, and Dakota glanced around. She was all in favor of adventure—but why couldn't it take place at ground level? Shannon and Andrew were wrapped in each other's arms, oblivious to the fact that the only thing between them and instant death was that puny fire that kept the bright red balloon aloft.

"Sure," she mumbled. "What do you care if I'm a fifth wheel in two centuries?" This was their destiny, after all. As far as Dakota could tell, she was just along for the ride, comic relief to keep them laughing as the decades whizzed by.

"You won't be here forever," Ginny had said a few days ago. Dakota had thought she meant the library where she worked. Why was it her psychic abilities were able to zero in on everybody else in the western hemisphere with laserlike precision but when it came to her own life, she invariably came up empty?

For instance, it would have been nice to have had some advance warning. If they were really traveling through time, she was going to need a make-over from Martha Washington as soon as they landed, because her dusty jeans, worn running shoes, and Jurassic Park T-shirt weren't going to win any fashion awards. Then again, neither was her coiffure. She reached up and touched the close-cropped mop of jet black curls that had probably never been in fashion, no matter the century.

Next to the beautiful Shannon with her elegant bone structure and glossy tresses, she probably looked like a boy with a severe water retention problem.

"I have a question," she said to the embracing couple who shared the basket with her. "How do we know if we're going the right way? I mean, this thing doesn't come with a road map. What if we end up back in the seventies or something?" A lifetime sentence of leisure suits and disco. It was enough to make her leap overboard.

"You are the one gifted with second sight, Mistress Dakota. Do you not know the outcome?" Andrew wasn't a handsome man by any account, but even Dakota had to admit he was quite something when he smiled.

"That's right," said Shannon. "You're psychic. You should know these things. We were counting on you to keep us on course."

"Just because I'm psychic doesn't mean I have a sense of direction," Dakota retorted. "You'd think there'd be some way to steer this thing." An odd prickle of apprehension twitched its way up her spine as she had a sudden and clear vision of thick woods and a child too young to find her way home.

"Dakota?" Shannon's voice reached her as if from far away. "Is something wrong?"

"I don't know," Dakota said. She shivered as a glimpse of tearstained cheeks and tangled hair spun past. "I must be flashing on last night." She'd spent the night in the woods with some residents of the battered women's shelter in an Outward Bound experiment, meant to enhance self-esteem and independence. Dakota had spent most of the hours after dark worried that one of the kids would wander away and get lost and she'd have to venture deeper into the bug-infested woods to look for the child.

"Mistress Dakota has no fondness for nature's wonders," said Andrew. "She was most distressed when a spider took up residence on her arm."

"You would've screamed, too, if you'd seen the sucker," Dakota said to Shannon. "The darn thing was the size of a blue jay."

Andrew held his thumb and forefinger an inch apart and Shannon laughed out loud. "Now you know everything you need to about Dakota. She hates spiders and loves jelly doughnuts."

"Raspberry-jelly doughnuts," Dakota said. "If you're going to spill my secrets, at least be accurate." She patted her hips. "I've worked hard for each one of these pounds."

Shannon executed a curtsy in her direction. "I stand corrected, Mistress Dakota."

Andrew's head snapped around. "I have not heard you speak thusly."

"'Tis time," Shannon said. "I must learn to fit into your world, Andrew."

Dakota watched, a huge lump throbbing in her throat, as the lovers took each other's measure and were well satisfied. Their auras shimmered like molten gold and Dakota found herself blinking back tears of joy... and envy. They said there was someone for every man and woman on the earth but at times it seemed to Dakota as if she were meant to go through life alone.

She'd been born with a wisecrack on her lips and cellulite on her thighs and that wasn't a combination destined to bring men to their knees. No, most men liked their women straight out of a Victoria's Secret catalog, demure and airbrushed to within an inch of their perfect lives.

She forced a saucy grin. "You're our time-traveling resident expert, Andrew. How long is this going to take?"

"You are wrong, mistress. I am no expert in such matters. 'Twill take as long as it takes."

"That's what my father used to say when we were halfway to Walt Disney World and had run out of comic books and candy bars."

Andrew met Shannon's eyes. "Walt Disney World?"

"You didn't tell him about Walt Disney World?" Dakota stared at her friend in disbelief.

Shannon shrugged gracefully, the way she did everything. You'd never believe her life had been anything but blessed. "We covered all major wars, important scientific advances and why Dick Clark still looks twenty-five when we all know he's one hundred and seven. I had to forget something."

"An unforgivable gap in your education," Dakota declared to Andrew. "Walt Disney World is a theme park."

Andrew looked at her blankly.

"A place where adults and children go to have fun," she explained, "and it all centers around a mouse named Mickey."

"'Tis a good thing I am leaving your time," Andrew said, shaking his head in amazement, "for your world is a place of uncommon strangeness."

Shannon went on in great detail about mice in short pants who always had a date for Saturday night, ducks with attitude problems and amusement-park rides whose sole purpose was to make grown men and women lose their lunches.

"Andrew is right," Dakota said, wiping away tears of laughter. "When you put it that way, it *does* sound strange. Maybe—" She stopped. "Did you hear that?"

Andrew and Shannon exchanged looks. It was obvious they had no idea what she was talking about.

"The magic fire," said Andrew, pointing toward the flame that kept the balloon inflated. "'Tis a distinctive sound."

"Not that," Dakota said with an impatient wave of her hand. "It's softer...more like a cry."

Shannon tilted her head to listen. "I don't hear anything, either, Dakota."

Dakota wrapped her arms around her chest as a blast of wind rocked the fragile gondola. The little girl knelt in front of her, crying brokenly over a tattered rag doll. The child's brown hair was tangled about her shoulders and was badly in need of a good shampoo and conditioning, while her cotton dress was woefully inadequate against the cold. The image was so clear, so real that Dakota wanted to reach out and wipe away the tears streaking down the girl's dirty face.

She hated it when the visions came at her like this, swift and hard as a punch to the gut, knocking the wind from her lungs and toppling her defenses. No matter how many times it happened, she never quite got used to this sudden stripping away of the shadowy barriers between the different levels of reality.

Most of the time she accepted her abilities the same way other people accepted a gift for music or a talent for drawing. They were part and parcel of the way she viewed the world and the way she viewed herself. But there were times, like now, when she devoutly wished she could be like everyone else and see life in only one dimension at a time.

The child's cries tore at her heart. "She's lost...she'll never find her way out of the woods." *It's too late, Dakota. You can't help her. Her time is spinning past....*

A stiff wind blew in from the west, rocking the basket as if it were made of tissue paper. The hairs on the back of her neck rose in response. *This isn't the way it's supposed to happen. Something's terribly wrong!*

"Dakota?" Shannon placed a hand on her arm. "Maybe you should sit down."

"I don't belong here," she whispered. "This is a mistake. I have to go back."

"Nay, mistress, 'twas no mistake." The basket lurched to the right and Andrew steadied her. "You are here because it was meant to be thus."

"We saw you, Dakota," Shannon said. "You were fading away right before our eyes. It was this or—"

Another gust of wind buffeted the balloon, to the left this time, sending the three of them smashing into the side of the basket.

"Andrew?" Shannon's voice sounded high and tight. "Is something wrong?"

"I do not know. My own journey to your time was most enjoyable. Indeed, I did not believe I had traveled anywhere at all until I found you and saw the newspaper."

I'm the reason things are going wrong. This trip should be as easy as the last. I'm the problem....

Dakota swallowed hard. Another blast of wind like that and they would all be tossed overboard like excess baggage. She closed her eyes, struggling to capture an image, a whisper, some indication of what was to come, but her thoughts were filled with the sight and sound of a little girl's tears.

"Look sharp!" Andrew's cry pierced through the roar of the wind. "To the left."

The cloud, an angular black mass, towered upward like a caricature of a twister. She didn't need second sight to know what it meant.

"Hang together!" Andrew called out. "We will—"

His words were torn apart by another vicious gust of wind that grabbed hold of the basket and threatened to flip it end over end. Her granny glasses slipped off her nose and blew away.

This is wrong, Dakota thought, clinging to the lip of the basket as the child's cries grew louder inside her head. Shannon and Andrew were meant to journey safely back to his time. The lives of Zane Rutledge and Josiah Blakelee, and the lives of their descendants, depended upon it. Wasn't she the one who'd found the proof in black and white on page 127 of *Forgotten Heroes?* The name Dakota Wylie didn't appear anywhere. She was the wild card, the X factor that changed the equation and threatened their future and she wanted to go home where she belonged right now.

The fire sputtered as the basket withstood another pummeling gust of wind. Shannon crouched on the floor, gripping the ropes that connected the gondola to the balloon itself, while Andrew reached out to Dakota.

"Grab my hand, mistress!" His voice rang out.

The basket tilted wildly to the right and she let out a scream as she fell to one knee.

"Now!" Andrew commanded. "We are dropping fast."

A few years ago she'd gone to the World Trade Center for dinner at Windows on the World when the elevator malfunctioned, dropping the car three stories in the blink of an eye. This was the same stomach-turning sensation, magnified a hundredfold. Was she dropping only through space or hurtling down through time, as well?

The towering black cloud enveloped them in a tunnel of darkness. She could hear Shannon's and Andrew's voices rising above the roar of the wind but it was impossible to see them.

The bottom of the basket made a sickening noise as it scraped the tops of the trees. Her nostrils twitched at the smell of pine and rich earth coming closer, closer.

"I hate you!" The child's voice trembled with pain. "I *hate* you!"

Dakota felt the little girl's pain in the center of her heart, in that place reserved for the children she would never have. *Go with it. You have no other choice.*

Whispering a swift prayer, Dakota climbed to the top of the basket railing and jumped.

1

It was said by the good people of Franklin Ridge, in the Colony of New Jersey, that Patrick Devane was the angriest man in four counties, and on that December afternoon he did nothing to dispel the notion.

His housekeeper, Mrs. O'Gorman, dabbed at her rheumy eyes with a wrinkled handkerchief. "'Tain't my fault, sir," she said through loud sniffles. "The child's willful as her mother and there wouldn't be a thing I could do to stop her."

"The child is six years old," Patrick snapped. "She requires a firm hand and a watchful eye, two things you are unwilling or unable to provide."

Mrs. O'Gorman's expression shifted from lugubrious to sly. "And a child needs a father, if I may be so bold, and it seems to me you been one in name only."

"Enough!" His roar rattled the walls. "You'll be out of my house by nightfall."

"And I'll be thanking the Almighty for that," Mrs. O'Gorman said, thrusting her chins at him. "I'd rather be workin' for Fat George in London than spend another day in this terrible place."

"Take care, woman, or I'll see that you get your wish."

Mrs. O'Gorman, no longer concerned with employment, was a woman unleashed. "'Tain't my wish that's comin' true, mister. 'Tis yours. The child is gone—just the way you wanted it—and if she has the sense of a mayfly, she won't be back here where she ain't wanted.''

With that the woman stormed from the library.

He swore softly at her retreating back. The truth ofttimes carried with it a scorpion's sting.

He'd heard them whispering belowstairs. How his cold heart had driven his warm-blooded wife into the arms of another man. And the way he treated the child was cause for scandal. He kept her clothed, fed and sheltered as was his duty as a Christian man. And now he would see to her education, as well. More than that he could not be asked to provide.

"'Tisn't natural to treat your own flesh and blood this way," Mrs. O'Gorman had said to her cronies the other day when she thought he could not hear. "All that money and not an ounce of warmth in his black heart."

"My papa is the best man in the world," Abigail had declared, biting Mrs. O'Gorman in her plump forearm.

Mrs. O'Gorman had tried to shake her off but the child had clung to her like a hound to a fox and it had taken three servants to finally pull her away.

"Poor little thing," Rosie, the scullery maid, had whispered loud enough to be heard in Trenton. "Him always treatin' her like a poor relation when it's his fault she's the way she is."

Abigail had rewarded the girl with a kick in the shins that had sent Rosie packing. If he did not put a stop to it, the child would drive every member of the staff from the house, nursing bite marks and bruises.

His hand had been forced and he was not ungrateful.

"This cannot go on, Abigail. Arrangements will be made for you to attend school in Boston."

"No!" Her gray eyes had darkened like the sky before a storm. She had spirit, this child. He would grant her that.

It would serve her well in the future, since she had not been granted beauty. "You cannot make me!"

He'd chosen to ignore the challenge. "The Girls' School of the Sacred Heart is a fine place. They will teach you the things a young lady must know to make her way in the world." The things a mother would teach her daughter, if the mother had seen fit to stay.

Her plain little face had crumpled beneath his gaze. So much power to have over one so small and defenseless. Better to break the cord between them cleanly and be done with it.

"I hate you!" she'd cried when he informed her that the matter was closed to further discussion. "I hate you!"

"I don't doubt that," he'd said, turning away. "There is little reason for you to feel otherwise."

She lacked her mother's beauty, but she had her mother's spirit, that fiery temper and pigheaded stubbornness, and for a moment he'd felt a stab of dark emotion in the center of his chest. How many nights had he stood over her cradle, watching the way her tiny fists pumped the air as she slept? *She's fighting the world,* he'd thought as pride filled his heart. Same as he'd fought the world as he struggled his way out of poverty. The notion of life renewing itself suddenly made sense to him in a way he'd never imagined.

What a fool he'd been.

He had loved once and deeply and he would never love that way again. Few who knew him today would believe him capable of so tender a sentiment, but there had been a time when his bitter heart had known how sweet life could be. A time when all things had seemed possible, if only because he knew how to make dreams come true.

"I'll build you the grandest house in the thirteen colonies," he had promised Susannah in the throes of new love. "You'll have servants and fine gowns from Paris, everything your heart desires."

His dreams were as big and untamed as the country that had given him birth, and with a woman like Susannah VanDorn by his side, there was nothing he couldn't do, no dream he couldn't make come true.

He'd built the house. He'd filled it with servants. He'd showered her with silk gowns and satin slippers and more love than any woman had ever known. For every dream he fulfilled, a new dream sprang to life, eager to take its place.

But those dreams were now long gone. Susannah had destroyed them the day she walked out the door and into the arms of another man.

The child. There is the child to consider. The child he had once believed the reason he had been put upon this earth. The sad-eyed little girl who looked to him to explain something even he didn't understand.

The truth was Abigail wasn't his child at all but the offspring of another man. Living proof that he'd been cuckolded, not just once but a multitude of times, by a wife as faithless as a stray cat.

"My parting gift," Susannah had called the revelation as she'd rolled her rings and earbobs in a long strip of velvet and tucked it into her satchel. "I had been with three other men the month she was conceived." Her full red lips curved upward in a smile. "The odds are not in your favor, my sweet."

He came close to murder that night. Blood lust flooded his brain, forcing out reason and sanity. With one blow he could snap her fragile neck and put an end to the pain and misery she'd caused him. Salvage what remained of his pride.

"Do it," she'd dared him, her eyes blazing. "Do it and pay for the action the rest of your pathetic life."

He'd let her live and regretted that decision every hour of every day since.

Not even Susannah's death one year later in a carriage accident had lessened his rage.

He saw their looks each time her name was mentioned. He heard the whispers when they talked about the child. Pious, sanctimonious bastards, the lot of them, feigning concern when all they cared about was lively gossip for their parties. Martha Washington's latest haircomb or his miserable plight—it was all the same to the good people of Franklin Ridge.

He knew more about the lot of them than they could ever imagine. He knew the spies and the traitors, knew how many guineas it took to sway a man's devotion to a cause. Every man had his price, whether it be silver coins or the golden glow of a woman's hair. He made it his business to know what that price was.

"Sir?"

He turned at the sound of Cook's voice in the doorway. Her full face was still flushed from the heat of the hearth fire. Her fingers, knuckles swollen with arthritis, twisted the coarse tan fabric of her apron.

"You wish something?" he asked. He saw to it that his tone did not betray his chaotic thoughts.

"The child," Cook said, meeting his eyes. "She missed the midday meal. My boy, William, from the stables and Joseph are willin' to lead a search for the wee one."

"This is not the first time she has done this and it will not be the last."

"But the sun will set within the hour and—"

"I know when the blasted sun sets, woman! Do you take me for a fool?"

She was wise enough to keep her own counsel. "Begging your pardon, sir. 'Tis dangerous times and many's the innocent who comes to a bad end. We love her like she's one of our own."

And for all he knew, she just might be.

"Have William saddle my horse," he roared, tired of the censure in their voices. "I'll search for the blasted child myself."

And when he found her he would see that she was on her way to the Girls' School of the Sacred Heart in Boston before the sun rose in the morning.

"I hate you!" Abigail Elizabeth Devane cried as she lashed out at Lucy with the toe of her leather boot. Her six-year-old heart was set upon murder. The doll's soft rag body tore at the seam beneath the right arm and a strip of pale green cotton poked through. Lucy was stupid, a baby's plaything, and Abby wasn't a baby any longer. That's what her father had told her that morning when he had said that she was to be sent away to school near a place called Boston.

She reared back and kicked the doll again, harder this time. A rip opened up on Lucy's left leg. Wads of yellow checkered cloth bunched through the opening. Good! That was better than blood, better than big pieces of broken bone. She wanted to throw Lucy into the river and watch her sink. She wanted to toss the doll into the cooking fire in the kitchen of the big house and smell the stink of burning cloth.

Grabbing Lucy by the right arm, she made to fling her against one of the big pine trees when she noticed that Lucy's head was hanging by a piece of yarn no thicker than a cat's whisker.

"Lucy!" All thoughts of violence forgotten, Abby clutched the doll to her breast and began to sob. The tears came all the way from the soles of her feet, big ugly gulps that would have embarrassed her had there been anyone around to hear. Big fat tears rolled down her dirty cheeks and she was glad there was no one there to see her wipe them away with the back of her arm.

The only person on earth who loved her was Lucy, and see what she had done to her. Everything Abby had suspected about herself was true, every terrible thing she'd heard whispered when they thought she wasn't listening. She was as ugly of spirit as she was of face, and even Papa was counting the days until she left for the Girls' School of the Sacred Heart.

"If only the little one was pretty," Cook had said the other night as she stirred the stew pot bubbling in the grate. "Pretty makes up for a multitude of sins. That might warm his cold heart some."

But Abby knew she wasn't pretty. Her hair wasn't shiny like gold coins or red as the leaves that had fallen from the trees. It was mud brown, as ordinary as the day was long. And instead of eyes as blue as the sky, hers were round blots as gray and ugly as winter rain. Was it any wonder Papa always looked away and frowned whenever she entered a room?

"I'm sorry, Lucy," she wailed, clutching the doll even tighter. She had a mean, wicked temper and now Lucy would be the one to pay the piper. It wasn't fair, it just wasn't—

She tilted her head to the left, listening. What a strange sound that was, a sputtering hiss that made her think of a big tomcat with his back arched, ready to fight. She knew by the strange clouds towering overhead that a big snowstorm was on its way, but not even the winds that howled down from the hills made such a horrid noise. Heart thudding inside her chest, she peered into the surrounding woods, afraid she might see a giant peering back at her with fire in his eyes.

Cook had told her a story about a ferocious mean giant who feasted on the bones of wicked Englishmen. Abby had the feeling a small girl from the Colony of New Jersey would make a tasty morsel.

She waited, but the woods remained still and silent. The noise sounded again, louder this time, and Abby wished she'd stayed closer to home. Hunters trapped bear in these very woods. She tried to imagine what she would do if a snarling, furry beast leapt out from behind a tree, ready to pounce. Maybe if she ran really fast she'd be able to make it back home before anything terrible happened to her.

She tucked Lucy inside the front of her cotton dress and was about to hike up her skirts and run when she saw the most amazing, the most splendid sight in the world! There, dancing across the tops of the trees, was a big red ball, so big that it blotted out the sky. It moved slowly, hissing as it did, swinging a funny-looking basket beneath it.

She watched, awestruck, as the bright red ball seemed to dip toward her in salute, then suddenly caught a breeze and rose higher and higher until it didn't seem big at all anymore.

"Oh, Lucy," she whispered, her temper and the frigid weather forgotten. "Did you ever see anything so beautiful?" It had hovered over the stand of pines just to the left of the clearing, as if beckoning her to jump into the basket and go off on a grand adventure. And she would have, too, if it hadn't floated away before she could run over and grab hold.

Short legs pumping fast beneath her skirt, she ran toward the trees. If the big red ball returned, she and Lucy would be there waiting and they wouldn't think twice before leaping aboard.

Papa would feel so bad that he'd forget all about that school in Boston and let her stay with him forever. And Mama would hear about her wondrous adventure and she would come back from heaven to stay and the big white house would be filled with laughter the way it used to be.

It wasn't as if Dakota had never been in a ridiculous situation before.

Just two months ago she'd accepted a blind date with the son of her mother's favorite tarot card reader from south Jersey, a guy named Brick who sold vinyl siding for a living and had all the creative imagination of his namesake. They'd spent a terrific hour and a half discussing the rela-

tive merits of faux cedar shakes before Dakota developed a
sudden headache and had to cut the evening short.

"You didn't give him a chance," her mother had said in
an exasperated tone of voice. "Elly read his palm a week ago
Thursday and she swears she saw your name scrawled across
his life line."

Which didn't surprise Dakota. Her name was scrawled
across the life line of every loser on the Eastern seaboard.
As bad as that blind date had been, nothing—not even the
time she'd trailed toilet paper from the ladies' room at the
swanky Palmer Inn—was worse than this.

You didn't need psychic powers to know nothing good
ever happened when you threw fate a curveball.

Anyone with a brain knew her destiny was clearly tied up
with Andrew and Shannon's. She'd been fading away like a
ghost in an old B movie and she had no doubt she would
have vanished into thin air in another moment if she hadn't
managed to scramble aboard with Andrew's help. Climbing into that gondola had been the equivalent of psychic
CPR.

She glanced at her hands. At least she couldn't see
through them. That had to be a good sign. Wherever she
was, she was solidly connected. But where was she? Where
were Andrew and Shannon? And, even more important,
when were they?

Her stomach lurched as she remembered the sickening
sound the basket had made as it scraped the tops of the
trees, and the look of fear in Shannon's eyes.

"They're fine," she mumbled. Their destiny had never
been in doubt. She was the one who'd been heading home
with a bag of jelly doughnuts, only to find herself propelled headlong through time.

*You panicked, kiddo. The second that balloon tilted, you
were ready to bail out.*

"Ridiculous!" She'd heard that little girl as clearly as
she'd heard her own voice and something, some suppressed

maternal instinct, had taken over and forced her to leap from the basket.

You leapt just before it went down, Wylie. You'd have been something on the Titanic.

So she was an idiot. Big deal. A few crossed neurons and she'd conjured up a lost little girl that only Dakota Wylie, Super Librarian, could rescue.

Now there she was, a good twenty feet off the ground, clinging to the branch of a naked maple tree that didn't look strong enough to support a blue jay, much less a plump American woman who believed in physical exertion only at gunpoint.

Of course, there was always the remote possibility that some kind soul with a reinforced aluminum ladder would come strolling through the woods in search of a damsel in distress.

Why on earth had she eaten that last raspberry-jelly doughnut anyway? Those few ounces of fat and sugar might be enough to send her crashing to the ground. She shifted her weight over to what she prayed was a sturdier limb.

The branch creaked loudly in protest but it held, and she breathed a huge sigh of relief. Somebody should invent a way to determine these things without offering yourself up as a human sacrifice.

As it was, if the fall didn't kill her, the weather might. The dark, jagged cloud cover that had rocked the gondola was gone now, replaced by heavy ivory-colored skies that promised snow. Lots of it. Goose bumps marched up and down her arms and her teeth chattered from the cold. Her T-shirt and jeans weren't going to cut it for very long.

Now you've done it, Wylie. Leave it to you to screw up the forces of destiny.

She clung to the branch as a furious blast of wind shook the maple. Maybe she wouldn't have to worry about climbing down from the tree. Another icy gust like that and she'd drop to the ground like an overripe peach. She longed for a

down-filled jacket and fur-lined boots. Hard to believe last
night she'd been praying for central air-conditioning and
something cool to drink.

*So now what, hotshot? How are you going to get out of
this one?*

She hadn't a clue. A lot depended on where—and when—
she'd ended up. What if she really had jumped out during
the seventies? She'd need a shoehorn to get her hips into one
of those slinky polyester dance dresses, the kind that required lots of attitude and breasts that saluted the sun.

Well, there was no hope for it. She couldn't hang there
like a bat for the rest of her natural life. Those snow clouds
lowering overhead meant business, and if she was going to
find shelter before nightfall, she'd better get to it.

In a nearby tree a woodpecker tapped relentlessly against
the hard wood. The machine-gun rat-a-tat-tat provided a
counterpoint to the din of two jays squabbling overhead.
Another, sweeter sound floated up toward her.

"Oh, Lucy...it was so beautiful!" A child's voice, high
and clear.

"Hello!" she called out. "Is somebody there?"

She waited, listening to the quality of the silence. Was she
crazy, or was it different than it had been a few moments
ago?

"I heard you," she continued, trying to sound as friendly
as the circumstances would allow. "Don't be shy. I need
your help." *And I need it now.*

She waited, scarcely breathing, as the branch she clung to
creaked ominously. Finally she heard the crunch of frozen
leaves underfoot as a little girl of no more than five or six
stepped into the clearing.

Her brown hair was plaited into two uneven braids that
drooped over narrow shoulders. She wore a heavy woolen
cloak that brushed her ankles and leather slippers that had
seen better days. The cloak was unfastened and Dakota

spied a plain cotton dress, faded from many washings. There was nothing of the twentieth century about the child.

Was this the little girl she'd heard just before she leapt from the gondola? She waited for the stirring of her blood, the rush of excitement that always accompanied a leap into another person's mind, but there was none.

The girl's narrow face was pale, her nose unremarkable; the last time Dakota had seen eyes that wide and round was at a revival of *Annie*. The child was a little slip of a thing with an air of sadness about her that Dakota could feel in her very bones without benefit of psychic help.

A coincidence, she thought, looking away. The woods were probably lousy with kids. Just because the Little Match Girl down there had popped up right on cue didn't mean she had anything to do with Dakota.

This couldn't be her destiny. Kids weren't part of her karma. She'd known that since she was fourteen years old, and she'd be willing to bet that not even the fact that she'd barreled through time like a human cannonball could change that fact.

2

"I'm up here," an unseen monster called out to Abby. "In the maple tree."

The monster could see her! It made Abby feel shivery inside, the way she did after Cook told her an Irish ghost story. Even though she knew she shouldn't, she turned toward the voice.

"The *maple* tree, little girl, not the chestnut."

"But the leaves are not—" Abby pressed her lips together to stop the flow of words. She didn't want the monster to know she couldn't tell a maple from a chestnut without their brightly colored leaves.

"Look right, then up! Believe me when I say you can't miss me."

Don't listen to the monster, Abby. You'll be gobbled up like one of Cook's apple pies.

Terrible things happened when you listened to monsters but she didn't know how to say no. Slowly, carefully, she peered up as ordered. "I still cannot see you."

"Don't you watch 'Sesame Street,' kid? I said look right." The monster didn't sound quite so friendly this time.

Abby popped her thumb into her mouth, the way she always did when she was afraid of something. Cook always said a little lady didn't—

"That's it!" the monster bellowed. "The hand you just used . . . that's your right. Turn that way."

Cautiously Abby did. Her eyeballs all but popped from their sockets at the sight of the creature with the black curls and white shoes. The monster wasn't so terribly large but it seemed to Abby she'd never seen feet so big in her entire life. Why, the soles of the monster's shoes were thicker than the feather mattress on her bed!

"So you finally found me."

"Ohh," Abby said as her breath locked deep inside her chest. The monster sounded like a girl but no one, not even a boy, would have such short and peculiar hair. "Oh, my!"

"Look," said the monster, just as pleasant as can be, "this isn't the most comfortable spot in town. Bring me a ladder and then we'll talk."

Abby took a step backward. "No."

"Help me get down from this tree and I'll give you something special."

"You are a monster," Abby said. "I want you to go away."

"Hey, I may not be a *Vogue* model, but isn't that monster business getting kind of personal?"

Abby clutched Lucy more tightly. She didn't understand everything the monster said but she had to pretend she did. You had to be clever to best them. "If you are not a monster, then what are you?"

Somewhere between "Hello," and "Bring me a ladder," Dakota had lost total control of the situation. The sky was growing darker, the wind was howling and, unless she missed her guess, those were snowflakes drifting past her nose.

"Listen, kid, think of me as your fairy godmother. Now, will you please find somebody to help me down from this tree?" Historically, fairy godmothers got good press, and from the look of interest in the kid's eyes she'd said the right thing.

"Are you a fairy godmother like in Cook's stories?"

"Absolutely."

Now all she had to do was provide some physical evidence. Whispering a silent prayer to the goddess of women stuck in maple trees, Dakota unloosed her death grip and waved her left hand in the air.

Her six silver rings reflected the fading light and she milked the effect for all it was worth, moving her hand in a wide arc like a crazed traffic cop. Her crystal bracelets proved even better. The kid seemed downright spellbound as the stones refracted what light there was into arrows of pure color. Too bad her granny glasses had disappeared. The lavender-tinted lenses—more fashion than function— would have blown the kid away.

For once she was glad good taste had never marred her talent for overstatement.

"Are they magic?" The child's tone was downright reverential.

In for a penny, in for a pound. "Yes, and if you help me get down from this tree, I'll prove it to you." How hard could it be to dazzle a little girl with an eye for gaudy costume jewelry?

"If they are magic, why can't they get you down from the tree?"

"They're a different kind of magic," she hedged. A logical kid. Just her luck. "They don't do tree magic."

"You are not a *real* fairy godmother."

Dakota tried to look demure. "Why do you say that?"

"Fairy godmothers are pretty."

"Like you're another Shirley Temple?" she muttered under her breath. She forced herself to bestow her best smile on the little darling. "Maybe I'm a different kind of fairy godmother."

"No." The child shook her head. "There is only one kind."

"Listen, kid, I'm trying real hard, but you're making it awfully tough to like you."

"I do not like you, either." The little girl's trembling chin punctuated the words.

Dakota cautiously shifted her weight over to a lower branch and pretended the creaking noise wasn't a portent of disaster. "You're not going to cry, are you?"

On cue the kid's eyes flooded with tears.

Dakota wrapped her legs around the trunk of the tree and eased herself down a good eighteen inches to another miserably scrawny branch. "There's nothing to cry about." *At least nobody called you a monster.*

The kid's mouth opened wide and she let loose a wail loud enough to be heard in the next county.

"Jeez." Dakota grabbed for the next branch down and breathed a sigh of relief when it didn't crack beneath her weight. "Crying never solved anything," she said. "Why don't you tell me what's wrong?"

The child clutched her pathetic excuse for a doll and mumbled something.

Dakota leaned forward. "What was that?"

"Papa does not..." The rest of the sentence was whispered into the doll's head and punctuated by noisy sobs.

Stay out of it, Dakota. Whatever it is, keep your nose out of it. Kids weren't her strong suit. Most people found their honesty charming; it scared the hell out of Dakota.

The branch creaked loudly. "What about your papa?" *Does he have a nice ladder I could borrow?*

The plain little girl fixed her with an unnervingly adult gaze. "Papa wishes I had never been born."

That was quite a non sequitur. It took Dakota a moment to get her bearings. "I'm sure you're wrong."

"Mrs. O'Gorman says it is so. And so does Rosie and William and Cook—"

"What does your father say?"

"He says, 'Abigail, you are incor—'"

"Incorrigible?"

The kid nodded. "And that I must leave tomorrow for the Girls' School of the Sacred Heart in Boston."

Dakota sighed. It was straight out of a segment on "Oprah." "And you were running away?"

"I will not go away to Boston. Mama ran away and that is when Papa stopped loving me."

The bastard. Dakota's heart lurched. *I don't want to hear this.* She had her own thwarted destiny to worry about. She didn't need the child's problems, too. Kids got annoyed with their parents every day of the week, then forgot their annoyance by bedtime. "Your mother ran away?"

"To Philadelphia."

Dakota took a deep breath. Now they were getting somewhere. "And where do you live?"

The child pointed beyond the clearing to the west. "The big white house."

"And where is the big white house?"

"It is—" The child froze and tilted her head.

"What's the matter?" Fear rippled up Dakota's spine. She'd heard the noise, too. "That's only the wind in the trees." She winced as the branch trembled. "Hey, wait a minute! Where are you going? Don't—"

Too late. The little girl vanished back into the woods as the branch Dakota was clutching groaned, cracked in two, then sent her crashing the rest of the way to the ground.

"I am sorry, Mr. Devane, but I fear we have not seen Abigail in weeks. Perhaps you did not know we have sent our dear Jonathan to his grandmother's in—"

Patrick cared little for the whereabouts of Mary Whitton's brat. "I regret the inconvenience, madam. I bid you good day." He inclined his head in the stiff and formal manner for which he was known, then turned sharply on his heel and headed for the door. The sun was dropping low in the sky and he intended to find the child before nightfall.

"Mr. Devane!" She stepped forward and placed a hand on his arm. "Have you spoken with Mistress Williams? Abigail oft spends time with Margaret's youngest... now, what is her name? Lily? Daisy? Rose! That is it. You must speak to Mistress Williams. I am sure that she—"

He neither slowed his pace nor met her eyes. "Thank you, madam. I will give your words the consideration they deserve."

With that he bounded down the porch stairs, mounted his chestnut stallion and was gone before the addlebrained woman could draw another breath.

It struck him how little he knew about the child's daily life, with whom she spent her time. He had assumed she passed her days alone, amusing herself either in the house or frolicking on the wide expanse of yard that was to have been Susannah's English garden. That she had companions was a revelation to him.

He was familiar with the Williams's house, a ramshackle bedevilment of wood and brick, situated on the other side of town near the encampment. That the child had managed to find it amazed him. She would need to traverse not only considerable open fields but a densely wooded area that many a learned man found challenging.

And there was the matter of twelve thousand troops, scattered from Morristown to Jockey Hollow to Franklin Ridge. They had felled trees, commandeered property and generally brought bedlam to the area. The men were ill-fed, ill-clothed and ill-tempered and he feared for the child's safety should she cross their path.

Still, she was a bright child with a talent for geography, unusual in one so young. He enjoyed a similar understanding of place, a knowledge of terrain that had stood him in good stead during his brief alliance with the Continental army. He wondered what other traits they shared, then laughed bitterly as he remembered that a shared bloodline was not among them.

Dakota lay facedown in a pile of leaves that smelled like wet squirrel. Not that she'd smelled many wet squirrels in her day but, like skunk, it was one of those things a woman never forgot. Her knee throbbed where she'd hit the ground, and she was reasonably sure her ankle was either broken or badly sprained.

Lifting her head, she looked up at the darkening sky. Fat white snowflakes landed on her cheeks and lashes and, if possible, it was even colder than it had been a few minutes ago. If she hadn't been so foolhardy, she'd be with Shannon and Andrew right now, facing their combined destiny like three time-traveling musketeers. She refused to believe her own destiny was to be found nose-deep in dead leaves.

Her psychic antennae were still all out of whack. Somehow she'd picked up on that little girl's temper tantrum and twisted it around until it became a plea for help. Pretty easy to see which one of them needed help. At least the kid knew what century she was living in.

"Damn," she whispered. If only she could home in on Shannon and Andrew's whereabouts. For weeks she'd felt as if they were Siamese triplets, attached at the psyche. But now there wasn't so much as a blip on her internal radar screen. The balloon had been in trouble when she bailed out. Were they in the same century? The same country? Dear God, were Shannon and Andrew even still alive?

She closed her eyes and emptied her mind of all but the image of her two friends. If they were anywhere nearby, certainly she'd pick up something. A vibration, a sound, a deep sense memory that could lead her to them.

The silence within was profound.

Her hands began to shake and she dragged them through her short, curly hair. *Calm down. This isn't the end of the world.* She'd just fallen out of a tree. That would be enough to shake up anybody's neurons. She'd try again in a few minutes. All she had to do was give her aura a chance to settle down and she'd be back in business.

Besides, she had more pressing problems to deal with. Survival, for one. If she lay there much longer she'd be a prime candidate for hypothermia. She had no intention of ending her days as a bear's Tastee-Freez.

She sat up, trying to pretend her ankle wasn't throbbing like crazy. Her immediate wish list wasn't that difficult. She needed shelter; she needed clothing; she needed to find a bathroom.

When she'd asked where the child lived, the girl had pointed beyond the clearing, toward the west. That was as good a place to start as any. She didn't know what she would say once she got there, but time was running out. Her earlobes ached from the cold; her fingers and toes were numb from it. Her brain would be the next to go.

She tried to stand, but her ankle gave way. "Damn," she whispered. "Damn, damn, damn." *Are you going to let a little thing like a broken ankle slow you down?* The snow was beginning to stick, both to the ground and to her person. *Think past the pain. The pain doesn't exist. Just get moving!*

She scrambled to her knees and was about to go for broke when she realized that wasn't a woodpecker she heard in the distance but a horse's hooves, and they were coming closer.

Dakota Wylie's First Rule of Survival: when in doubt, run for cover.

She dived into a huge pile of leaves and began to pray.

Patrick's chestnut hated the snow. The stallion was skittish at the best of times, and the accumulating snow made him almost impossible to manage. Patrick breathed a sigh of relief when they left the town proper and plunged into the woods. The multitude of evergreens formed a natural shield from the worst of the storm. The nervous beast quickly calmed.

Moments later, to Patrick's dismay, a white-tailed deer leapt from the bushes and bounded across the path, directly in front of them.

The chestnut whinnied and reared; Patrick fell backward and landed in a huge pile of leaves.

The chestnut, unperturbed by his predicament, stood a few yards away, rooting through another mound of leaves in search of something edible.

"Watch it!"

Patrick tilted his head. The voice sounded to be that of a female, but there was something sharp about the tone that was most unattractive. A young man, perhaps. One too youthful to grow whiskers but too old for the nursery. The chestnut rooted more deeply into the leaves, tail twitching with interest.

"Cut that out!" The accent was reminiscent of his own, yet different. A Marylander, perhaps.

Spies abounded everywhere. They worshiped at the First Presbyterian Church; they lifted a glass to General Washington's health at Arnold's Tavern; more than one had dined at his own table.

And unless the chestnut had developed the power of speech, one was hiding in the leaves.

Dakota held her nose as warm equine breath gusted toward her. *Haven't you ever heard of dental hygiene?* And the breath was nothing compared with the thought of big yellow horse teeth poking at her ribs. Did horses bite? Except for the appendix, nature rarely gave creatures body parts they didn't need. Those teeth were probably huge for a reason, and she'd bet it wasn't just to eat carrots.

And that wasn't the worst of it. Unless she'd dropped down onto the Ponderosa, horses didn't wander around without riders, and she'd bet her last jelly doughnut that this horse's rider was somewhere close by.

She lay there scarcely breathing, listening to the sound of her heart beating in her ear...and footsteps crunching through the snow, heading straight toward her. A nervous laugh struggled to escape.

The footsteps sounded angry and male. Brimming with testosterone. She tried to focus in on those footsteps and conjure up a picture of the man responsible for them, but her mind screen was still blank.

For the first time in her life, she was on her own.

Patrick Devane was no man's fool. These were dangerous times. A body did not hide himself in a pile of leaves unless he wished to escape notice. He cursed the fact that he'd left his pistol in his study. The Colony of New Jersey was a hotbed of infidels and opportunists and the best way to deal with any and all of them was from the right side of a weapon.

He stepped between the chestnut and the coward who lay quaking beneath a pile of brittle maple leaves.

"Show yourself, man!" His voice filled the clearing. No boy still wet behind the ears would best him, no matter the situation.

The leaves fluttered, but there was no response. A wry smile twisted his lips. The sorry bastard was trembling, more likely than not. An unworthy opponent, but he would see it through. He dug the toe of his riding boots beneath the leaves and nudged the coward.

"My patience grows thin," he warned, thinking of the encroaching darkness and the missing child.

He nudged harder.

"Once more and you lose the foot," came the voice from the leaf pile.

He watched, openmouthed, as a person of indeterminate age and gender sat up in the fallen leaves and stared at him.

"Sweet Jesus!" He stepped back. His eyes darted from one indescribable part of the stranger's body to another. Black hair shorter than a newborn babe's. Trousers of faded blue material. A thin shirt with odd words embroidered across the breast. The stranger wore enormous silver earbobs that dangled on its shoulders, their lacy pattern looking for all the world like tracings of ice on a windowpane.

He narrowed his eyes. The breasts seemed too full to belong to a boy but not full enough to belong to a grown woman. Still, he was reasonably sure the stranger was female.

"You're staring," the stranger said.

"I am," he said, not seeking to avoid the truth, "for I have not seen the likes of you in this or any other life."

3

"Thanks a lot," Dakota said, sitting in the leaves like a toadstool. "I'm going to take that as a compliment."

"It was not meant thus."

"You don't do irony," she noted. "I'll have to remember that."

He was the kind of man who'd gone out of fashion about two hundred years ago and somehow continued to thrive in the romantic imagination of women on every continent.

Take a good look at him, Dakota. This is the stuff dreams are made of. Tall, lean and harboring major attitude. He wore tight, tobacco brown breeches that were tucked into high boots, an ivory-colored shirt and a flowing black wool cape that fell from shoulders as wide as an NFL linebacker's. His dark brown hair was pulled straight back and tied in a ponytail. He should come with a warning label attached: Danger! Foolish Women Proceed At Your Own Risk.

Late eighteenth century, she thought, heart pounding. Both the clothes and the man. And, dear God, what a man he was.

Unfortunately he was staring at her breasts and it was painfully clear he wasn't sure if he should be attracted or concerned.

"Stop it!" she ordered, attempting to take control of the situation as romantic conjecture swiftly gave way to reality. "You're being rude."

"Explain your meaning."

"Tell me which word you didn't understand and I will."

His jaw tightened. "Your words are not the problem, madam. Your appearance is." He stripped off the cloak and tossed it to her. "Cover yourself."

A man of few words and all of them were orders. She considered tossing the cloak back to him, but death seemed too high a price to pay for the pleasure. "One size fits all," she remarked, pulling the cloak around her shivering body.

"Madam?"

"Private joke."

Somehow he didn't look like the type who cared for jokes, private or otherwise.

"How do you call yourself?" he asked.

She'd never seen anyone bristle with menace before, but darned if the guy wasn't doing exactly that.

"Who's asking?"

The look of surprise on his gorgeous face was priceless. It was obvious the man was accustomed to being obeyed. "Patrick Devane." He executed a curt bow, more a knee-jerk response than a display of polite behavior. "And I am addressing—?"

Great posture, she thought as he straightened. You didn't often see posture like that on anything but a department-store mannequin. "Dakota Wylie."

His frown deepened. "What manner of name is that?"

"What manner of question is that?" she parried, cursing herself for not inventing a nice normal name like Mary or Sarah. "It's a . . . family name."

He nodded. "Stand up, madam."

"I don't think so."

"I am not a patient man."

"So I've gathered." She rubbed her hip. "Those boots of yours are lethal weapons."

"Stand," he repeated, "or I will not be held responsible for my actions."

His hands were huge. Big, workman's hands that were at odds with his elegant dress and carriage. She wondered how those hands would feel against the bare skin of her back . . . or wrapped around her throat.

"Now, madam!" he roared.

So much for fantasy. "I can't."

He moved toward her, those big hands clenched into fists. *He means business, Dakota.* She'd better curb her tongue or he'd curb it for her permanently. This wasn't the nineties. She glanced at his attire. At least, not the 1990s. Historically, smart-mouthed women earned themselves a one-way ticket to oblivion and she wasn't about to let that happen. Not with Andrew and Shannon's destiny at stake.

"M-my ankle," she said with a pathetic attempt at female vulnerability. She wondered if she should bat her eyelashes at him, then thought better of it. She might have traveled through time but she still had her scruples. "I—I fear I've sprained it."

A ruse, Patrick thought, and a most unconvincing one. This odd-looking female must take him for a fool.

"And how did you sprain your ankle, madam?" He wondered if she concealed a weapon in the pile of leaves in which she sat. Surely she did not intend to defend herself using only her wits.

Still, there was something about her countenance that made him wonder if she did not intend exactly that. She was no coy miss, deferring to a man for the very air she breathed. Both wit and intelligence were evident in the dark eyes that dominated her pale moon of a face. Her skin was smooth and unblemished, an unusual sight in a woman beyond childhood. No scars from smallpox. No ruddy cheeks or broken veins from hours spent tending a hearth. Perhaps with a more womanly toilette she would appeal to a man, but Patrick found himself unmoved by the dimple that appeared in her left cheek as she offered up an uncertain smile.

"I—I fell from a tree."

He said nothing. Her smile faltered, then faded to memory.

"The maple tree," she said, pointing.

"And why is it you were in the maple tree?" he asked, not knowing why it was he chose to indulge this particular flight of imaginative fancy. The women of his acquaintance did not make a habit of climbing trees.

"A bear," she said, then nodded as if pleased by her words. "I feared for my safety."

He took stock of the immediate vicinity. Only human footprints were visible in the thin crust of yesterday's snow. "I see no tracks."

"Well, I didn't actually *see* a bear. I heard one."

"And you sought shelter in the maple tree."

"Exactly." Her smile reappeared. Her teeth were remarkably white and even. He wondered where she had purchased them. "Better safe than sorry."

"And where is the bear now?"

"Beats me."

"Madam?"

"I don't know where the bear is."

"Mayhap there was no bear."

"Look," she said, dark eyes flashing with sudden anger, "if you're going to do something awful, then just do it. The suspense is killing me. If falling from a tree is a capital offense around here, then do what you have to and get it over with." She struggled to her feet, then, with a yelp, sat back down again. "I think it's broken."

He bent down next to her. "Show me."

"You don't believe me?"

"I do not believe you."

She pulled up the leg of her peculiar garment and exposed a badly swollen ankle. "Do you believe me now?"

"The evidence seems irrefutable." In truth, her action surprised him. Displaying her limbs to all and sundry as if doing so were an everyday occurrence. Another woman would have swooned at the thought. Had the woman no modesty?

Indeed, it was a most pleasing ankle and that surprised him most of all. There was little else about her person that spoke of femininity.

"Do you think it's broken?" she asked, her tone subdued.

"I cannot tell through observation alone."

She pulled up the other leg of her garment. "Look at the difference."

He did. The uninjured ankle was delicate, almost fragile. The skin was pale and smooth, and a most unexpected feeling heated his blood. Leaning forward, he encircled the uninjured ankle with his hand, then attempted the same with the other.

A hiss of pain issued forth.

"I meant no harm, madam."

"I know," she said. Nothing more than that. Again he was struck by the differences between this stranger and other women of his acquaintance.

"A nasty sprain," he said at last, rocking back upon his heels. "One that will require attention."

She scowled at him. "Why don't you just climb on your horse and get lost? I was doing fine before you showed up."

"You have an uncommon sharp tongue, madam, for one in so precarious a position." A plain woman with the fiery spirit of a beauty and the speech patterns of a learned man. It was a combination Patrick did not happen upon every day of the week. He was intrigued despite himself.

"It will be dark in a matter of minutes," he stated. "You will not make it through the night out here."

"I have no intention of staying here all night," she retorted.

"And where is it you intend to stay?"

She pointed across the clearing in the direction of his house. "I plan to stay with friends. They're expecting me."

He arched a brow. The situation grew more strange with each revelation. "I am not familiar with this town," he said blandly. "Where do your friends reside?"

"They live in a big white house," she said. "Darling little Abigail said—"

One second Dakota was seated in a pile of leaves, the next she was dangling in the air, nose-to-nose with the angriest man on the planet.

"What on earth—"

"Abigail." You could actually growl a word. She wouldn't have believed it if she hadn't heard it with her very own ears. "If you know anything of her whereabouts, speak now, madam, or speak to your Maker before the moon rises."

"Too late." The words popped out before she could stop them. Talk about a death wish. "The moon's probably already up." Though you couldn't see it for the storm.

He pulled her close to him until she could feel the horn buttons on his coffee brown waistcoat pressing against her belly. He held her fast with just one arm—a remarkable feat considering the fact that her bathroom scale issued daily warnings. She felt downright petite and delicate, the way she had when he'd encircled her ankle with his hand. She'd always daydreamed about having a man span her waist with his hands, and this was about as close as she was likely to get unless she met a guy with hands the size of a cherry picker.

Too bad he had to go and ruin the moment by wrapping one of those big hands around her throat and squeezing.

"I will continue to apply pressure, madam, until you tell me what you know about the child."

His fingers pressed harder on her windpipe. Good thing she'd had her tonsils removed when she was three years old, otherwise they'd be popping out the top of her head.

Your smart mouth's going to get you in trouble one day. If she'd heard it once, she'd heard it a thousand times. Looked as if her mother was right. She was about to give her life for a one-liner.

"You are moments away from unconsciousness," he said calmly. "Consider your options swiftly."

"C-can't talk." She pointed to her throat. "C-can't breathe, either."

"Be quick, madam, or face my wrath."

Who does your dialogue? she thought. *Rafael Sabatini?*

"Where is the child?" he repeated.

The pressure eased and she gulped in a deep breath. "I don't know." The pressure returned briefly, a subtle reminder of who was in charge. "She ran off when she heard you approaching." *And now I know why.*

"Where did she run?"

"Into the woods." She watched, astonished, as the expression in his dark blue eyes changed from anger to fear. He was the kid's father. "What on earth did you do to that child?" she berated him, hanging from his arm like an overcoat. "She said you wished she'd never been born."

He met her eyes. "The child is right."

The son of a bitch. What a way to build a kid's self-esteem. "No wonder she ran away."

"Abigail does not wish to attend school in Boston. That is the reason she fled."

"So you're blind as well as obnoxious. What a marvelous combination."

"Madam, we have yet to explore your own virtues."

He threw her over his shoulder and started toward his horse. Damn the luck. He had her cellulite in a death grip.

"Put me down!"

He ignored her.

"If you don't put me down I'll scream loud enough to wake the entire town."

"We are at war, madam," he retorted, not breaking stride. "A scream in the night is a frequent occurrence."

Her breath caught inside her chest. At war! Dear God, could it be? Had she somehow tumbled into the very place she needed to be? She struggled to stay calm. "How goes the fighting? I have had no news in days." Not bad. She sounded like a cross between "Masterpiece Theatre" and *Poor Richard's Almanack*.

"Clever, madam. A simple request for information." She felt his chest rumble with laughter. "These are dangerous times. Spies come in many guises, some more memorable than others."

"You think I'm a spy?"

"I have yet to make that judgment."

"Trust me," she said. "I'm no spy. You have nothing to worry about on that account."

They reached the horse. He swung her up onto the saddle as if she was a child, then took his position behind her.

"You're making a mistake," she said. "There's nothing I can do for you."

"You will help me find the child, Mistress Dakota Wylie." He grabbed the reins and they were off in a swirl of snow and leaves.

Twenty-four hours ago she'd been camped in the woods with a bunch of women and kids, wondering if she was doomed to spend the rest of her life with people who couldn't remember her name. They'd called her Utah, Nevada and Montana and she supposed she should have been grateful they'd restricted themselves to states west of the Mississippi.

Now there she was, galloping through the woods with a man who not only remembered her name but was able to carry her in his arms without turning red in the face or gasping for air.

Too bad it would probably end up with her in the town jail before sunrise.

She smelled better than a woman so strangely attired had any right to smell. There was about her person the scent of something floral and sweet, a scent at direct odds with her masculine attire and unusual haircomb. It rose up from her hair and skin, discernible even through the cold, wet smell of snow. Indeed, he could remember few women who smelled as enticing, especially when not fresh from bathing.

Susannah. The way the sun played off her lustrous golden hair. The laughter like a carillon of bells.

The heart of stone.

And you, madam? he thought, glancing down at the woman cradled against his chest. *What manner of treachery are you about?*

She could be a spy, sent by the British in New York to acquire information to help them in their cause. She could be a patriot, determined to discover where his own loyalties rested. She could be a good wife who had followed her husband into battle, only to find herself lost and alone as a storm approached.

Good wife. The words sounded false to his ears. There was something most peculiar about the woman and he would be damned if he let her out of his sight until he determined exactly what it was.

"Stop!" Her voice sounded urgent.

He did as requested. "You are in pain, madam?"

"Over there." She pointed down and to her right. "That's Abigail's doll. Or at least part of it."

He turned to look. "I see naught but rags."

"I know that striped cloth," she persisted. "It was poking out from the doll's shoulder."

He had not realized Abigail possessed a rag doll. "This is no revelation, madam. No doubt both Abigail and her doll have traversed these woods with great regularity."

"She's here now."

"You cannot know that with certainty."

"Yes, I can."

"You are uncommonly stubborn, madam, or blessed with second sight."

"Do you want to argue with me or find your daughter?"

He dismounted. "I wish to put an end to this encounter as swiftly as possible."

She lowered her voice to a whisper. "Then listen to me. Abigail is behind the holly bushes about fifty yards from here. The hem of her cloak is showing."

He grabbed the peculiar woman by the waist and swung her down from the saddle.

"You can't expect me to walk with this ankle. Put me back on the horse."

"That would be most unwise."

"Don't be ridiculous," she said. "Where am I going to go?"

Grimly he tossed her over his shoulder like a sack of flour.

"You didn't really think I was going to run away?" Her voice was muffled by his back.

"Draw your own conclusions, madam, from the evidence at hand."

"Trust me, you didn't have to worry. Horses and I don't get along. When I was a child I never . . ."

She talked more than any three women of his acquaintance, but it was she who had spotted the hem of Abigail's cloak. That truth rankled as he strode toward the bushes with bleak determination.

Of course, Dakota had lied to him when she said she had no intention of escaping. She'd had every intention of digging her heels into the horse's flanks and galloping hell-bent for leather as far away as she could possibly get.

Which, all things considered, would have been a mistake. Maybe all the blood rushing to her head as he carried her was helping to clarify the situation.

Dakota supposed any woman in her right mind would be royally insulted at being draped over a man's shoulder like a mailbag. An hour from now she would probably be furious, too, but right now she was enjoying the whole thing immensely. There was something to be said for feeling like a fragile flower of femininity. She wouldn't be surprised if her T-shirt and jeans were morphing into a satin ballgown. Even her hair felt longer and straighter.

Still she refused to believe her destiny was tied up with Devane and his daughter. This whole adventure was nothing more than the equivalent of taking the wrong exit on the highway. You mutter a pungent phrase or two, then get back on the highway and try again. Of course, it would help if you had someone to give you directions.

Too bad Patrick Devane didn't seem the helpful type.

You're a smart one, she thought. *I'll give you that. You're not going to make this easy on me*.

He might be smart but she was smarter. She had two hundred years of additional evolution on her side and she had the feeling she would need every one of them.

4

Abigail peered out from behind the holly bush at the astonishing sight. Papa had killed the monster and was carrying the body home so everyone would know how brave he was. The monster didn't look half so fierce draped over Papa's shoulder. It looked little and weak, and Abby felt sad that it had come to such a terrible end.

"Abigail!" Papa's voice rang out. He sounded angry, the way he had when Mama left with the soldier.

She ducked deeper in the bushes, holding back a sneeze as icy snowflakes tickled her nose.

"Now, Abigail!"

Maybe if she crouched down low and didn't so much as breathe he wouldn't realize she was there.

"This is stupid!"

Abby's head popped up at the second voice.

"The poor kid's scared to death of you."

The monster was alive! How could that be?

Papa stepped forward until the toes of his black leather boots were close enough to touch. Her nose twitched from the smell of polish and earth.

Her teeth were chattering like marbles on a tin roof and all she could think of was Cook's tasty mutton stew, all piping hot from the hearth. *Don't be a baby, Abby! If you go home Papa will send you away to Boston.*

She had to stay there in the woods even if she was afraid the bears would find her and grind her up for dinner.

"Abigail!"

He grabbed for her sleeve, but she was too fast for him. Clutching Lucy, she darted out from the bushes and ran deeper into the woods. She wasn't afraid of anything, not wolves or bears or monsters. If Papa was going to send her off to school in Boston, first he'd have to catch her.

The kid ran as if the hounds of hell were at her heels. Those short legs managed to eat up an incredible amount of ground, and in an instant she vanished into the woods with her father close behind.

She had to hand it to the man. He somehow managed to run as if he weren't lugging a full-grown woman for ballast. Maybe cross-training had started a lot earlier than she'd first thought.

"Whither thou goest," Dakota muttered as Devane leapt a fallen tree like an Olympic hurdler. Too bad his boots hadn't been fitted with shock absorbers. Her teeth rattled with every step he took and her midriff smarted from banging against his rock-hard shoulder. It was pretty obvious he was going to catch his daughter or kill himself in the attempt.

Her psychic antennae might be down but her imagination was up and running, and every scenario she came up with cast Patrick Devane as the villain. Not that the kid wasn't showing a marked tendency toward villainy herself—apparently tantrums had been invented long before child psychologists.

Father and daughter had some pretty strange family dynamics going on between them, and if this were the twentieth century she'd say they were prime candidates for therapy.

They must have been halfway to the next state by the time they caught up with the kid. Abigail had stumbled over a rotted log and was scrambling to her feet when Devane found her.

"No!" the girl shrieked as he scooped her up with his free arm. "I will not go! I will not! You cannot make me!"

He strode toward his horse with Dakota tucked under his right arm like a football and Abigail under his left.

"Not a word," he said, "from either one of you. We ride in silence."

He swung Dakota up onto the horse.

"About this horse stuff," she began.

"Silence."

His look was almost enough to do the trick. "I came close to falling off before. Maybe—"

There it was again. The Look. Okay, so maybe silence wasn't such a bad idea.

Was she imagining it or did a smile flicker briefly across his handsome face?

No matter. It was gone before she could be certain.

"No!" Abigail shrieked, clutching her father tightly about the neck as he swung her onto the saddle in front of Dakota. "I will not! You cannot make me!"

"Enough!" he ordered in a voice that brooked no argument. "Isn't it enough that you waste my time with your foolish tantrums?"

"She's only a child," Dakota piped up. "Why don't you—"

"Your opinion is unwelcome, madam."

"Are you joining us?" she asked sweetly as she patted the saddle in invitation.

By way of answer, he took up the reins and started walking toward the clearing.

Abigail cast a series of worried glances over her shoulder, as if she were calculating her odds of survival.

"Enough with the dirty looks," Dakota said. "We're both freezing to death. Why don't you sit back and share this cape with me?"

"N-no!" The kid's lips were turning blue from the cold but she had her righteous indignation to keep her warm.

"I don't like this any more than you do, but I'm willing to share."

She could see the wheels turning inside the poor kid's head. Freeze to death or cuddle up with a monster? Talk about a tough choice. Against her better judgment her heart went out to the kid once again.

"I promise I won't bite."

Obviously that was the wrong thing to say because the kid opened her mouth wider than Dakota would have thought humanly possible without a submarine sandwich in the vicinity and screamed.

"Damnation!" Devane roared. "What in the name of God is going on?"

Dakota fixed him with an evil look. "She thinks I'm a monster."

He stared at her, uncomprehending.

"You heard me," she snapped. "Your daughter thinks I'm a monster right out of a fairy tale."

Abigail bristled with indignation. "*You* said you were my fairy godmother."

"I was being sarcastic. As you pointed out, fairy godmothers are pretty."

"Great God in heaven, cease your infernal racket!" Devane bellowed. "Is it not enough that a blizzard is unleashing its fury upon us?"

"A blizzard?" Dakota looked up toward the sky. "What do you mean, a blizzard?"

"You are unfamiliar with the word?"

"Get real."

"Madam?" How he managed to put such a disagreeable spin on a lone word was beyond her.

"This is a minor snowstorm, not a blizzard." She couldn't contain her snicker of amusement. "I just can't believe you'd call a few snow flurries a blizzard."

* * *

Her words were innocent but Patrick knew her meaning was not. Had no one ever told her that a pleasant temperament was a most agreeable quality in a plain woman?

"The signs are inarguable, madam."

"*Un*arguable," she said. "Trust me on this one."

She infuriated him beyond endurance. "I graduated William and Mary," he said through clenched teeth.

"Did you see *1776,* too? That's exactly what Thomas Jefferson said."

It was not the response he expected. First she asked about the year of our Lord 1776, then she compared him to the farmer from Virginia. At no time did she express regard for William and Mary. The mere mention of the illustrious center of classical education should render a normal man or woman speechless with admiration.

"You have heard of William and Mary, have you not, madam?" Mayhap she was from the country and ignorant of such things.

"Of course I have," she said, as if astonished he could think otherwise. "I graduated—" She stopped abruptly, pressing her lips together until they formed a thin line.

"Do not stop, madam," he urged as they reached the edge of his property. "From which esteemed academy of learning did you graduate?"

She glanced toward Abigail, who was wide-eyed at the exchange, then back again at him. "It's a good thing your daughter is here, Mr. Devane, or I'd give you a piece of my mind."

"I do not doubt that," he drawled. "But have a care, madam, for soon you will have given all away."

Pompous dimwit.

As if graduating from William and Mary made him master of the universe. She'd come this close to telling him she'd graduated Harvard. The words had been burning a hole in her tongue and it had taken every single ounce of self-control she possessed to hold them back.

Oh, what she would have given to see his smug and perfect face go slack with disbelief. Too bad it would be another two hundred years until women would be admitted to the university's hallowed, lousy-with-Y-chromosome halls.

He was a disagreeable, argumentative sort without a sense of humor. She couldn't imagine going through life without, at the very least, a healthy sense of the absurd. But not Patrick Devane. He was humorless, literal to the extreme and quite obviously heartless, as well.

Still, his daughter loved him. She supposed that was a point in his favor, even if he treated the child as if she was so much excess baggage. *Don't you know what you have?* she wondered. *Don't you know how lucky you are?* A child's love was a precious gift. He should be down on his knees thanking God that he was lucky enough to be Abigail's father. She was a brat, but she was *his* brat. They were so much alike that Dakota felt sorry for the kid.

"Papa!" Abigail cried out. "Look!"

Dakota twisted around in the saddle and looked in the direction the child was pointing. Two men on horseback galloped toward them. The combination of darkness and driving snow made it difficult for her to see more than that.

Devane swore under his breath and abruptly stopped walking.

"What's wrong?" Dakota asked. "Are we in danger?"

He ignored her question.

"Soldiers," said Abigail, casting a look in her direction.

"Our side?" Dakota asked, not sure she wanted to know the answer.

"Papa hates soldiers," the little girl confided. "He says..."

The child's words faded as a buzzing sounded in Dakota's head. Squinting, she tried to focus through the snow on the approaching riders, but without her glasses it was all but impossible. *Contact lenses,* she thought. Now she understood why people loved them. At least contacts might have survived the trip. Even though her glasses were more for fashion than function, she would have welcomed the edge they provided.

Men in uniform had never done much for her on a personal level, but she had to admit the sight was pretty darned impressive. They sat tall in their saddles, which made her wonder if perfect posture was the norm around there rather than the exception it was in her own time. Both wore buff-colored breeches and waistcoats, high boots and a navy coat with turnings at collar and lapels of the same buff-colored material as the breeches.

She knew those uniforms. Just last month she'd helped put together a new display at the museum. She'd dressed three aging Princetonians in reproductions that had been authentic right down to the worked buttonholes.

"Halt!" The soldier on the right angled his horse across the roadway some ten feet in front of them, blocking their way. "Who goes there?"

Devane dropped the reins and stepped forward. "You trespass, sir. State your business."

The soldier's hand hovered near the hilt of his sword. Dakota tensed, drawing the cloak more tightly around herself and Abigail in a gesture more instinctual than practical.

This isn't a re-creation, she told herself as the two men faced off. The two soldiers were patriots. Every freedom she took for granted had been hard won by men and women just like them. And, unless she missed her guess, it was all happening right now before her very eyes.

Devane's voice pierced the cold. The man really was good at growling his dialogue. "... will not allow my home to be turned into a Continental circus!"

Abigail started to speak but Dakota placed a hand over the child's mouth to stop her. She couldn't afford to miss a word of this.

The second soldier dismounted. Dakota spotted a green ribbon pinned to his waistcoat. She was fairly sure that meant he was an aide-de-camp but wished she'd paid more attention to detail when she'd had the chance.

The soldier nodded at Devane. "You will ask your family to dismount."

Family? She swallowed hard. If Devane turned her over to the army she'd probably end up hanged for treason, sold into indentured servitude or enlisted. The thought of trying to explain her attire—not to mention her haircut—was enough to make her weep.

Why shouldn't he turn you over to the army? He can't wait to get rid of his own daughter. He'll be ecstatic to get rid of you.

"I will not inconvenience them."

"We must insist."

Abigail squirmed and the cape shifted. Dakota managed to pull it back into position a millisecond before the words *Jurassic Park* were exposed to one and all. She met Devane's eyes and he held her glance. His eyes were beautiful, a dark and wondrous shade of blue, but she could read nothing in them.

Time slowed around them.

One of the horses whinnied with impatience.

Say something, Wylie. This is your chance. At least she knew which side the soldiers were on, which was more than she could say about Devane.

His expression gave away nothing. Would he hand her over to the soldiers? Leave her alone in the woods to fend for herself? Take her home and lock her in the attic like the mad wife in *Jane Eyre?*

Drawing in a deep breath, she willed herself into his head, but all she could hear was the sound of her heart beating and her own jumbled thoughts. Nothing in his expression betrayed his thoughts and she found herself longing for the abilities she'd taken for granted.

The second soldier dismounted and started toward Dakota and Abigail.

"No." One word. A single syllable. But the power in Devane's voice stopped the man in his tracks.

"My wife and child are tired and cold. You will not inconvenience them with your nonsense."

My wife?

We've hit the jackpot, Ma, she thought. *And I only had to travel two hundred years to do it.*

The second soldier bowed low to Dakota and the child, then held out his hand. "Madam, I will assist you and your daughter as you dismount."

Abigail, as if on cue, burst into noisy, shrieking tears that made both soldiers wince.

You're good, kid. Shirley Temple couldn't have done better herself.

Dakota whispered a silent prayer, then plunged in. "It has been a difficult journey," she said with the proper amount of deference, "and I have an injured foot. I beg your indulgence, sir, just this once."

The two soldiers looked at each other.

"A terribly difficult journey," she repeated, wishing she had her sister's talent for crying on command. To think she used to believe speaking French was more important.

"We will grant your request," the first soldier said with a neck bow.

"Move," Devane commanded. "You have wasted enough of my time already."

"There is still the matter of housing to be considered," said the first soldier. "His Excellency regrets any inconvenience to you and your—" he cast a peculiar look in Dakota's direction "—family, but the housing problem in Morristown—"

"Hang Morristown and hang the lot of you! You will leave my property now."

The original alpha male, Dakota thought. Defending turf, protecting women and children, acting like a horse's ass.

"His Excellency's orders are clear." The second soldier met Devane's eyes. "You have no choice in this, sir."

"I'll torch the damned place before I'll have the vermin-infested lot of you beneath my roof again."

Pretty clear on which side of the war his loyalties rested. Wasn't it just her luck to whiz through the centuries only to land in the lap of a Tory sympathizer?

The first soldier reached inside his cloak, then removed an envelope. He handed it to Devane, who regarded the seal with something close to disgust.

Dakota craned her neck to get a better look at it. The wax was thick, a deep shade of cranberry that approached maroon. It made a satisfying crack when Devane lifted the flap. He unfolded the letter, read swiftly, then crumpled it in his hand.

"Stop!" she cried out. "That's a letter from George Washington!" *Father of our country. Slayer of cherry trees. The guy on the dollar bill!*

"And a most unusual event," Devane said, his deep voice rich with sarcasm. "If the man spent as much time with the sword as he does with the pen, his cause against the British would be greatly advanced."

He tossed the crumpled letter to the ground the way another man would toss a cigarette butt. She considered leaping from the horse and making a grab for it, but the way her ankle was throbbing she'd probably end up in an ungraceful heap on the ground.

The soldiers looked at each other, then back at Devane. Dakota held her breath. The male ego was a force to behold.

"His Excellency's most esteemed colleague General McDowell requires two front rooms and the second-floor bedrooms for his use. You and your family may enjoy the remainder.''

"Hang General McDowell!''

"Papa's angry,'' Abigail whispered.

"I know,'' Dakota whispered back.

It was an awesome sight.

His jaw was set in stone. His thick dark brows met in a square knot over his nose. His blue eyes burned with a fury she was glad was not directed at her.

"May you and General Washington rot in hell.''

Grabbing the reins of the horse, he headed up the hill the rest of the way to the house.

A small farm south of Franklin Ridge

Emilie Crosse Rutledge watched as her husband buttoned the heavy black wool cape at his throat.

"Look at you,'' she said, reaching up to tuck his shirt collar inside the cape. "Can't even manage to get dressed on your own.''

"Everything's going to be fine, Em,'' he said, drawing her into his arms. "Josiah and I will be back by morning.''

She tried to smile but failed. "I don't know what's the matter with me,'' she said, pressing her forehead against his shoulder. "All day long I've had the strangest feeling that something terrible is going to happen.''

He inclined his head toward the staircase. "Something terrible's going to happen, all right. In about ten minutes Andrew and Sara are going to wake up from their naps and all hell will break loose.''

Not even the thought of her beloved children could wipe the fear from Emilie's mind. "Be careful,'' she said, cupping his face between her hands. "Nothing is worth losing you.''

"It's a simple drop," Zane said. "We ride to the White Horse Tavern near Jockey Hollow and leave the blankets with the owner. What can go wrong?"

"I don't know," Emilie said, "but I'm afraid something will."

"You didn't embroider the wrong codes in the binding, did you?"

She shook her head. "Of course I didn't. I'm the one who originated the idea, remember?"

"Then there's no problem."

"That inn is dangerous," she said, trying desperately to shake off the feeling of dread building inside her heart. "What if the Tories figure out you're really a counterspy? They hanged three men last week, Zane. How do you know Patrick isn't part of it?" She'd heard the gossip about him, how his loyalties had shifted to the British when his late wife ran off with a Continental army officer. They said he had a heart of stone and that not even his little daughter could make him smile.

"Remember Philadelphia," she warned. The Tories had stolen their farm away from them, but not before they'd seen Devane in the company of Benedict Arnold and his young wife, Peggy Shippen, on more than a few occasions. You didn't have to be a rocket scientist to know what that meant.

"They won't figure out a damn thing," Zane said, his jaw set in lines of granite. "Patrick's a good man. He wouldn't put us in any danger."

This time it was Emilie's jaw that turned to cement. "I don't like him."

Her husband laughed. "You don't really know him."

"I don't care," she said, waving a hand in dismissal. "I didn't like him when we lived in Philly and I don't like him now. He's a cold-hearted rat and I'll bet you my last packet of pins that he's working for the British."

"He's a patriot."

"I wish I could be as sure of that as you are."

"Trust me, Em. The guy's on our side."

Josiah Blakelee, a huge bear of a man, appeared in the doorway to the parlor. "The horses are saddled and ready," he said.

Zane nodded while Emilie struggled to compose herself. She looked up at Josiah. "Where is Rebekah?"

"She will not come down to bid me farewell."

"I know exactly how she feels," said Emilie. When they first joined the spy ring three years ago, it had seemed exciting, but now that she was the mother of twins she knew only terror.

The war was everywhere. It sat at your kitchen table while you drank hot cider instead of tea; it climbed your stairs as you searched for an extra blanket to give to a freezing soldier asleep on your porch; it crawled into your bed at night and colored your dreams.

The war was fought in front yards and village greens. Mothers brought buckets of water to sons as those sons battled to hold on to the hill where they had played as children. Even knowing that the war would soon end and that their side would be victorious, Emilie experienced moments of fear so powerful, so deeply visceral, that it made her wonder if her heart would stop beating.

All day long she'd been filled with profound dread, and now that it was time to say goodbye to her husband, she wanted to throw her arms around him and beg him to stay home where he was safe.

"Godspeed," she whispered, touching Zane's cheek with her hand.

"I love you, Em," he said quietly. "I'll be home before dawn."

She stood by the window and watched as the two men trudged through the snow to the stables where their horses waited.

Be careful what you wish for, she thought with a bitter-sweet laugh. She had wanted a husband who understood the meaning of commitment to something greater than himself, and in this second marriage to Zane she had been granted everything she'd ever wanted.

The man she'd loved then divorced all those years ago no longer existed. He had been replaced by a man of vision and commitment, a man whose loyalty to country was second only to his loyalty to the woman he loved and the children they shared.

They both belonged to this time and place. Their children were the children of two centuries, conceived in the twentieth and delivered in the eighteenth, and she marveled at the miracle fate had wrought from nothing more than a man and woman in love.

She'd fallen in love with a rogue only to have him turn into a rebel hero, and there were times late at night, when her fears ran free, that she would trade the hero for the rogue in an instant if it meant she could keep him safe.

She waved farewell as Zane and Josiah rode off down the lane. Snow had begun falling an hour ago, gentle flakes that softened the edges of everything they touched, even the ugly reality of war. She turned to leave the window when something caught her eye in the sky above the stables.

"Oh, God," she whispered. Her pulse beat hard at the base of her throat. A jagged tower of black clouds rose up in the distance toward Franklin Ridge, obscured by the snow. Three years ago she'd seen a cloud formation just like that and it had changed their lives forever.

"No," she said, stepping back as if she could put distance between herself and her fears. It couldn't be. Not again.

Not now. Not when victory would soon be within reach.

She knew all about that cloud formation, knew exactly what it meant. The first time it had appeared, it had carried her and Zane back through time in a crimson hot-air balloon to this place where they'd found happiness. The second time it had appeared, Andrew McVie had flown off in the same bright red balloon to meet his destiny.

She peered into the gathering darkness, straining for a glimpse of crimson silk against the snowy sky, praying she wouldn't see it. The clouds were nothing without the balloon, nothing but a lot of bad weather.

As long as there was no balloon, she had nothing to worry about.

Nothing at all.

5

The house rose up through the snow like a mirage. Two stories of beautiful Georgian architecture, untouched by time. The Colonial era's love of symmetry was apparent in the way the house grew outward from the center, with an equal number of windows to either side of the front door. The building boasted a fresh coat of whitewash. The shutters that framed each of the twelve windows were painted a dark forest green. Snow blanketed the shingled roof, while four tall chimneys puffed white smoke into the evening sky.

I know this place, Dakota thought. Everything about it seemed familiar, from its front door with the brass knocker to the huge expanse of land on which it had been built. The area was too hilly to be Princeton, too wooded to be the Shore, but she knew it was New Jersey because it felt like home.

In many ways the place reminded her of the Ford Mansion in Morristown. She'd worked there as a docent during summer vacations, handing out brochures and keeping her eyes on squabbling kids determined to bounce on the bed where George and Martha had slept during the infamous winter of 1779-1780.

Most people thought the Valley Forge winter was the worst of the war, but 1779 had it beaten. The snows started early and came often, twenty-eight blizzards by the coming of spring.

"Abigail," she said, "has it been snowing a lot lately?"

The little girl, who apparently had decided Dakota wasn't a monster after all, twisted around to look at her. "Don't you know?"

Dakota shook her head. "I am new to the area."

"It snowed for my birthday," Abigail said. "Cook says she cannot ever remember such an early snowfall."

"Your birthday," Dakota persisted. "When would that be?"

The little girl's forehead puckered in a frown much like her father's. "In September," she said, then held up ten fingers twice.

Good grief, Dakota thought. The twentieth of September. That was an early snowfall for Nome.

A young boy rounded the side of the house and raced toward them.

"William!" Abigail cried out. "We saw soldiers in the woods!"

William skidded to a halt next to Devane. "They said they had the right to take over the house, but Ma turned them out on their ears." His jaw dropped open when he spied Dakota. Splotches of bright red spread across his cheeks.

"This is my fairy godmother," said Abigail. "I thought she was a monster but she isn't."

If possible, William looked even more astonished. Devane's patience snapped.

"Look sharp, boy!" He handed the reins to William then wheeled and started up the stairs to the house. "Do not move until you're told to."

"Hey!" Dakota called out. "Aren't you forgetting something?"

He didn't break stride. "I will send Joseph to help you."

She wished she had a tomato to lob at his fat head.

"Who's Joseph?" she asked the boy.

"M-my pa."

"Where is he?"

"I don't know," said William.

"It's freezing out here."

"Yes'm."

"Maybe you should go look for your father. We don't want Abigail to get sick, do we?"

"No'm."

"So why don't you go get him?" she asked sweetly.

"Cannot. The mister said he would do it."

"Mr. Devane will understand. I'll explain it to him."

"Papa will be real mad if you do that, William," Abigail piped up.

Score another one for the kid. William maintained his tight grip on the reins while Dakota struggled to keep a tight grip on her sanity. More than anything she wanted to kick William, then the horse, and gallop off into the storm.

But even Dakota knew better than that. You don't run away from hot food, warm clothing and shelter on a cold winter's night. She must have been crazy to even think about it.

Patrick flung open the front door, then strode into the main hallway. "Mrs. O'Gorman! Damnation, where are you, woman?"

Cook bustled into the room, face flushed as always from the hearth fire. "Begging your pardon, sir, but you let Mrs. O'Gorman go this afternoon. Right after the wee one disappeared."

He'd put it from his mind in the uproar surrounding the child. "And Rosie?"

"She'd be gone, too. Said she wouldn't be working with a child what bites. I been expectin' my niece Molly to lend a hand, but what with the storm blowin' in, I don't think—"

"Then it falls to you." He had no time for her domestic intrigues.

Cook eyed him with some suspicion. "Begging your pardon, but a lot be falling to me of late. I'm not as young as I used to be and getting older every day."

"As are we all. A guest will be staying with us overnight. You'll see to it that the rear bedroom is ready."

"The rear bedroom? Nobody's been in that bedroom since—" She looked away.

They both knew what she had been about to say. *Since the missus ran off with the soldier.* Susannah's paramour had stayed in that room.

"She is outside," he said, striding toward the library with the housekeeper hard on his heels. "Her ankle is sprained. Send Joseph to assist her."

Cook was a good, hardworking woman. As a rule she did as told with little by way of complaint or question. This time she stood her ground. "And who will fetch wood for the bedroom fire? A body can do just so much, sir."

"William is a strong young man."

"Yes, sir." Her round features clearly expressed her displeasure.

The rum on the sideboard beckoned to him. "Is there anything else, Cook?" He doubted there was enough rum in the Colony of New Jersey to slake his thirst.

"Your visitor," she said, aquiver with curiosity. "Would this be the next Mrs. Devane?"

His pithy response sent the poor woman scurrying for the safety of her kitchen.

There would never be another Mrs. Devane, of that he was certain. He poured himself some rum, then filled his belly with the potent liquid. One attempt at matrimony had forever rid him of the desire to take a woman to wife. There was more honor among thieves than had existed between himself and Susannah. And, he was certain, a great deal more respect.

At least there was no danger of matrimony with Mistress Wylie. No, he thought as he poured himself another rum, he could not imagine a more unlikely prospect. Her manner of dress was most peculiar: she wore leggings like a man, a printed undergarment over her breasts, and shoes the likes of which he had never imagined. They were constructed of heavy white cloth with soles thick as a feather pillow. He wondered if her feet were outsize or in some way malformed, for certainly no woman would choose to wear such enormous footwear.

And then there was the matter of her hair. Cut short and close to her head, the dark curls were uncommonly shiny and lustrous and, in their own way, quite suitable to her face. He found that last fact most disconcerting. A luxurious mane of hair was a woman's most visible asset, yet Mistress Wylie did not seem to require such bounty. Susannah had prided herself on her spill of golden waves. He remembered the way she'd sit before the glass each night, drawing her brush through the silky mass over and over again until she'd accomplished one hundred strokes. In their bed, he had—

He swallowed the last of the rum, eager to burn the image from his brain.

Yes, there was no denying the powerful beauty of a woman's hair. No woman would willingly sacrifice so wondrous an asset unless she had good reason. He'd heard tales of wives who, driven by the need to be with their husbands, had disguised themselves as men in order to fight the enemy at their beloved's side.

He paced the library, his boots leaving wet stains on the dark rose-and-green rug. Such a thing would explain her mannish attire, as well as her combative demeanor. It took a most unusual woman to garb herself as a man and take up arms against the enemy, all in the name of love.

Of course, there also was the possibility that she had been afflicted with head lice and had had to shear off her tresses in the name of good health.

"Damnation," he muttered, wishing he had more rum. Her attire and haircomb were of no consequence. There was something most peculiar about the woman, something that went beyond the way she looked. Spies abounded in the Colony of New Jersey and he had best look sharp lest he find himself dangling from the hangman's noose in the town square.

"Can't we go in the front door?" Dakota asked as Joseph led her around the side of the mansion. The throbbing pain in her ankle had subsided, replaced by a dull ache. She thanked God it wasn't broken.

"Begging your pardon, mistress, but those wouldn't be the clothes most of our guests be wearing when they come calling."

"So where are you taking me?"

"Servants' entrance, right near to the kitchen."

A round-faced woman with a sweet smile and a mobcap on her head waited in the open door. "Have a care, Joseph," she chided the man. "The poor thing looks half-frozen."

She leaned on Joseph as he helped her up the three stone steps and into the kitchen.

"Now out with you, Joseph," said the woman named Cook. "Fetch some wood for the bedroom while I see to our visitor." She turned her attention to Dakota. "Don't you worry. I promise you'll be all toasty in two shakes of a lamb's tail."

"It's so warm in here!" Dakota exclaimed as soon as the door closed behind Joseph.

"That it is," said Cook, hanging her cloak on the wooden peg by the door. "We tend the fires day and night."

Dakota stood before the hearth and rubbed her hands together. The blast of heat from the fire was almost painful against her skin. The kitchen was all stone and heavy wood saved from depressing darkness by the blaze of fire and candles everywhere. The ceiling was constructed of exposed dark pine beams with bunches of dried herbs and flowers hung at random intervals. The air was fragrant with wood smoke, roasting meat and the pungent smells of rosemary and thyme.

"Hot cider if you'd be of a mind," Cook said.

Dakota offered the woman a shivery smile. "I'd be of a mind, thank you."

"And some clothes, missy. Makes a body cold just to be lookin' at you."

Dakota waited, fully expecting a question or two about her strange attire, but there was none. Cook plucked a ladle from the rack hanging above the massive stone hearth. Bending forward, the older woman dipped the ladle into a metal pot that rested on the ledge, then poured the contents into a pewter tankard.

"Drink up and warm your bones."

"My bones could use it, I assure you." Dakota accepted the tankard gratefully. "How wonderful! I can't remember the last time I had hot cider."

Cook's eyebrows disappeared up into her mobcap. "Like mother's milk to me." *And to everyone else in the world,* her look all but screamed.

Details, Dakota reminded herself. Wasn't it always the tiny details that tripped a person up? She cast around for a safer subject. "It's so quiet in here. How many people work for De—Mr. Devane?"

"Not half enough," said Cook. "Not that he'd be asking me my opinion."

"This is an enormous house. I would think you'd have considerable staff."

"Getting and keeping are two different things, missy."

Dakota nodded. "He must be a difficult man to work for." She'd known him less than an hour and she would've bet the farm on that fact.

"Oh, he is that," Cook agreed, "but it's the wee one what's driving them away."

"Abigail?"

"Four housekeepers in as many months. Mrs. O'Gorman packed her bags and left this very day, with Rosie right behind her."

"All because of Abigail?"

The woman nodded. "Now me, I have a soft spot for the poor little thing, but not all have my way with the children." Cook lowered her voice and leaned toward Dakota. "Needs a mother's touch, that's what I say."

A mother's touch. A wave of sadness broke over Dakota, surprising her with its force. *Oh, Ma,* she thought. *You knew this was going to happen to me, didn't you?* Her mother's ESP had zeroed in on her daughter's future, the same way it had zeroed in on her weight problem and lack of male companionship. Dakota and her mother had spent the better part of Dakota's life getting on each other's nerves, and lately it had escalated to a particularly annoying battle of wills.

For the past few weeks Ginny had taken to popping up unannounced at the library, making bizarre pronouncements about Dakota's future. She'd all but told her daughter to pack her bags and say goodbye. Dakota had been ready to declare herself an orphan.

Strange how it took a little thing like a two-hundred-year separation to make a daughter realize that it had all been part and parcel of the mother-daughter bond. The criticizing. The bitching. The endless search for approval. All of it tangled up with love Dakota had somehow never found time to express.

Cook placed a hand on her forearm. "Look at me, talking like an old fool, and you standing here all cold and wet. Come with me, missy, and we'll find you some warm clothes."

Dakota was so pathetically grateful that her eyes filled with tears. There had to be a catch somewhere, but damned if she could find it. If the woman had questions about Dakota's appearance, she was keeping them to herself.

Which was more than Patrick Devane was likely to do.

Cook showed her to a bedroom on the second floor. It was a small room by late-twentieth-century suburban standards, but quite pleasant. The bed dominated the room with its thick feather mattress and canopy, complete with bed hangings to ward off the cold.

"Joseph will be up directly to light the fire," Cook said, smoothing a hand over the heavily embroidered spread. A tree of life, worked in shades of earth and berry and moss, spread its branches from one side to the other. "Won't take but a few minutes to take the chill out. Himself is many things but he sees to it we're warm."

"Does he have guests often?"

Cook's laugh held the bite of sarcasm. "No, he's a solitary one since the missus—" Her words stopped abruptly and she busied herself picking imaginary pieces of fluff from the spread.

"Since the missus what?"

Cook glanced toward the door. "Begging your pardon, missy, but it ain't like me to speak out of turn. I've already said more than I should."

Dakota feigned interest in the dark pine armoire in the corner. "Abigail mentioned that her mother lives in Philadelphia." *Perfect.* The statement was so casual that Cook would never suspect that she was bursting with curiosity.

There was no mistaking the look of disgust on the woman's face. "A fine how-do-you-do that was. Sneaking out in the dead of night like a thief and all the time they'd been carrying on in this very room while her husband slept—"

Cook stopped abruptly. Dakota nearly wept with disappointment.

Don't stop now. This is better than "Hard Copy."

" ''Tain't Christian to speak ill of people,'' Cook said.

Sure it is, Dakota thought. *Gossip transcends religion.*

"Let the dead rest in peace, I always say."

"Dead?" Dakota's voice rose in surprise.

"Well, sure she's dead, missus, otherwise you wouldn't be here, now, would you?" Cook said with a bawdy laugh.

Divorce had yet to become the national pastime it was in the latter part of the twentieth century. She'd have to remember that.

Cook flung open the wardrobe doors. "She left her things behind. Now, I couldn't be squeezing myself into any of her gowns, but you're a slip of a thing. You'll do fine."

God bless you and your poor eyesight, Dakota thought as she gaped at the array of outfits. She'd been called many things in her life, but a "slip of a thing" wasn't one of them.

The gowns were utterly magnificent. Dakota had been around many reproductions of eighteenth century garb, but even the fine work done by the Princeton Historical Society left her unprepared for the splendor of the real thing. The absent Mrs. Devane might have had questionable taste in men, but her fashion sense was beyond reproach. Gowns of vivid scarlet, sky blue, lemon yellow the color of sunshine on an April morning—the beauty stole Dakota's breath away.

"Six ballgowns," she said, turning toward the older woman. "Did she do anything besides dance?"

Cook's round face crinkled with laughter. "One other thing," she said, eyes twinkling, "but I'd be too much the lady to tell you what it was."

To her surprise, Dakota felt a twinge of sympathy for Devane, but Cook's next words dispelled that emotion.

"You can't be leavin' a young and beautiful girl alone like that," the woman said as she supplied Dakota with a pitcher of water, a basin and soft cloths. "Flowers need tending, plain and simple, or else they find some place else to bloom."

It was as good a rationalization for infidelity as Dakota had ever heard. Still, whatever had happened between Devane and his wife, it must have been volcanic because no woman in her right mind would leave these treasures behind.

Cook excused herself and went back downstairs to tend to supper, leaving Dakota alone with six gowns, eight day dresses and the slim hope that one of them might actually fit.

She rummaged behind two exceptionally gorgeous satin numbers with bodices cut down to there and settled on a flower-sprigged muslin in shades of butter yellow and antique gold that would probably look like hell on her but was too spectacular to ignore.

She kicked off her running shoes, unzipped her jeans, then pulled her T-shirt over her head. Clad in cotton bra and panties, she stared at herself in the cheval glass then sighed. She was glad she didn't have her glasses. She doubted there were enough whalebone stays in the world to cinch in her waist tightly enough to fit into Mrs. Devane's clothing, but she'd give it her best shot.

"Easier said than done," she muttered a few minutes later. The full skirt did hide a multitude of sins but the bodice revealed her lack of assets. She ended up ripping the sleeves off her T-shirt and using them to provide what nature had forgotten.

The waistline was too snug for comfort but as long as she didn't breathe too deeply she'd survive. Besides, what was one popped button when there were four hundred more where that came from? As far as she could tell, the average woman had to get up three hours early just to be dressed in time for breakfast. She peered into the mirror. But maybe it was worth it. The bodice laced up the front and did a spectacular job of making very little look like a lot.

"So who needs a WonderBra?" She vamped in front of the mirror, enjoying the illusion of cleavage, when she noticed Abigail standing in the doorway.

"How long have you been there?" she asked in what she hoped was a pleasant tone of voice.

Abigail pointed toward Dakota's shoulder "What's that?"

The tattoo. "You don't like the dress?" *When your back is against the wall, play dumb.*

Abigail shook her head. She stepped into the room, a tiny commando on a search-and-destroy mission. "I saw a picture on your shoulder."

"You must mean my birthmark."

"It looked like a heart."

"It's a family trait."

Abigail looked at her with those sad gray eyes but she didn't pursue the issue. Still, Dakota felt as if the child had her dead to rights.

"Papa wants to see you in the library. Cook said to tell you because she's only one woman and can't do everything." The last was delivered with Cook's intonation, right down to the vaguely Irish lilt to the voice.

"Thank you." Dakota wished the kid would stop looking at her as if she expected Dakota to sprout fangs and breathe fire. "I'll be down shortly."

"Papa doesn't like to be kept waiting."

And I don't like being ordered around. "I won't keep him waiting long."

Abigail wandered into the room and sat on the foot of the bed. "I know how you came here."

Dakota's spine stiffened. "Sure you do," she said easily. "We shared a saddle on your papa's horse."

"No," said Abigail, fixing her with a look. "It was that big red ball in the sky."

Oh, my God! "I—I don't know what you're talking about."

"That big red ball floating over the trees. I saw it."

"And you think that's how I came here?" Her heart was beating so hard that her ribs hurt.

Abigail nodded her head. "When I saw it, I wanted to fly away in it."

"What a funny idea." She hated herself for lying to the child, but there was no alternative.

"It was not funny," Abigail said, eyes narrowing. "'Twas real."

"I'm sure it looked real."

"It made a funny sound." She mimicked the intermittent hiss of the propane tanks.

Dakota almost choked on her own saliva. How was she going to convince the kid she'd been hallucinating?

"Were you scared up there in the sky?" Abigail persisted.

"I'd love to talk to you, Abigail, but your papa is waiting for me downstairs and you know he doesn't like to be kept waiting."

"My mama had a dress like that," the child said in her serious way.

"I, uh..." Dakota's voice trailed off. This was even more dangerous territory than hot-air balloons.

"You look pretty."

Definitely a day for surprises. "You called me a monster before, remember?" *Good going, Dakota. You can't even take a compliment from a six-year-old.*

The kid's lower lip trembled. "*You* said you were a fairy godmother."

Dakota sighed, then caught herself. Another sigh could cost her five or six buttons. *I really don't want to like you, kid, but you're starting to get to me.* "So we both made mistakes," she said after a moment. "Maybe we should start all over again."

Abigail's forehead puckered in a frown. She really was the image of her father. "I do not understand."

Dakota extended her right hand in greeting. "My name is Dakota."

"M-my name is Abigail Elizabeth Devane and I'm six years old." Cautiously the child extended her hand until their fingertips touched.

"I'm happy to meet you."

Abigail removed her hand from Dakota's. "That's Mama's dress, isn't it?"

"I needed something to wear."

"Where are your shoes?"

"I took them off." Running shoes didn't make quite the fashion statement she was looking for.

"You have to wear shoes."

"I'll find something."

"Mama's shoes are still here."

"I know, but your mama had smaller feet than I do."

"Cook has shoes."

"I'll see if she has an extra pair."

Abigail nodded as if satisfied. Dakota was about to congratulate herself on surviving questions about tattoos, shoes and transportation, but Abigail wasn't quite finished.

"When will the big red ball come back?" she asked in a matter-of-fact tone of voice.

"Honey," she lied, "I just don't know what you're talking about."

"Yes, you do," Abigail said sagely, "and when it does, I'm going to fly away."

6

Abigail's words lingered with Dakota as she hurried downstairs to the library. The last thing she needed was for the child to tell anyone else about the hot-air balloon. How could you possibly explain something that hadn't been invented yet?

Still, Abigail was on to something, no doubt about it. She was only six years old, but she held Dakota's eyes with her own in a way that was almost eerily adult. *As if she knows what I'm thinking...*

"Ridiculous," she murmured as she limped her way, barefoot, through the long hallway to the library in the front of the house. If the girl knew what she was thinking, she'd know that Dakota had been lying through her teeth.

Just as she intended to do with her father.

"You wanted to speak with me?"

Patrick turned from the window where he'd been looking out at the drifting snow. Dakota Wylie stood in the doorway, clad in one of Susannah's dresses. The skirt was too long for her, as were the sleeves, but on the whole it was a most pleasing sight. A fact that annoyed him immeasurably.

"Come in." He motioned for her to take a seat in front of the fire. "You have eaten, I assume."

"No, actually, I haven't." She sat on the chair then leapt back up to rearrange her skirts. She mumbled something under her breath but he couldn't make out the words. Then she sat down again.

"I will ask Cook to prepare a plate."

"Don't go to any trouble on my account. I'll help myself."

"That is her job. She will see to it."

"Doesn't she have enough to do? Your housekeeper's gone, half of the maids have quit—"

"Damnation, woman! You have been under my roof for one hour and you presume to tell me how to run my house?"

There was nothing deferential in the way she looked at him, nothing feminine or ladylike. Her gaze held both challenge and reproach and he found himself oddly stirred by it.

Her bosoms rose and fell as she drew in a deep breath. Odd, he thought. The right one seemed larger than the left.

She was a most unusual woman.

"All I'm saying is that Cook has enough to do without making her wait on me. I'll take care of myself."

Words he had never heard Susannah utter.

He looked down at her feet, then looked again. They were bare. Her toenails were painted a vivid shade of red. He had never seen a more astonishing sight. "Your shoes, madam?"

"I didn't want to make Mr. Blackwell's list."

He did not know who this Mr. Blackwell was but did not wish to reveal his ignorance. "You require shoes, madam."

She glanced down at her bare feet. "I'll find something."

"I will see what I can do."

It would not be an easy task. Much of George Washington's army went barefoot these days. There were those who said you could observe their progress by following the trail in the snow left by their bloody feet. Shoes for a mere woman would be difficult to find, for few would condone the waste of good leather when there were valiant soldiers in need of boots.

She rose from the chair. "Well, if that's it, I think I'll see about dinner."

"Sit down."

She did not. "I'm tired and I'm hungry," she said in an even tone of voice. "I appreciate your giving me a place to sleep and I promise that I will be gone by daybreak tomorrow."

"You are going nowhere, mistress."

Fire flashed in her dark brown eyes. She truly did have the spirit of a beauty. "I do not appreciate orders, sir."

"You are in my house. You will do as I say."

"So this is how it is? You fight British tyranny only to inflict your own form of tyranny on your household." The fire flashed brighter. "Or is it you find no problem with tyrants?"

"Angry words, madam. Watch what you say lest you find yourself cast out into the snow."

And you'd do it, too, Dakota thought.

One look at that stubborn jawline and she could imagine him dragging her through the hallway, then booting her butt out into the night.

You're blowing it, Wylie. Get a grip on your temper and think before you shoot off your mouth!

She was two hundred years away from home and smack in the middle of a revolution. This was no time to congratulate herself on her snappy comebacks. A little humility. A touch of vulnerability. That was the secret to success.

Even if she choked on it.

"My apologies, sir," she said, gazing up at him through lowered lashes. "It has been a most difficult day."

Is that humble enough for you, Devane? That granite jaw softened the slightest bit as she sat back down. *See? We can get along. All I have to do is turn into a mindless twit.*

"You were on my property," he said without preamble. "I demand an explanation."

She gave him her best wide-eyed and innocent look, the one that had never worked on her boss at the library. "You own the woods?"

"I own the town."

"An overstatement, I'm sure."

"An understatement, madam. I am a wealthy and powerful man."

"Don't forget modest," she murmured.

"Say again."

Not on your life. "If I trespassed, I apologize." If he lived in the twentieth century he'd probably install a surveillance camera in the highest pine tree and monitor the deer.

She watched his face, waiting for a reaction to her apology. If there was one, she couldn't see it. *Remind me never to play poker with you, Devane.*

"What is it you sought in the woods, madam?"

The sixty-four-thousand-dollar question. Now all she had to do was come up with an answer. "It was a difficult journey," she said carefully. "I lost my way."

"Where is it you wished to go?"

"I—I do not know."

"You try my patience, madam. Do not play the fool, for I will not allow it."

"I tell the truth. I do not know my destination."

If possible, his glower grew even more threatening. *Go ahead,* she thought. *Hook me up to a lie detector. I'm giving it to you straight.*

"You are in the habit of wandering the woods, half-dressed, in a blizzard?"

"That's about the size of it."

"An unusual expression, madam. Where did you come by it?"

She ignored the question and plunged ahead. "I have lost the people near to me." The quaver in her voice surprised her; it was the real thing.

"You have lost them to death?"

She looked away. "I do not know." The balloon had been in dire trouble. Although it terrified her to think about it, anything was possible. "My family is gone. My friends are lost to me. I do not know where I am, only that I am probably in New Jersey."

"Franklin Ridge," he elaborated. "In the house of Patrick Devane."

"I have traveled long and far. I do not even know the day of the month."

"The first of December, madam." A hint of a smile flickered across his face. "The year of our Lord seventeen hundred and seventy-nine."

The thundering in her head drowned out everything else. 1779 ... the worst winter of the war. Before the month was out, snow would drift past the first-floor windows, choking the roads, killing the soldiers, making her escape impossible.

"Madam?" Devane stepped closer to where she sat. "Are you unwell?"

"Yes—I mean, no."

"You are trembling."

"The cold." She leaned back into the chair.

"This room is warm."

"I'm cold," she repeated.

"That is a trait we share in common."

"I was speaking of the temperature."

"As was I, madam." His expression betrayed nothing, but she had the oddest sense that he had revealed himself to her in an intimate, if puzzling, way.

They fell quiet as Cook's husband, Joseph, entered the room, bearing an armful of wood. Working swiftly, the gray-haired man added the logs to the fire, pumped the bellows a half-dozen times, then bowed and left the room. Her mind raced, leaping between possibilities, dodging probable land mines, searching for something—anything—to say that this suspicious man might believe.

Devane waited until Joseph's footsteps faded down the hallway, then he turned to Dakota. "Your story, madam," he said without preamble.

"My husband was a simple man...."

She lies, Patrick thought, watching the play of light and shadow on the woman's face as she wove a story of sorrow and loss. He was not a man who put much stock in second sight, but there was no denying the strong feeling inside him that all was not as it seemed.

Not that her story wasn't most believable. The woman wove a canny tale, designed to bring a hard-hearted man to tears. A loving husband whom she had joined in battle, only to lose to a Lobsterback's bayonet. Faithful friends had opened their heart and home to her and she had found a measure of contentment under their roof until they were routed by British General Gage's men.

She spoke with animation. At times her voice shook with emotion. From another woman, at another time, he would have had no reason to doubt her veracity. When she told him about the stagecoach accident along the Millstone River and the blow to the head that had rendered her unconscious, he had felt her pain.

At least, he had felt her pain until he remembered that the stagecoach had not run along the Millstone River in many months.

You are a liar, madam, he thought, watching as her dark eyes shimmered with tears. *And a most accomplished one.*

Dakota Wylie was a spy. Of that he was certain.

The question now remained—to which side did she belong?

He's buying it, Dakota thought gleefully. *Hook, line and sinker.*

The more outrageous the story got, the more certain she became that he believed every single word. So far, she'd created a martyred husband, saintly parents in New Hampshire and wonderful friends whose sole purpose in life was to see to her comfort and happiness. She was even pretty darned certain she'd noticed a single tear forming at the inner corner of his right eye as she described her loneliness at being separated from people who meant so much to her.

For a woman who'd never told a lie in her entire life, she was showing an appalling talent for tall tales. She hoped the fact that it was a life-or-death situation would make up for it later on.

And it *was* a life-or-death situation.

If Devane found out she was lying, she had no doubt he'd kill her.

The guy simmered with rage. It was in the look in his eyes, the way he carried himself, that low growl of a voice. No wonder his wife had run off to Philadelphia. Being married to Patrick Devane had to be like sleepwalking through a minefield.

"Begging your pardon." They both turned toward the doorway, to find Cook standing there. "I fixed a nice plate for the lady. Fresh bread right from the oven and my own cider to wash it down."

"That sounds wonderful." Dakota rose from her chair. "I'm on my way."

She made to leave the room but Devane blocked her way. "We have not finished our conversation."

"I think we have," she said.

"There is still the question of your future plans."

She looked up and met his eyes. "I don't see why my plans should be any concern of yours."

"You are in my house and that makes you my responsibility."

"Sorry," she said lightly. "I'm not buying that."

"Madam?"

"I don't believe you. Be honest with me, Mr. Devane—you do not care what happens to me, any more than I care what happens to you. You offered me your hospitality for the night and I accepted. Beyond that, you owe me nothing at all."

"Look." He strode toward the window. How he managed to pack such a testosterone punch into such a simple gesture was beyond her. He drew the drapes back. "A blizzard, Mistress Wylie. You will not be going anywhere tomorrow or the day after."

"Oh, God," she said, peering through the frosty glass at the Currier & Ives scene in front of her. "I may not be going anywhere until spring."

Their eyes met. If possible, he was even more devastating by firelight, with the angles and planes of his gorgeous face chiseled to perfection by light and shadow and one damn fine set of genes. It was one of those Kodak moments diehard romantics celebrated in greeting cards and sappy love songs.

A magnificent man.

A lonely woman.

A roaring fireplace.

Anything seemed possible.

The tight waistband of her gown must be cutting off circulation to her brain. This wasn't the "Love Connection." For one thing, there wasn't the slightest hint of attraction between them. Suspicion, yes. Curiosity, definitely. But attraction? Not on your life.

Still, there was no denying that everything about the man had been designed to get a woman's attention. What was it about bad-tempered macho types that set a good woman's blood racing?

"Excuse me," she said, turning away from the window—and from temptation. "Cook must be wondering where I am."

He didn't move aside. Somehow she wasn't surprised. Crowds probably parted for him like the Red Sea for Moses.

"I will have my answer," he said. "Make no mistake about it."

"I have told you all there is to tell."

"I fear I do not believe you, madam."

"And I fear that is your problem, Mr. Devane."

Getting out of here is mine.

7

No matter how hard Abby tried, she couldn't fall asleep.

Papa had sent her to her room without dinner—punishment, he'd told her, for running away from home. "Disobedience will not be tolerated," he'd said in his angriest voice. "If I cannot teach you, the good sisters will."

Her stomach rumbled and she shifted position, drawing her knees up close. Papa thought that being hungry would teach her to behave, but so far all it had done was make her even angrier. Papa still thought she was a baby. He didn't realize she knew exactly where Cook stored wondrous things like leftover stew and bread, and as soon as the house fell quiet, she would sneak down the back stairs and eat to her heart's content.

She wondered when Papa and the lady from the maple tree would stop talking and say good-night. Abby would give anything to know what they were saying. She couldn't remember the last time a stranger had spent the night in the big white house, especially not a stranger as peculiar as Dakota Wylie.

She pulled the coverlet up over her shoulders and made sure Lucy was tucked in safe and snug. She had said terrible things to the lady, calling her a monster and saying she wasn't pretty when in truth she was. Abby's cheeks burned as she remembered her words. It was just that she had never seen a grown woman sitting in a maple tree before. And she surely had never seen one wearing breeches or with hair so short that it made her look like a child.

In truth, Dakota didn't look anything like a monster, but Abby knew that monsters came in many guises and she was smart enough to be careful.

It seemed as if Papa and Dakota had been talking for hours. She wondered if they were talking about her. Maybe Papa was telling Dakota about the Girls' School of the Sacred Heart in Boston and Dakota was telling Papa why he shouldn't send his little girl so far away.

Sometimes when she closed her eyes and made her mind go all dark and empty, she could see what was going on in other parts of the house, really see them, same as if she were standing right there in the room. But tonight she just couldn't make the pictures appear inside her head. She squeezed her eyes shut as tightly as she could and waited, but she didn't see or hear a thing.

A very long time ago she'd asked her governess why it was she heard people talking when they didn't even move their lips. The governess, a sour-faced young woman from New Hampshire, had given her a peculiar look then laughed and said that Abby had something called an imagination. But when Abby told the governess that she really shouldn't think such peculiar things about the way Cook's son looked without his breeches on, the governess had let out a shriek, then rushed up to her room to pack her bags.

Abby never talked about it again with anybody.

Abby wasn't like the others. Mama had known it and that was why she'd left. Papa knew it, as well, and that was why he was sending her far away to school. Other boys and girls laughed and played and had parents who loved them more than anything.

She threw off the covers and shivered as a cold draft ruffled the hem of her nightdress. When she'd seen that bright red ball dancing over the tops of the trees she'd been possessed of a feeling that something wonderful was right around the corner, something so splendid and unexpected that all the sad things that had come before it would be forgotten.

But then she'd found Dakota in the maple tree and thoughts of the big red ball had been pushed aside by silly talk of monsters and fairy godmothers.

She wrapped her arms about her knees and sighed. She wasn't entirely sure about monsters, but she knew fairy godmothers were only in stories. If fairy godmothers really existed, she wouldn't be forced to leave her home and everything she loved in order to go to some dreadful school in faraway Boston. If fairy godmothers really existed, Mama would still live in the big white house and Papa would be happy again and Abby wouldn't be sitting there in the darkness, feeling cold and hungry and lonely.

Gently she plucked Lucy from under the covers and cradled the battered rag doll against her chest. She guessed it must be near to midnight. Surely Papa and Dakota had finished talking by now and it would be safe to sneak down the back stairs to the kitchen.

She tiptoed across the room, making sure to avoid the squeaky floorboards near the rocking chair. Easing open the door, she stepped into the hallway. There wasn't a sound to be heard. If she was very quiet and very careful, she could sneak downstairs, find some bread or stew to fill her belly, then be back in her bed before anyone knew she was missing.

She crept past Papa's room, then was about to slip past Dakota's when a sound caught her attention. She held her breath and listened. *Oh, Lucy! She's crying.* Abby could scarcely believe her ears. Grown people didn't cry. Sometimes their eyes got all watery, but they never cried the way she did when she was sad.

Her heart ached as if someone had grabbed it with a giant fist. *She's lonely,* Abby thought, then wondered how it was she could know such a thing about a stranger. The woman missed her mother same as Abby did and was afraid she would never see her again. *Don't be sad,* Abby thought. Dakota's mother loved her and held her close to her heart and one day they would be together again—something Abby knew would never, ever happen for her.

"Oh, Mama," she whispered, her lips pressed against the soft top of Lucy's head. "I miss you so."

Patrick muttered a curse, then stepped deeper into the shadows at the top of the stairs.

Damn Susannah. Damn her cheating soul. The child deserved better than either one of them had been able to provide.

It is for the best, he told himself as the child wiped her eyes with the sleeve of her nightdress. Sending her away was the only solution. There was nothing for her here but loneliness and pain and even danger. To keep her here with him was to do her a disservice. The child was the only true innocent in the situation, and he prayed the good sisters of the Sacred Heart would keep her that way.

Hardening his heart once again, he moved toward her.

"Abigail."

She started in surprise, her gray eyes wide and fearful in her tiny face.

"To bed, Abigail," he said, pushing away the memory of how she'd lain in his arms as a newborn. So deeply wanted. So well loved.

"Papa," she whispered, "the lady is crying."

He started to say he thought that prospect highly unlikely but then, in the brittle silence of his house, he heard the sound of a woman's tears. He found it difficult to imagine Mistress Dakota with her sharp tongue and peculiar ways indulging in something as soft and vulnerable as tears.

"To bed," he repeated, placing a hand on her shoulder. "The hour is late."

"She is sad," the child said softly. "She misses her mother."

Her words startled him. "You and Mistress Dakota have talked of such things?"

Abigail shook her head.

"Then how is it you know this?"

Her brows slid together into a knot over the bridge of her upturned nose. He waited as she struggled to find the words to explain her flight of imaginative fancy.

"She comes from far away," Abigail said at last, sounding suddenly far older than her half dozen years. "And she can never go back."

A changeling, he thought. The child was unlike anyone he had ever known. Certainly nothing like himself.

She shivered and he noticed her feet were bare. "To bed with you," he said, his voice gruff. "You cannot travel to Boston if you are sick."

"Good," she said, lifting her chin in defiance.

Did she have to look at him like that, as if he were sentencing her to a life of indentured servitude? "I was sent to school at your age, Abigail. It is a good thing, not a punishment."

Her gray eyes flashed. "Mama wouldn't have sent me to Boston."

He felt his temper rise. "Your mother is not here, Abigail."

"I hate you!" Abigail kicked his ankle with her small bare foot.

He watched her run down the hall to her room. There were no dark secrets hiding in the corners of his loneliness. Nothing to rear up, stare him in the eye and force him to see things the way they really were. He knew the breadth and depth of it and somehow the knowledge sustained him.

It was the unexpected that had the power to destroy.

The child's tears were no business of his.

Nor were the tears of the woman on the other side of the closed door.

Turning, he headed for the stairs and the other life that awaited him miles away from this house of pain.

Dakota's breath caught in her throat at the sound of his retreating footsteps.

She leaned back against the door and closed her eyes, waiting for her heartbeat to return to normal. "Ridiculous," she said aloud, her voice breaking the quiet of her room. As if it mattered, what he thought of her.

When she'd first heard Devane and Abigail whispering in the hallway, she'd been too caught up in her own woes to pay much attention. But that was before she realized they were talking about her.

Scarcely breathing, she'd pressed her ear to the closed door and tried to make out their words. The sounds were hushed, almost inaudible, but she'd caught enough of it to know that Devane was a hard-hearted bastard and that one day Abigail would thank her lucky stars that she had lived with him for only six years.

She'd had a good mind to fling open the door and tell him that, too. The man needed to have his butt recalibrated and she was in the mood to do it for him. At least then she'd be doing something, not staying cooped up in a strange room, crying from fatigue and frustration.

Her fingers had curled around the latch and she had been about to swing open the door and surprise the living hell out of him when Abigail's clear, sweet voice had floated through the heavy wood.

She could still hear the words. *She is sad...she misses her mother.*

That was impossible. Dakota hadn't been gone twenty-four hours yet. Ginny's last "You've gained weight and you're still single" remark was still fresh in her mind.

Sometimes a week or two went by when she didn't talk to Ginny at all, and she enjoyed every day of it.

No, the kid was wrong. Right now the only things she missed were indoor plumbing, Letterman and possibly her sofa bed with the fluky spring and the tendency to open itself up without human assistance.

She was a firm believer in destiny, confident that nothing in life happened without a reason, but darned if she could figure this one out. No one had ever accused her of being a closet Mary Poppins. And, even if she was dying to be someone's nanny, the kid was being shipped up to Boston tomorrow, so she'd end up being unemployed in two centuries without even trying. That alone could win her a spot on "Nightline" when she got back to where she belonged.

She comes from far away and she can never go back.

Dakota shivered and wrapped her arms across her chest.

Maybe you're right, Abigail, she thought as she moved away from her own door. Maybe the plain little girl with the big gray eyes had zeroed in on the truth that Dakota wanted to avoid.

Suddenly it seemed so clear to her that it took her breath away.

The spider plant in her bathroom would probably die from neglect. Her mail would pile up and everybody would know she didn't just read the *National Enquirer* in line at the supermarket, she actually subscribed to it. Her landlord would call the sheriff to break down her door and instead of her dead body propped up in a chair with a container of Häagen-Dazs clutched in her rigor-mortised hand, they'd find a couple of centuries' worth of dust balls.

Tears welled and she didn't bother to blink them back. What if she couldn't go back? Just because Andrew had been able to get back home didn't mean she'd be that lucky. The tears flowed more freely and she made one attempt to stem the tide, then realized it made no difference at all. There was no one there to see her. No one to give a damn if she never watched the home shopping channel again or ate a Big Mac or sat with her family over Thanksgiving dinner and explained why she still wasn't married.

She used to believe she thrived on adventure, that she'd be the first to leap aboard a UFO and fly off to parts unknown. "Footloose and fancy-free," she'd called herself. Ready to kick over the traces of her everyday life at a moment's notice.

So much for what she used to believe. She was turning out to be a gutless wonder, one of those passive people she despised who waited for life to do its worst.

Instead of sniveling alone in her bedroom, she should be downstairs searching for a map, a newspaper, anything that would help her pinpoint her location. Once she figured out exactly where she was, how hard could it be to find Andrew and Shannon?

Andrew and Shannon were the key to everything. This was their destiny, after all, not Dakota's. As close as she could tell, her only purpose had been to return Abby to her father. Beyond that, she was as useful as a VCR in a world without television. If she could find Andrew and Shannon, she could find the balloon that had brought them there and once she found that balloon, she'd be halfway home.

So what're you waiting for, Wylie? There was no "Nick at Nite" to keep people up late. They went to bed early and they stayed there, mainly because there was nowhere else to go.

She wiped her eyes with the back of her hand and straightened her spine. Why wait for tomorrow and have to worry about dodging Devane? He was probably tucked away in bed like a good little dictator. This was the perfect time to do some sleuthing.

It was at least seven hours until dawn. You didn't have to be a budding Jessica Fletcher to be able to get the goods on someone in that amount of time.

8

They met in the shadows behind Arnold's Tavern in Morristown, shielded from the snow and cold by naught save the bare branches of dormant oaks and maples.

"Victory is at hand," said the youngest of the three, "but at what cost? Six lives lost and maybe more and now our two best are at the mercy of the British."

"The cause is all," said the peacemaker of the trio. "'Twas understood by each before the campaign was engaged. Sacrifice is both honorable and necessary."

Their words reached Patrick through the dark cloud of despair that had enveloped him since learning Blakelee and Rutledge had been taken prisoner by the British. They had supped at the White Horse Tavern and made to leave the embroidered blanket with the tavern owner when a pair of British soldiers had arrested them on charges unspecified. And they wondered how it was the Americans fought so hard for their rights....

"Aye," the peacemaker was saying, "but still the goal remains elusive."

"Always the goal," said the youngest. "What of the cause which brings us here?"

"We have no time for philosophy," Patrick said over the howling of the wind. "We will meet again tomorrow, for there is still much to do."

He turned to leave, but the peacemaker stopped him. "There is another matter. A most peculiar sighting to the west."

He thought of the towering cloud formations he'd noted upon leaving Mrs. Whitton's home. "The storm," he said, dismissing the man's words. "'Tis nothing but a strange new pattern."

"Not the clouds," the man persisted. "Something far more strange than that."

Patrick listened to the story, then threw back his head and laughed. His colleagues looked at him, openmouthed, for he had never laughed before in their presence. This story, however, merited little else.

"A large red ball seen bouncing over the treetops?" he asked for once forgetting the anger in his belly. "Mayhap our good soldiers should reconsider their love of rum and the grape."

The peacemaker shook his head. "'Twould seem so, but 'twas not the case. All were teetotal."

"A trick of those clouds and the setting sun," Patrick said, determined to find a reasonable explanation. Nonsensical stories such as this one ofttimes destroyed the most carefully wrought plans. Better to stop it now.

"His Excellency himself laid claim to the sight," said the peacemaker.

Patrick arched his brow. "This story stops now," he ordered. "It serves no purpose, save to foster unrest."

The youngest of the three opened his mouth to speak, then closed it again.

"Say your piece, man," Patrick ordered, noticing the man's unease. He wondered if the innocent face hid the heart of a traitor. "Have done with it now, then get on with the business at hand."

"There are those who say a man and two women floated from a basket suspended below the big red ball and that the man was Andrew McVie. "

"Yes," said Patrick, ruing the day he'd thrown in his lot with beggars and fools. "A most likely occurrence." McVie had vanished three summers ago and Patrick had every reason to believe him dead and buried.

"A farmer near to King's Crossing claims to have seen them sail off behind the hills then disappear. A shopkeeper in Morristown says the Lobsterbacks brung them to the ground and threw them in jail."

The peacemaker laughed. "Next we'll hear that King George was with them, drinking tea."

Could the gentle-voiced man be the one who sold their secrets to the enemy?

"Nonsense, all of it," Patrick stated in a tone that brooked no argument. If Andrew McVie was alive and anywhere in the thirteen colonies, he would know about it. "Put an end to conjecture and concentrate on the job at hand."

He turned once again to leave.

This time no one stopped him.

Dakota quickly discovered that the man of the house was pathologically tidy.

His desk top was a testament to anal-retentive decorating. The blotter was perfectly centered. A chunky glass inkpot was situated at the upper right-hand corner. Two quills rested next to it, points aimed toward the door.

If he had any personal effects, he kept them well hidden. No miniatures of the wife and kid. No busts of either of the Georges, Washington or king. It wasn't as if she'd been expecting to find a framed eight-by-ten glossy or manila folder filled with carbon copies of his correspondence, but she'd certainly figured to uncover more than this.

She tried the top drawer but it was locked. So were the other three. Devane didn't strike her as the kind of guy who would take the time to lock his desk, then hide the key under the blotter. He probably slept with the damn thing under his pillow.

The thought made her laugh out loud, and she stifled the sound with her hand. She could just imagine herself slipping back upstairs, sneaking down the hallway to his room, then trying to inch her hand under his pillow. He'd probably shoot her dead before she made it back out the door.

So that left the books themselves. Maybe he had a map or a copy of some incriminating correspondence tucked between the pages of Aristotle or Shakespeare's sonnets.

She paused, waiting for that tingle of energy that she knew so well, but nothing came. It had been so easy with Andrew McVie. The image of the book *Forgotten Heroes* had come to her so clearly that she'd never doubted its existence—or that she would find the passage that spoke of Andrew's destiny, saving the lives of his friends Rutledge and Blakelee.

But it was different this time. Her mind was empty of everything but the terrifying notion that her world had suddenly gone from Technicolor to black and white. If this was how the rest of the world went through life, she wasn't impressed. Instead of relying on those mysterious inner voices, she was reduced to using logic.

"No use whining about it, Wylie," she said with a sigh. The clock was ticking and if she didn't want Devane to catch her in flagrante delicto, she'd better get cracking.

She thanked her years of library science classes as she climbed the ladder and reached for the copy of *Aesop's Fables*. Librarians knew how to handle books. She could make her way through Devane's entire library in a few hours and he'd never even know she'd been there.

The first thing Patrick noticed as he approached the house was the light burning in the library window.

"Bloody hell," he swore under his breath. The dark-haired wench was up and about. He should have realized she would not miss an opportunity to pry into his affairs. He was grateful he had remembered to lock his desk drawers and secret the key upon his person.

He reined in the black stallion that had been Susannah's favorite and dismounted. The beast was high-strung and possessed of a foul disposition, yet he feared nothing. Patrick's own chestnut had patently refused to venture into the storm.

Quietly he led the horse back toward the stable and settled the animal in for the night. He had given William permission to sleep in the main house during the winter months, as much for his own convenience as for the boy's comfort.

Of late he and his companions had enjoyed much luck in their endeavors, despite the traitor among them who oft fed information to the other side. They moved swiftly and secretly about the countryside, gathering information, freeing innocent men held against their will. And with every day, every raid, he came closer to his goal.

He slipped into the kitchen and shut the door behind him. The hearth fire was banked, but warmth still rose up from the embers. His body registered the heat, but he took no pleasure from it. He allowed himself to think of naught save stopping the short-haired wench before she stumbled upon the truth.

The library door was closed. The yellow glow of candlelight spilled through the cracks and out into the darkened hallway. Mistress Wylie had a great deal to learn. A more experienced member of a spy ring would have known to block the escape of light with cushions or books.

Grim faced, he reached for the latch.

"The man's a sociopath," Dakota muttered as she slid a heavy leather-bound tome back onto the shelf. It was bad enough that Devane didn't have any fascinating knick-knacks scattered about his library, but she'd at least hoped his choice of books would shed some light on the man.

You'd have to check into the morgue to find a more deadly dull collection of books. Where were the hand-drawn maps? The letters from family and friends? The telephone wouldn't be invented for another hundred years, for heaven's sake. If you wanted to get in touch with someone, you wrote a letter, but so far Dakota hadn't found one single shred of information that would give her even the slightest idea of where she was or what was going on around her.

If she didn't come up with some answers soon, she'd be forced to do the unthinkable and ask him.

She knew that asking questions made you vulnerable; it provided your enemy with a road map of all your weaknesses. But when you came down to it, what choice did she have? It wasn't as if she could turn on CNN to catch up on things.

If nothing else, she finally understood why the heroines of the Gothic novels she'd devoured as a teenager never asked questions. She couldn't count the number of times she'd flung a poor unsuspecting book against the wall and snarled, "Why didn't you just *ask*?" at the hapless heroine. Now she knew. If the heroine had uttered so much as "Where am I?" the antihero would have known she was ripe for the taking.

No, she'd have to find a more subtle way to get at the truth.

She was considering that when something caught her eye near the corner of the room. A piece of paper stuck out from beneath the lush Persian carpet. Quickly she crossed the room and grabbed for it.

Pay dirt!

It was a list of some kind. Two columns of names written in a strong, masculine hand. She scanned the long left-hand column and saw the names McDowell, Grant and Arnold. Her eyes shifted to the right-hand column, where the names Rutledge and Blakelee leapt out at her. Her heart pounded wildly and she had started to zero in on the others when she heard footsteps in the hallway. She barely had time to stash the slip of paper back underneath the carpet when the door swung open and Devane loomed in the doorway.

"What in bloody hell are you doing in my library?" he roared.

"Trying to figure out where in bloody hell I am," she roared back.

The room fell silent.

It was the *hell* that did it, she thought. The look of utter amazement on his face was priceless. It was almost enough to make up for the fatal error she'd made. Now he probably thought she was a fallen woman on top of everything else.

She took a deep breath and squared her shoulders. "So where am I?" she asked.

"Franklin Ridge," he said after a pause. "You asked that question before, madam."

"Are we near Princeton?"

"You do not know?"

"If I knew, I wouldn't be asking you."

"Is it that you have no sense of geography or are you not from this colony?"

"A little of both."

He stepped into the room and closed the door behind him.

The library suddenly got a lot smaller.

Her dark eyes held a fierce glitter within their depths, but was it the glitter of madness or commitment? He needed to find out.

"We are a half day's ride from Princeton to the north," he said.

"Near Morristown?"

"A stone's throw."

"And where's the closest jail?"

"Sweet Jesus, madam, but you try a man's patience beyond endurance."

"You're not a walk in the park yourself."

Again the words were recognizable but the pattern was not.

He closed the distance between them. "It is now my turn to ask the questions and, by all that is holy, you are to answer with the truth."

"And I've told you the truth. My name is Dakota Wylie. I have no sense of direction and, believe me, I'm not from around here."

"And where are you from?"

"I told you before, sir, or were you not listening?"

She was a canny wench, one not easily bested, but he was not a man easily deterred by a challenge.

"New Hampshire, did you say?"

She hesitated. It was clear she did not remember what lie she had perpetrated upon him.

"Or was it Boston?" he prodded.

"It is none of your business, Mr. Devane."

"But I think it *is* my business." He moved closer. "I find you on my property. I find you in my library. If not mine, then whose business is it?"

"This is getting ridiculous." She stepped backward.

He stepped forward.

"If you're trying to intimidate me, it won't work."

"I am trying to obtain an answer to my question, madam, and if intimidation is the means by which I will succeed, then we will soon find out who the victor is."

"Move out of my way," she ordered. "It's late. I wish to sleep."

He blocked her passage. "You had your chance to sleep and it has passed."

"No wonder your wife left you," the woman snapped. "The only thing that surprises me is the fact that she made it past the honeymoon."

* * *

Uh-oh, Dakota thought as she watched a human face turn to granite before her very eyes. *Wrong thing to say.*

She gauged the distance between herself and the door and considered making a run for it. *Right, Wylie. Like you have a chance in hell of outrunning the guy.* The last time she'd done any running it was to grab the last bag of chips at the supermarket. As it was, he looked as if he wanted to wrap his enormous hands around her throat again and throttle her.

"You will not talk of my wife or my marriage again." His voice was low, menacing. "Not in this house. Not with anyone."

She lifted her chin and met his eyes. "Why?" she asked, sounding braver than she felt. "Got something to hide?"

"That is not your concern."

"I'm not the one who goes sneaking around at night during a snowstorm." She grinned as he glanced down at his snow-covered cape and the pool of water forming at his booted feet. "Didn't think I'd notice, did you?" she asked, reveling in his surprise. "Details, Mr. Devane. It always comes down to the details."

She had to hand it to him, however. He dissembled faster than a speeding bullet. "What did you seek to find in my library, madam?"

"A map," she said, opting for the truth. "I needed to know my location."

"And what will you do now that you have found your location?"

"I'll leave tomorrow at dawn."

"To find your husband?"

She nodded. "Yes. And to find my friends."

"Tell me their names," he persisted, stepping into her space. "Mayhap I have some knowledge of their whereabouts."

"You wouldn't know them." *Trust me on that one.*

"Their names," he persisted.

No way, Devane. That's the last thing I'm about to tell you. She was unimportant in the scheme of things but Andrew and Shannon had a destiny to fulfill. "I don't see what—"

"Their names."

"Ronald and Nancy Reagan."

He considered her words. "I do not know them."

She bit the inside of her cheek. "I didn't think so."

He studied her carefully. The last man to study her so carefully had the initials OB-GYN after his name. "And you last saw them—"

"In the snow," she said, feigning a look of deep sadness. "In the woods."

He took another step toward her. She took another step backward. The edge of his cherrywood desk bit into the back of her thighs. "And what of your husband, madam? When last did you see him?"

"The same time," she said, her heart thudding painfully inside her chest. "I—"

He pinned her hands behind her back and pulled her against him. If he hadn't looked bent on murder, it might have been exciting. "You lie, madam." His voice was low with menace.

"N-no," she stammered. "I'm telling you the truth."

"The grieving widow had best get her story straight."

Widow? Oh, God... She'd totally forgotten the glib story she'd spun for him in this same library a few hours ago. She tried to look suitably mournful. "I—I am terribly tired, sir. A slip of the tongue, that's all." *Think, Wylie, think! What tall tale did you foist on the man?* "We were walking—"

"You were in a stagecoach."

"Near Princeton—"

"Millstone."

"And we had an accident."

"At last," said Devane. "You have stumbled upon the truth."

"Okay," she said, utterly exasperated. "So I lied to you. Can you blame me?"

"And what else have you lied about, madam?"

"Nothing," she lied. She summoned up a weak and guilty smile. "You are a stranger to me. These are, as you have said, dangerous times. Would you have bared your soul to the first person to come along?" She was on a roll. "I think not. I think you would—"

9

Her mouth was full and inviting and, had the situation been different, he might have taken advantage of that fact.

"Say nothing," Patrick murmured, almost brushing her lips with his. "We are being observed."

She lashed out with her foot. He angled his body away from her and pulled her even closer.

"Careful, madam." He cupped her face with his hands and met her eyes. She looked flushed and ruffled, eminently desirable. "You may yet sign your own death warrant."

"Don't tell me what to do. I'll—"

"Soldiers," he said in a low voice as he brought one hand to her throat as a warning. "At the window."

She threw back her head to scream but he quickly moved his hand to her mouth.

"Sweet Jesus!" he muttered as she kicked him then darted toward the door. He tackled her about the waist and lifted her off the floor. "You will regret this."

"Let me go! If you think I'm going to let you bully me into—"

The pounding at the front door drowned out her words.

"Choose sides carefully, madam," he warned as he dragged her across the hall. "Your situation is most unusual and few would be so tolerant."

They reached the door as the Continental soldiers kicked it open.

"The list grows," Patrick said, eyeing the damage with some disgust.

The young officer, in full uniform despite the hour and the weather, bowed curtly to Patrick and more cordially to Dakota, who stood behind him.

Patrick recognized the man as one of the soldiers they'd met earlier.

"We heard a...commotion," said the soldier, his expression bland. "I wish to inquire of your safety."

"How kind of you," Dakota said, stepping forward. "As it happens, I need—"

"Privacy," Patrick interrupted. He gestured toward the door. "If you would take your leave, sir, we will retire once again."

The soldier made no move to leave. "While it was my wish to express concern for your well-being, sir, I fear that 'twas not the sole reason for this visit."

"Out with it, man," Patrick ordered. "The hour is late."

"'Twas our hope you would experience a change of heart, sir, but it becomes imperative that we take such matters into our own hands."

"What's he talking about?" Dakota's voice rose in question.

He shot a quelling look at the short-haired woman, but doubted it would have the desired effect. Was she the only citizen of the thirteen colonies who did not understand the gravity of the situation?

"This house remains private property, sir," Patrick said to the soldier. "I wish you godspeed in securing another property for your needs."

"Your good wishes are unnecessary, sir." The officer reached inside his coat and withdrew a letter, complete with that all-too-familiar seal. "We have secured that which we require right here."

"George Washington again," Dakota whispered as the soldier extended the letter toward him. "This place is a gold mine."

Ignoring her, he folded his arms across his chest and glared at the young officer. "You are not welcome here."

"That may be, Mr. Devane, but still we are come to stay." He nodded toward Dakota, who now stood next to him. "We shall not inconvenience you and your wife."

"I'm not—"

He drew Dakota to his side. It would not go well for either of them if she chose this moment to inform the officer that they were strangers to each other.

Patrick placed a hand at her waist. "We are just wed, sir. This is not a time for company, even of a patriotic sort."

The officer's expression remained carefully blank. "The matter is beyond my power, sir. I offer you most humble apologies, but beg your indulgence as we prepare for the general's arrival."

"The general!" Dakota's heart was beating so fast she thought she'd pass out. What red-blooded American woman wouldn't be thrilled by the thought of actually meeting the father of her country? Certainly her excitement had nothing to do with the fact that Devane had almost kissed her. "Is George Washington coming *here?*"

The young officer looked at her and smiled, the first real smile he'd offered since noticing her hair. "An honor it would be, Mrs. Devane, but His Excellency enjoys fine accommodations with the Widow Ford and her children."

She could barely contain her disappointment. "What general, then?"

"General McDowell, madam, His Excellency's most trusted colleague and friend."

"A braggart and a coward," Devane said. "Unworthy of the command given him."

The officer's jaw tightened visibly. "An untoward comment, sir, from one who has chosen not to serve."

"Let General McDowell stay with the Widow Ford and her brood if the accommodations there are to everyone's liking."

"Would that it were possible, sir, but with Lady Washington's arrival imminent, there is no room for General McDowell."

"You bleed me like a stone with your taxes, then take what you want from my home. Is there no end to the Continental treachery?"

"Take care, man," the soldier warned, "for your reputation precedes you. 'Tis a short leap from debate to treason."

Treason? Had she missed something? She thought they'd been having a discussion about closet space. She bit back a sigh. What she wouldn't give for five seconds inside Devane's head, just five measly little seconds and she'd at least have a handle on what was going on.

"Are you calling me out, sir?" Devane's voice rippled with menace.

The soldier took a step forward, his gloved hands clenched into fists. "If that is what you—"

The thought of physical violence made her go weak in the knees and she allowed herself to tumble in a heap at Devane's booted feet. She would have two-stepped to a chorus of "Disco Duck" if she'd thought it would break the tension but, given when and where she was, swooning seemed a safer bet.

The fact that she'd managed to stay upright this long was more of a miracle than she dared to contemplate. His touch had unraveled her defenses. Maybe if she'd been touched more often—and more recently—she wouldn't have reacted so strongly to the feel of his fingers against the skin of her throat.

He stared down at her.

She fluttered her eyelashes in a pathetic attempt at wielding her feminine wiles, praying he didn't leave her curled at his feet like a stray cat.

After what seemed to be an eternity, a grim-faced Devane swept her up into his arms. A bizarre feeling of relief washed over her and she almost laughed at the absurdity of it all.

He didn't owe her anything at all. In fact, she wouldn't blame him if he handed her over to the soldiers and washed his hands of her.

"The hour is late," Devane said in that deadly tone she was coming to know. "My wife is exhausted."

Dakota stifled a yawn. Some might call it overacting but it seemed like a nice touch.

After what seemed an eternity, the officer nodded. "We will limit ourselves to the main floor for the night."

"You will limit yourselves to the main floor for the duration of your stay," Devane said.

"The general's wife will be joining him by week's end. Her requirements are quite specific."

"Hang the general's wife!" Devane roared.

Dakota laid a hand against his stubbly cheek. "Darling, you're tired," she said, praying he wouldn't stare at her in openmouthed astonishment. "You can see to this tomorrow."

He started to erupt again, but she increased the pressure on his cheek.

"The matter is not resolved," he said instead to the officer. "We will continue this discussion in the morning."

"As you wish, sir." The young officer bowed deeply from the waist. "But our position will not change."

"Shut up," Dakota whispered in Devane's shell-like ear. "Two guys with really big muskets are standing near the library and they don't look friendly."

She could almost feel the adrenaline flowing through his body as she spoke. The guy really liked a challenge, she had to grant him that.

I could get used to this, she thought as he carried her up the staircase in a major display of machismo. This was Rhett and Scarlett and her big wide smile the morning after. Of course, she didn't exactly have Scarlett's eighteen-inch waist, but she could cop an attitude with the best of them.

"Wait a minute!" she protested. "That's my room you just zoomed past."

"You forget, madam," he said through gritted teeth. "We are on our honeymoon."

"That was your idea, not mine. The soldiers are downstairs. They'll never know the difference."

"You believe that to be true?"

"Absolutely."

"Then you are a fool, madam, and all the more reason to keep a close eye upon your activities."

"My activities are none of your business."

He pushed open the bedroom door with the tip of his boot. "As long as we are husband and wife, they are most definitely my business."

Her pulses leapt. "I think you've lost your mind, Devane. We're strangers."

He kicked the bedroom door shut after them. "That no longer matters."

He strode toward the bed. It was big, wide and too darned inviting.

"Don't even think about it," she warned.

"Trust me, madam." He continued through a side door and into an anteroom that was outfitted as a small bedroom, then deposited her in the middle of the feather mattress. "It is the last thing on my mind."

She scrambled to her knees, sinking into the softness. "If you think I'm sleeping in here with you, you're crazy."

"I will be in my own bed, madam, and of no danger to you."

"I want my own room."

"You cannot have it."

"Then I'll sleep downstairs with Cook."

"Where a score of suspicious soldiers in need of a woman rest, as well."

"Then let me go back to the room you gave me in the first place."

"Most married couples do not sleep in separate rooms."

"But we're not married."

"They believe so."

"Look, I appreciate what you did before, pretending I was your wife and everything, but enough's enough. This joke is getting out of hand."

He gripped her by the shoulders. "You have thrown in your lot with a dangerous man, madam. They will be watching us closely."

"What do you mean, dangerous? I know you're not the friendliest guy in town, but..." Her words trailed off.

"I will spend the night in the main bedroom. Your virtue will remain unassailed, madam."

That's a good *thing,* Dakota reminded herself as he bowed and left her alone.

For a split second she'd been ready to toss reason aside and fling herself at him the way she'd previously only flung herself at Mrs. Fields's chocolate chip cookies, but twenty-six years of caution washed over her like a cold shower, bringing her back to reality.

He was a hunk. That much was a given, assuming you liked them tall, dark and dangerous, which she did. Thank God he found her about as appealing as a kid sister or some other annoying relative you couldn't wait to get rid of.

This wasn't a romantic encounter. She was only using his house as a colonial Motel 6, a place to crash until the snow stopped falling and she could set out to find Shannon and

Andrew and the hot-air balloon that had carried them across the centuries.

Nothing about the experience felt right. She couldn't shake that sense of going from a Technicolor world to a black-and-white landscape. Her thoughts were chaotic and one-dimensional, her emotions were out of control, even her skin seemed as if it belonged to someone else. Shannon and Andrew had an eighteenth-century destiny to fulfill. All Dakota had was the feeling that she'd overstayed her welcome.

She'd crammed more excitement into the past twenty-four hours than the law allowed and, while she didn't regret a moment of it, she was ready to go back where she came from, back to the twentieth century with all of its problems. Back to her chaotic but loving family.

Back home where she belonged.

The farm

The evening seemed endless to Emilie. The twins were in a rambunctious mood, not that unusual for a pair of two-year-olds, and she breathed a sigh of relief when she finally got them put down for the night in the trundle bed by the fire.

"I know, I know," she said to Rebekah, who sat in the rocking chair, nursing her newest child. "They will not be two years old forever."

"Nay," said Rebekah, adjusting the light blanket draped across her shoulder, "they will not. By the time they have attained five or six years, you will find yourself longing for these days when they belonged to you and you alone."

Tears burned behind Emilie's eyelids and she made a pretense of yawning. "It has been a long day."

"And 'twill be a longer night," Rebekah said. "I fear I do not rest well when Josiah is away."

"It is the same for me when Zane is away."

She curled up on the hearth rug near her friend and prayed the warmth would seep through to her bones and burn away the terrible sense of dread that had taken hold. "How did you manage, Rebekah?" she asked. "When Josiah was in prison, how on earth did you get through the days?"

The babe in her arms whimpered as Rebekah moved him to her other breast. "I had the children," she said after a long silence. "They gave meaning to my days."

"But the nights," Emilie whispered. "Not knowing where he was or if he was even alive—" She shivered violently and drew her shawl more tightly about her shoulders.

"I always knew," Rebekah said fiercely in a tone of voice Emilie had never before heard her use. "His heart beat within mine, and as long as it did, I knew we still shared the same world as before. The Almighty would not take him before his time."

Emilie arched a brow. "You believe that?"

Rebekah met her eyes. "I believe that."

"Oh, 'Bekah..." Emilie buried her face in her hands. "I'm so scared."

Rebekah murmured soothing words of comfort, much as she would for one of her many children, but Emilie was beyond their reach. Her friend thought she worried about the mission Zane and Josiah were on, but that was the least of it.

I'm afraid it's going to happen again, Rebekah. I'm afraid that bright red balloon is going to swoop down on Zane and he won't be able to resist.

It wasn't as if it hadn't happened before. She and Zane hadn't planned to make their life together in the eighteenth century. They didn't wake up one morning and say, "Hey, we're tired of the old neighborhood. Let's try something around 1776 on for size." The moment she had climbed into the basket of that hot-air balloon and Zane had leapt in after her, their future had rested in the hands of destiny.

And destiny had been kind to them. Theirs was not an easy life, but it was a good one. They had a home of their own, two healthy children and the Blakelees, dear friends with whom to share it all. She thought of Andrew McVie and his longing for the world she'd left behind and wondered if destiny had been as kind to him, as well.

One of the twins sighed softly and Emilie rose to her feet to see if all was well. She touched her lips to her daughter's soft pink cheek, kissed the top of her son's fair head and told herself everything would be all right.

There was nothing dangerous about clouds, not even when they towered overhead like dark and forbidding cliffs. In a few hours the clouds would drift away. Zane would come home and he would climb into bed beside her and her fears would be forgotten.

10

Abby woke at first light.

Shivering in the morning chill, she ran to the window, pushed aside the heavy curtains and peered through the heavily frosted glass. She whooped with delight at the splendid sight below.

"Oh, Lucy!" She leapt back into her warm bed and pulled the quilts up to her chin. In her whole life she'd never seen so much snow. "Now we don't have to go to Boston."

The snow was piled higher than the front steps, higher than the bare rosebushes lining the walk. Papa would never send her away in such a terrible storm.

Oh, yes, she thought, burrowing deeper under the covers. She had the feeling it would snow all winter long.

"Don't mind tellin' you I've never seen a storm like this in all my born days." Cook set a bowl of oatmeal in front of Dakota and pushed a pitcher of molasses toward her. "Will said he fair to disappeared in a drift out by the stable this morning. Looks like my sister's girl Molly won't be around here to lend a hand until the thaw."

Dakota stared at the older woman in dismay. "It's stopped, hasn't it? I mean, the storm *is* over."

"Over?" Cook threw back her head and laughed. "Missy, it's like to snow till Christmas."

Dakota tilted the jar of molasses over her oatmeal and watched as a stream of brown goo rained down. "I don't suppose you have any Oreo cookies, do you?"

Cook looked at her, obviously puzzled. "If you give me the receipt, I'd be pleased to make them for you."

Dakota smiled up at the woman. "That's okay. I don't know what made me think of them, anyway." Other than the fact she felt like going on a twelve-day chocolate bender.

"Ahh," said Cook with a wink. "How long will it be?"

Dakota swallowed a spoonful of cereal-flavored molasses and grimaced. "How long will what be?" she asked.

"The baby," said Cook. "The signs are plain as the nose on your face."

Dakota did a spit take Robin Williams would have envied. "Baby? What baby?" *I'm fat, lady, not pregnant!*

"You and the mister." Her round face beamed with delight. "He's a sly fox, he is, keepin' the good news of your wedding from those of us few what care for him."

Dakota suppressed a groan. Word certainly traveled fast around Happy House. "We, um, we were going to make an announcement tonight at dinner but I guess . . . I suppose—" She looked up at Cook. "How *did* you find out, anyway?"

"Soldiers talk, missy."

"Oh, God." Who would have figured that whey-faced soldier would have such a big mouth?

"Don't be shy with me," Cook admonished. "Joseph and I been married twenty-five years. There's nothing new under the sun to me."

Dakota buried her face in her hands. *Quiet, Cook! Please don't tell me that you and Joseph swing from the chandeliers.*

"Wouldn't have figured you for a shy one, but the world's full of surprises."

"Oh, yes," said Dakota, choking back a laugh. "The world's definitely full of surprises."

"So when is the little one due?"

"I don't...I mean..." She struggled to find the right words.

"There, there." Cook patted her on the shoulder. "An early baby's something to celebrate."

Dakota took a deep breath and plunged ahead. "I'm not with child, Cook."

The woman's face fell. "Don't you be worryin', missy. 'Twill happen before you know it."

No, it won't, Dakota thought. She could travel through time, but she couldn't do the one thing that every woman on earth took for granted. It seemed such a simple thing. A man and woman come together and from their love a child is conceived. Rich or poor, smart or slow. It didn't matter. The miracle was there for the asking.

But not for Dakota.

Each time she thought she had moved beyond the pain, it rose up from deep inside her soul and stole her breath away. Such a small thing to ask from life. And so impossible.

"I hope you wouldn't be holding it against me," Cook was saying. "All that talk about the other missus."

"Of course not," Dakota said, cheeks flaming. "You were only answering my questions."

She pushed her chair back from the table and rose to her feet. Her ankle still throbbed and she wished she had some Advil. She thought about Shannon and the bulging tote bag she'd brought with her on the hot-air balloon and wondered what latter-day miracles she'd managed to pack.

"Have you seen Abigail?" she asked, pushing away thoughts of her friend.

Cook nodded. "She gobbled up her breakfast and went outside to watch the soldiers set up camp."

"We have not told her yet about our...marriage. We think it best to wait until she gets to know me a bit better."

Cook winked at her. "Don't you be waitin' too long, missy. Better she hears it from you and the mister."

Better I throw myself into a snowdrift, Dakota thought as she made her way down the hall toward the library. This was a terrible thing to do to a kid, even one as feisty as Abigail. Her mother was a bolter. Her father was as demonstrative as a hollow log. The best thing that could happen to the kid would be to go off to school and bond with a group of other lonely kids who'd provide the family she needed.

Not that it was any of her business. Abigail could go off and join the circus for all she cared. Devane could declare himself the next king of England. She didn't belong there and she wasn't going to stay one moment longer than necessary.

You didn't feel that way when you thought he was about to kiss you.

"Baloney," she muttered. She knew a business kiss when she got one. He'd been trying to shut her up so she didn't tell the soldiers they really weren't married. Although why he'd told them that in the first place was beyond her. Saving her sorry fanny wasn't his first priority.

Which meant that he had another, more personal reason.

Don't flatter yourself, Wylie. He's just never seen anything quite like you before.

Short-haired, tattooed women weren't exactly a dime a dozen around there. She was bound to make an impression. A pair of lips. An almost-kiss. Just because it had made her downright dizzy with excitement was no reason to think it had rocked his world.

You're an idiot, Wylie. Maybe if she had a few more kisses under her belt and a few less jelly doughnuts she wouldn't find her head turned by the first bad-tempered Colonial landowner to come along.

The hallway was littered with military gear—everything from rolled-up blankets to muskets to dispatch boxes lined her path. Uniformed soldiers with ramrod-straight posture carted firewood and odd pieces of furniture. The beautiful entrance hall had been reduced to an eighteenth-century version of Grand Central Station.

A young soldier nodded at her as she approached the front door. A wicked-looking bayonet rested near him. She noted a slight twitch in his left cheek. He probably didn't like that bayonet any more than she did.

"So," said Dakota, smiling, "is it cold enough for you?"

He didn't so much as blink. "Yes, ma'am."

She sighed. Poor guy didn't get the joke. Give him another couple of hundred years and he'd be as sick of it as she was.

Still smiling, she swung open the door. *I have to get out of here,* she thought as she stepped past the guard. Another bad joke and she'd end up on the business end of one of those bayonets. Maybe Cook had been exaggerating. One woman's blizzard was another woman's flurries. Weather didn't faze her. It would take more than a lousy storm to stop Dakota Wylie.

Still smiling, she stepped out onto the front porch. Her smile quickly faded.

The snow was level with the top step and still falling.

The worst winter of the century was under way.

Patrick swore as he paced the length of the library. The bloody beggars were everywhere. General McDowell's men had taken over the two front rooms, plus the servants' quarters on the first floor, and plans were afoot to build an additional kitchen before the arrival of the general's lady. Cook and Joseph had been forced to move their belongings up to a tiny attic room, while William was once again relegated to the barn. The other servants slept crowded together in the kitchen and pantry.

He had refused to allow the interlopers access to his library or to the room he now shared with Dakota Wylie, but he knew that when the general arrived, the argument would resume.

And then there was the issue of Abigail. Her room afforded a splendid view of the yard and the road beyond it. The general's aide-de-camp had earmarked it for the general's use, but once again Patrick refused to yield. As long as the snow made her departure for Boston impossible, he would not have Abigail banished from her room.

Quite the altruist, Devane. Such concern for the welfare of a child.

The truth was an uncomfortable fit. He wished the child well. He prayed her life would be a long and happy one, but no longer would he allow emotion to determine his fate.

In truth, it served his purpose to allow the child to stay. The child's presence would distract the soldiers from what he was about. There was still much to be accomplished and time was growing short.

Dakota Wylie presented a problem of a different sort. She said she was a widow, who once had disguised herself as a man in order to fight side by side with the man she loved. A noble sentiment, to be sure, and one that would explain the odd manner in which she wore her hair. Torn by grief at her husband's death, routed from her home, she was traveling with friends toward some unknown safe harbor when she was separated from them and thrust into her current circumstances.

He might have believed her story had she not contradicted herself last night upon questioning.

His eye was caught by movement outside the library window. Soldiers, some young enough to be his sons, struggled against the fierce snow and wind as they dragged newly felled trees across the yard. Their uniforms were a pathetic mix of tattered breeches, worn coats and anything else they could find to protect them from the cold. Half went shoeless. The footprints in the snow were tinged red with blood.

All morning he'd heard the muffled thuds of falling trees as the soldiers systematically cut down the finest pines and maples to turn into makeshift shelters while the officers slept peacefully in feather beds. Many of those young men would be dead before the winter was over.

Patrick didn't give a tinker's damn what happened to the fat and happy officers, but he cared a great deal what happened to the young boys and old men they sent into battle.

He turned away from the window and thought again of the woman. Would her heart break at the sight of those hapless young men or did she conspire to send them to their deaths?

"Stop it!" Dakota said as she stared out the front door at the steady fall of snow. "Enough's enough."

She turned at the sound of a childish giggle.

"Think it's funny, do you?" she asked Abigail, who was sitting near the hearth, her bedraggled rag doll firmly in hand. "I'll bet you never had to shovel the stuff."

"Who were you talking to?" Abigail asked, those big eyes of hers wide with curiosity.

"Myself."

Abigail considered her for a moment. "I talk to Lucy."

"Lucy? Who—" She stopped, then nodded. "Your doll?"

Abigail hugged the doll close to her narrow chest. "Mama gave her to me."

Dakota's interest was piqued. It was hard to imagine the kind of woman Devane had been married to.

"Better be careful," she said, crossing the stone floor to where the girl sat. "Her stuffing's coming out."

Abigail shied away from Dakota.

"I'm not going to hurt her. I want to help."

The child gave her a sidelong look that seemed terribly adult coming from someone so young. "Lucy has a hurt shoulder."

"I know," said Dakota. "I think she needs a Band-Aid."

Abby's brow puckered. "A Band-Aid?"

Uh-oh, thought Dakota. *Culture shock.* "She needs to be repaired."

"You can do that?" Abby asked.

"If you find me a needle and thread I can."

"Mama had a sewing kit in her room. I can show you where."

"Sounds good to me." She followed the kid to the back staircase, wondering if she'd lost what was left of her mind. She sewed about as well as she sang coloratura. But, damn it, there was something about the look in the kid's eyes that made her want to help. It felt strangely like a maternal instinct and Dakota didn't like it one bit.

They passed three perfectly uniformed officers in the upstairs hallway. The men stepped aside to make way for them, which seemed a polite enough gesture, but Dakota was aware of their intense scrutiny burning a hole in her back. *Take a good look, fellows,* she thought as Abby pushed open the door to Devane's suite of rooms. *You've seen the future and I'm it.*

Not that they'd believe her. In truth, she didn't totally believe the whole thing herself. She'd half expected to wake up this morning in her lumpy sofa bed with the bad spring, serenaded by her mother's voice floating through the answering machine.

"Mama's sewing box is in here," Abby said, snapping Dakota from her reverie. "She forgot it when she left."

"Smart woman," said Dakota, without thinking. "Why sew if you can buy retail?"

"What's ree-tail?" asked Abby.

"A new kind of cloth," she said after a moment. These cultural references were going to trip her up sooner or later.

Abby nodded as if it all made perfect sense and Dakota felt like the rat that she was.

"I know," said Abby.

Dakota frowned. "Know what?"

"That you feel bad because you're not telling the truth."

11

If Dakota had had dentures, they would have dropped to the floor. "I—I mean, you don't . . ." She came to a rolling stop. "How did you know?"

The child shrugged her shoulders. "I just did."

Dakota chose her words with care. Her thoughts, however, were beyond her control. "I'm sorry I didn't tell you the truth, Abby. I should have."

"Yes," said Abby solemnly, "but grown people never do. I hear them in my head and I know that."

"Of course you hear them," Dakota said easily. "Most grown people talk too loud."

"No." Abby tapped her temple with a forefinger. "I hear them up here."

"Are their lips moving?" A basic question, but important, given the circumstances.

Abby shook her head. "No, but I hear them anyway."

Oh, God, Dakota thought. Was it possible she and the kid had more in common than gender? "Can you hear me that way?"

Abby considered her for a moment. "Sometimes."

"Can you hear me now?" *Row, row, row your boat . . .*

"No," said Abby. "I can't hear you at all today."

"So how did you know I wasn't telling the truth?"

"I felt it."

"In your bones," Dakota whispered as a shiver rippled up her spine.

"Yes!" The sorrowful expression in Abby's eyes vanished, replaced by something close to joy. "Way down deep inside."

Dakota had been called crazy, high-strung, a compulsive liar—and that was on the eve of the millennium. She could only imagine how Abby would be treated less than one hundred years after they'd burned witches at the stake in Salem. "Have you told anyone?"

"Mama," she said, her gaze never leaving Dakota's face.

"And what did she say?"

"That I was a wicked girl and I should never talk of such things again."

Considering what she'd heard about Mrs. Devane, it was about what Dakota had expected. "And your papa?"

Abby shook her head. "Not Papa, but I told a governess once and then she screamed and ran away."

"My aunt did that." Impulsively she smoothed the girl's plain brown hair. "Screamed so loud her wig fell off and scared the cat."

Abby giggled. "You hear things, too?"

"Yes," she said. "At least, I used to."

"You don't hear them anymore?"

"Not in a while."

"Why don't you hear them?"

"I don't know, Abby."

"Will I stop hearing them?"

She sighed. "I'm afraid I don't know the answer to that, either."

The child thought about that for a moment. "I know lots of things," Abigail said, with a kid's leapfrog logic that never failed to disorient Dakota. "I know where Papa hides special treasures."

This is none of your business, Wylie. You'll only end up getting the kid in trouble. Devane seemed to think little enough of his daughter as it was. If he found her leading Dakota on a scavenger hunt, he'd hit the roof. She opted to change the subject.

"Lucy is looking pretty sad," Dakota said, pointing toward the doll clutched in Abby's arms. "I think you should get the sewing basket so I can fix her up."

"Here," said Abby, handing the doll to Dakota. "You hold Lucy."

The doll was as scruffy as her owner, a skinny little thing stuffed with rags and dressed in them, as well. It was painfully obvious that Abby loved the toy, and Dakota wondered if anyone had ever loved Abby half as much.

Abby fixed her with a look. "You're crying."

"No, I'm not."

"Your eyes are red."

"I didn't get much sleep."

"I know that," said Abby. "You and Papa were talking until very late."

Dakota looked toward the window. She was only two floors up. If she jumped, the snow would cushion her fall. "How do you know that?"

"I could hear you."

"Did you really hear us or did you just feel like you heard us?"

"I—"

"Abigail!" Cook's clarion call rang out from the downstairs hallway. "I'm givin' you the count of ten, missy, before I toss your stew to the pigs."

"Cook gave William's supper to the dogs last week," Abby said in a horrified tone of voice as she turned toward the door.

"Wait a minute!" Dakota said. "What about the sewing basket?"

"In there," Abby said, pointing toward a large cherry-wood armoire.

She ran from the room in a flutter of pigtails, leaving Dakota alone in Devane's bedroom.

Talk about temptation.

"No," she said out loud. Talking to herself was getting to be a habit. "I don't need to know if he wears boxers or briefs."

No, she didn't *need* to have that bit of information, but that didn't mean she wouldn't give ten IQ points to know the answer. But at least she knew her limitations. If she so much as touched a knob on that armoire she'd be sunk.

What she should do is walk through the adjoining door to her room and lock it after her and forget all about that armoire and whatever secrets he had hidden inside.

What about Lucy? The doll's lucky if it makes it to the end of the week.

"What about her?" she muttered. It's not as if the doll was entered in a beauty pageant. It wouldn't kill Lucy if she waited a while longer for cosmetic surgery.

But think about poor little Abby. Wouldn't she just love to come back and find Lucy as good as new?

Sooner or later Devane was going to pack Abby off to that boarding school in Boston, and the only thing the kid would have to remind her of home was this sorry-looking hunk of rag and wool.

She eyed the armoire. Who said she couldn't open the doors, remove the sewing basket, then close the doors again without taking a peek at whatever else was stowed away in there?

It wasn't exactly a Herculean task.

All it called for was a little self-control. Certainly she could muster up enough to grab a sewing basket.

"Okay," she told herself. "In and out."

She opened the doors and was greeted with an array of drawers and cubbyholes that reminded her of a rabbit warren. The first drawer she tried was empty. So was the second one and the third. And the fourth. Every single drawer was empty.

What on earth was with the man? Didn't he believe in personal possessions?

She peered inside the cubbyholes at eye level and below, then reached up and stuck her hand into the cubbyhole on the upper right-hand side. The flimsy interior of the armoire surprised her. She'd always believed shoddy construction was a product of the age of indifference.

Her fingers closed around a cold piece of metal that felt like a drawer pull or latch of some kind. She tugged, but met with considerable resistance. Curious, she raised up on tiptoe, changed her grip and—

"What in bloody hell do you think you're doing?"

Devane! Her heart almost burst through her chest. "Don't you know better than to sneak up on people? You almost gave me a heart attack!" She sounded amazingly defiant, considering the fact she was up to her guilty elbows in his stuff.

She withdrew her hand from the cubbyhole, then pointed toward the rag doll resting on the foot of his bed. "I'm looking for the sewing basket. Lucy needs some repair work."

"Take care what you say, madam. You are not speaking to a fool."

She marched toward the bed and grabbed the rag doll. "Look for yourself. Her head's falling off, her shoulder's ripped."

"And how is this your concern?"

"It isn't," she retorted, "but it should be your concern. This doll is your daughter's favorite thing in the entire world and it's falling apart."

"You are a seamstress then, madam?"

"No, I'm not a seamstress, you—" She stopped. Calling him a supercilious jerk didn't seem a wise thing to do.

"Finish your sentence," he ordered, arms folded across his muscular chest. "I am sure I have been called worse."

"Don't bet on it."

The wench had a marked affinity for danger.

Patrick wondered how it was she had managed to live so long.

The last time he had encountered such ferocity, his opponent had topped six feet in height and carried a loaded musket. In truth, he considered himself lucky that Mistress Dakota did not have access to arms, for he had no doubt she would use them against his person.

He met her fury with anger of his own.

"Explain yourself, madam, if you can."

"I did explain myself." Her words were clipped. "Perhaps if you paid more attention to your daughter and less to yourself, you'd understand how important Lucy is to her."

"The child is no concern of yours."

"And apparently she is no concern of yours, either."

"Tread softly, madam, for you are on dangerous ground."

She poked him in the chest with a beringed forefinger. "I don't care what you think of me, Mr. Devane. I'm going to be out of your life as soon as the snow stops. But Abigail is your child and you owe her better than this."

"Abigail is not—" He stopped. What was it about the woman that brought his emotions so quickly to the surface?

Her gaze never left his and he had the unsettling feeling that she saw into his black soul.

Still, there was something strangely appealing about the woman who stood before him, prepared to do battle. Her soft dark eyes were lit from within, burning with the fires of righteous anger. She was a woman of passion, this short-haired wench with the sharp tongue and quick wit. A man would be well-served to have such a partner at his side.

Susannah had cared for little but her own immediate pleasures. French perfumes. Fancy dresses made of satin and lace. Endless hours spent primping before the glass in her dressing room. The sweetness of her disposition had been directly related to the number of compliments he saw fit to bestow upon her. The thought of the beauteous Susannah trudging through mud and snow to follow him into battle was as laughable as it was unlikely—for many reasons.

He had oft heard stories of women whose courage matched or surpassed the courage of men in Continental uniform. Women who donned masculine garb and followed their beloveds into the fray. Until this moment he had not believed such a woman existed.

There was much about Dakota Wylie to make him believe.

She had known Abigail for less than twenty-four hours, and already she'd risked his considerable wrath in defense of the child. Abigail's own mother had not seen fit to do that.

An elaborate ruse, a voice inside him cautioned. *She seeks to insinuate herself into your household for her own nefarious purposes.*

Her story had been rife with inconsistency. At one point she had seemed to forget the very husband she'd claimed to have loved and lost. Yet the one thing that never varied was her desire to find her friends—and the passionate determination with which she said it.

Her arrival was well-timed, the voice continued. *She appeared with the storm that keeps her captive in your home.*

A coincidence or the carefully laid plan of a woman more cunning than any he had ever known?

Grimly, he determined to uncover the truth.

"Don't you dare walk out on me!" Dakota snapped as the louse turned away.

If that arrogant stinker actually thought they were through talking, he had another think coming. She hadn't traveled two hundred years to be insulted by a man who didn't even know the name of his daughter's favorite doll.

He continued toward the door with the stride of a man who knew what he was about. The nerve of him. She might not be a raving beauty who brought men to their feet, but she was a human being and she deserved at least a modicum of respect.

"Devane! You can't leave before I—"

"Once again you speak too soon, madam." He slammed shut the door to the bedroom, then turned back toward her.

Life as she knew it ground to a sudden stop. "Wh-what do you think you're doing?"

"I am doing as you ordered me to do, madam." He strode toward her, all menace and—to her dismay—devastating sensuality.

"You haven't heard a word I've said."

"I have heard all of the words, Dakota Wylie, and the time has come for silence."

"I don't believe in silence," she said as pulse points sprang to life all over her body. "Silence is vastly overrated."

"And how would you know that, madam, when you practice it so rarely?"

"I'm a talker," she agreed, taking a step back. "Talking's good. Talking bonds people together."

He moved closer still. "There are other ways to bind a man and woman together."

"What?" She tried to take another step backward but found herself pressed up against his bed.

The expression in his eyes was nothing short of dangerous. "You play the innocent," he observed. "An interesting diversion, but unnecessary given the circumstances."

She scrambled onto the mattress and scooted toward the other side. "I'm in mourning," she reminded him.

"Are you, madam?"

"Of course I am." She summoned up a suitably mournful expression. "I would appreciate it if you left me alone now."

He arched a dark brow. "Moments ago you wished me to remain."

"I've changed my mind," she said. "Feel free to go."

"Your company intrigues me. I choose to stay."

"I want to be alone." It had worked for Greta Garbo. Too bad she didn't have as much success. She reached the other side of the mattress, only to find herself wedged between the bed and the window.

He rounded the foot of the bed. "A husband should know certain things about his wife."

"I'm not your wife." Talk about stating the obvious.

"To the soldiers you are."

"Fine," she said. "I'll remember to look subservient when I'm downstairs."

"Your late husband," he said, moving closer. "Did he find your sharp tongue an obstacle to happiness?"

"My husband loved me as I am." Or he would have if she'd ever managed to find herself one.

"And how long were you married to this patient man?"

"Your own tongue is sharp as well, Mr. Devane."

"You have not answered my question."

"My marriage is none of your business." Her back was pressed against icy-cold panes of window glass. Talk about a metaphor.

"*You*, madam, are my business."

Not in this lifetime, she thought. "Don't be absurd. As soon as the snow stops, I'll be out of your hair."

"You have an unusual manner of speaking, but your meaning is clear."

"Good," she said. "Then we have no problem."

"No problem at all," he said smoothly. "You will leave when I say it is time for you to leave and not before."

"Excuse me, but you don't have any rights over me."

"This is my house. That gives me the right."

"No wonder you hate those soldiers downstairs," she snapped. "If they win the war, you won't be able to pretend you're king anymore."

"A man will always be king in his own house."

She choked back her laughter. "Oh, Mr. Devane, how I wish I could see your face when you find out."

"Explain your meaning, madam."

Once again she'd taken things a step too far. Women's liberation was still a long way off— "I'm tired," she announced with as much haughty disdain as she could manage. "I wish to rest."

His gaze drifted toward the bed. "Your idea has much to recommend it."

She watched, astonished, as he stretched out across the bed, his huge leather boots stark against the embroidered spread, and patted the spot next to him. She had a quick vision of herself arranged amid the bedcovers, looking all soft and feminine and artfully backlit, while he dropped to his knees in speechless adoration.

"Join me, madam. This is a most comfortable bed. You will rest easy here."

"I'd rest easier on a bed of nails," she muttered.

"You are alone," he continued, "as am I. We should take our comfort where we can."

This isn't funny, Devane. I'm not a charity case. Unexpected tears burned behind her lids and she prayed she wouldn't start to cry. Crying would show him she was vulnerable, and that was the last thing she wanted him to know. "I will find all the comfort I desire when I rejoin my friends."

"These friends of yours," he said slowly, arms crossed behind his head. "Could it be they do not exist?"

"Believe what you will," she managed to say with as much dignity as she could muster. "It is of no concern to me."

He met her eyes. "A man and woman were found dead this morning," he said in a tone of voice much softer than any he had used before.

The room began to spin and she clutched the bedpost for support.

"They were near to Morristown," he said, watching her closely. "A man of some two score and ten and a woman of the same years. Are they the pair for whom you search?"

She lowered her head as a powerful wave of relief rocked through her body. "They are not my friends," she said after a moment, "but I thank you for the information."

He inclined his head, an absurdly formal response from a man stretched out on a feather mattress like a *Playgirl* centerfold. A few less-than-innocent fantasies played themselves out as heat gathered inside her chest. She was shocked that desire was so close to the surface.

"Abigail is waiting for me to repair Lucy," Dakota said, aware that she was suddenly babbling like a fool. "She must be wondering what is taking me so long."

"Cook called the child to her midday meal."

"Unless it's a ten-course feast, she must be finished by now." His eyes narrowed, and instantly she regretted her flip tone and sharp-edged words. If she ever made it back to her own time, she was going to write a handbook on how to hook a man, and the first rule would be "Smart-mouthed dames need not apply."

She started toward the door as fast as her dainty size eights would carry her.

Before she knew what he was about, Patrick reached out and encircled her narrow wrist with his fingers. Again he was struck by the softness of her skin, and he willed himself to ignore the perfumed sweetness that rose up from her person to ensnare him. He had known women far more beautiful than this odd, dark-tressed creature, but something about the woman reached deep into his black soul and touched his heart in a way he did not understand and, most assuredly, did not want.

She met his eyes. Another woman would have recognized the moment and used her feminine charms to dissuade him from his purpose. At the very least, he would have seen a spark of recognition that they were a man and a woman alone together with all the possibilities such a combination entailed.

Not Dakota Wylie. He saw fear in the ebony depths of her eyes, and he saw something else, as well: a strength of character—a sense of resolve—that he had believed to be solely the province of men. For a moment he hesitated. He had lived so long amidst liars that perhaps he had lost the ability to recognize truth when he heard it spoken. Was it possible she was indeed the grieving widow of her story, a good wife with a heart that yearned for the husband she had lost to the capricious whims of fate?

Or had he finally lost his mind?

12

They said position in life was everything, and for the first time in her life Dakota agreed. The world looked entirely different from her position underneath Patrick Devane.

One minute she'd been striding toward the door, Lucy in her hand, and the next she was on the feather bed and Lucy was lying near the door. It occurred to her that maybe she should have put up some kind of struggle, that surrender really wasn't a viable option for a twentieth-century woman, not even one who'd found herself living and breathing in 1779. She was smart enough to know better, but there was something deeply pleasurable about the idea, something dark and dangerous and so compelling that twenty-six years of independent thought were in danger of going up in a haze of erotic smoke.

He cupped her face in his hands. "How long has it been, Dakota Wylie, since a man held you like this?"

All my life, she thought. No one had ever looked at her with such intensity before, as if he could see her heart beating beneath her skin. Drawing in a breath became a supreme act of will.

He stroked her cheek with the pad of his thumb. His fingers were callused from riding. The roughened skin sent a thrill of excitement rippling up her spine and she shivered involuntarily. She met his eyes but could read nothing in his expression.

"Don't," she whispered, sounding painfully vulnerable to her own ears. She heard the loneliness beneath the words, the aching need, and she closed her eyes, praying he wouldn't know the effect his touch was having upon her.

"Be still," he said, spreading his hands along the base of her throat, her collarbones. "You are a woman. You need the touch of a man."

Inflammatory sexist claptrap, she thought, but sadly— painfully—true. His touch made her feel dizzy, as if she'd climbed to the top of the tallest tree and was falling, falling through sweet green leaves.

"Beautiful eyes," he murmured, caressing her shoulders, her upper arms. "I have never seen a color such as that before."

"It's called brown," she said, trying to remember that this wasn't real. He wasn't her friend and he wasn't her lover. He wasn't anything to her but the man who stood between her and the world she'd left behind. If she believed it was real for even a moment, she would be lost.

"Midnight black," he said. "Dark as ebony."

"Ebony?" She had to be dreaming. Didn't he know she wasn't the kind of woman a man whispered insincere compliments to?

"It is as if you hear the words for the first time," he mused, cupping her elbows in a way that was illegal, or should be. "Your husband must have told you these things."

She struggled to remember her fictional husband, old what's-his-name. "H-he was a man of few words."

Those few words had barely escaped her lips when he lowered his head, bringing his mouth closer to hers, then closer still. He had a beautiful mouth, full and perfectly formed. She couldn't believe that mouth was only inches away from hers.

"No more words," he said, eyes glittering dangerously.

"But—"

He claimed her mouth as if she'd given him the right, as if everything that had ever happened in her life had given him that right. His touch was gentle at first, his lips moving against hers with a subtle, coaxing motion that weakened what remained of her defenses. She exhaled on a long sigh and as her lips parted, he deepened the kiss.

Nothing mattered but the feel of his mouth on hers. He tasted of oranges and cherry tobacco and some sweet, sweet narcotic that was slipping into her bloodstream in a flood of heat, making her forget how she had come to be there in his arms.

She yielded to him with an eagerness that was almost his undoing. He grew hard and he made no attempt to disguise the desire he felt for her. Everything about her person pleased him. Her soft skin. The scent of flowers that surrounded her. The gentle curves of her woman's body as she lay beneath him. He could imagine her naked, skin gleaming in the firelight, as she welcomed him into the haven of her arms.

Were she not a liar and a spy sent to thwart his cause, he might have pressed his advantage, but Patrick Devane had had enough prevarication to last him his lifetime. He had made a costly mistake with Susannah. He would not make another one now when there was so much to lose.

"The grieving widow," he murmured, breaking the kiss. "I think it is not for your husband that you grieve, madam. I think it is for your freedom."

Her ebony eyes fluttered open and she met his gaze with a forthrightness that once again surprised him. "I—I don't know what you're talking about."

He kissed her again, hard and long, and she arched against him. "That is not the response of a good wife who mourns the passing of her husband."

"You know nothing of my response," she snapped in a voice of surprising vigor. "A man who must entrap a woman for his own amusement is not one to judge the quality of a kiss."

Had he imagined the heat of her response? There was nothing of the supplicant in either her voice or manner.

Irritated, he gathered her wrists in one hand and pinned them over her head. He placed his other hand at her throat where her pulse beat heavily against his palm.

"There is no dead husband, is there, *Mistress* Wylie? No beloved companions whose loss you mourn."

"I have told you my intentions," she said, neither flinching nor looking away. "As soon as the storm ends, I will be on my way to find my friends."

"And I will find the truth," he warned, his grip on her wrists tightening. "Better to unburden yourself now than to risk my anger later on."

"How courageous," she said, her tone heavy with irony. "You threaten a *mere* woman but refuse to take up arms against the enemy." Her eyes narrowed as she looked ever deeper into his soul. "Or is it that you're having trouble deciding which side you're on?"

So that's *a glower,* Dakota thought as his expression darkened. She'd always wanted to see one somewhere besides a comic strip. The man had a quicksilver temper. Sooner or later he was going to explode like Mount St. Helens, and she didn't want to be around when it happened.

He straddled her, knees pressing against her hips. She wondered if he'd believe she padded her petticoats the same way she boosted her bodice. She didn't know whether to laugh or cry. To think she'd believed for even one second that they had some chemistry going between them. He was about as attracted to her as she was to "Beavis and Butthead," and it was time she remembered that.

"Get off me!" she ordered.

"Tell me the names of the friends for whom you search and I'll do as you ask."

"I already told you their names."

"I grow forgetful. Tell me again."

She could do what she did the last time, toss out the names Ronald and Nancy Reagan and be done with it, but she no longer felt either flip or funny. Andrew and Shannon were out there somewhere in that storm and she knew if she didn't find them soon, she'd be trapped there forever.

She could be walking straight into the jaws of a trap, but it was a risk she had to take.

"Whitney," she said after a moment. "Shannon Whitney."

" 'Tis an odd name."

Not where I come from. "She is traveling with a man named Andrew." If Devane's dubious loyalties lay with the British, betraying Andrew McVie's identity could compromise his safety, and Shannon's, as well. "I do not know his family name."

"He is your friend and yet you do not know his full name?"

"Shannon is my friend. Andrew is her companion." She struggled for the properly archaic way to express herself. "I have only recently made his acquaintanceship."

"Andrew." He seemed thoughtful, almost pensive. "No," he said, more to himself than to her. "It is not possible."

"What is not possible?" she asked, almost afraid to hear the answer.

He parried with a question of his own. "This Andrew you speak of—what is his association with Shannon Whitney?"

"They're lovers, not that it's any of your business."

To her amazement, his cheeks reddened and she was reminded once again of the differences between her world and his. *So you're human after all,* she thought. Who would have imagined a man like Patrick Devane had sensibilities? Her innocent words must have sounded shockingly blunt to him, and she couldn't quite hide her smile.

"You find humor in the situation?" he asked.

"Yes," she said, meeting his eyes. "I'm afraid I do."

Their gazes held while the room did a slow fade until there was nothing but the big feather bed and the ragged sound of their breathing.

"You are a puzzle to me, madam. I know beyond doubt that you weave a fabric of lies, but still I find myself unable to determine clearly if you are friend or foe."

"I am neither," she said, her voice husky. She tried to ignore the way his big strong body felt covering hers. "I'm nothing to you at all. Once I leave here, you'll never see me again."

His expression softened and he touched her cheek in a spontaneous gesture unlike the calculated kisses and caresses of moments ago. She felt as if he'd somehow reached into her heart and discovered a place no one knew existed, the secret place where she kept her dreams. His hold on her wrists loosened, until it was more caress than bondage and she wondered if—

"Papa, is it true?" Abigail's voice shattered the spell.

They both jumped, startled to find the little girl standing in the open doorway with a tattered Lucy clutched to her chest. Her eyes were huge in her narrow face as she stared at the sight of her father and Dakota entwined on the feather bed.

Devane rose easily from the bed as if his daughter found him lying on top of a woman every day of the week. No doubt about it, the man was one cool customer. Dakota, on the other hand, felt as if she'd been caught swinging naked from a chandelier. She couldn't have felt guiltier if they'd actually been doing something—which they hadn't been, but that fact somehow seemed beside the point.

She sat up and tugged at the bodice of her gown, praying the rolled-up sleeves of her dinosaur T-shirt didn't choose that moment to make an appearance. That would really put a lid on what was turning out to be the weirdest day of her life.

Devane stood in front of his daughter. His back was ramrod straight, in marked contrast to the rumpled look of his shirt and waistcoat.

"How long have you been standing there, Abigail?" he asked the child.

If Dakota hadn't known better, she'd have thought he was talking to a stranger rather than his own flesh and blood.

"I saw you kissing her," Abigail said with the alarming directness most kids lost around puberty. The child approached the bed where Dakota sat with her feet on the floor and her hands primly folded on her lap. "Cook says you're my new mama."

Dakota felt as if she'd been hit in the stomach with a two-by-four. She looked toward Devane, whose face had gone ashen. His spur-of-the-moment statement to the young soldier had come back to haunt them both. Why hadn't Devane realized the impact it would have upon his daughter?

"You can answer this one," she said to him, thankful for the opportunity to pass the buck.

"Did Cook say anything else to you, Abigail?" he asked in that same maddeningly bland tone of voice.

"She said it was time that a woman warmed your bed. But I told her grandmama's quilt was in the—"

"Oh, God..." Dakota sank back onto the mattress and wished she could disappear beneath the covers.

Abigail's steady gaze pierced her heart. "Is that why you and Papa were lying here together, to warm the bed?"

Dakota could count on the fingers of one hand the times she'd been struck speechless. The glib remarks that usually flowed from her lips like mineral water at a trendy restaurant dried up and disappeared. She wasn't given to saccharine displays of affection toward children, but there was something about the little girl that inspired the oddest emotions. She didn't particularly like kids, but she wanted to gather this one into her arms and make her smile. Go figure.

Abigail climbed up onto the bed and looked Dakota in the eye. "Tell me!" she demanded in her childish voice. "Are you my new mama?"

Dakota met Devane's eyes. The warm fire she'd noticed before in their indigo depths had been extinguished. His expression was as cold as the bitter winter winds that rattled the windows and whistled down the chimneys.

What do I do? she pleaded silently. *How can we lie to her about this?*

He nodded curtly, a quick dip of the head, and her heart sank. He actually expected her to say something to Abigail. But what?

She tried to speak but the words wouldn't come. They were trapped behind a wall of regret so high and wide she wondered if she would ever be able to break through.

She cleared her throat, praying that whatever she said wouldn't hurt the child any more than life had already hurt her.

"Your papa and I—"

"Yes," Devane broke in, reaching for Dakota's hand and clasping it in his. "Dakota is your new mother." He paused, meeting Dakota's eyes with a glance that warned her not to disagree.

Abigail's light brown brows slanted toward the bridge of her tiny nose.

Smart kid, thought Dakota, squirming beneath the weight of the child's scrutiny. *I wouldn't believe this bilge water, either.*

The child spoke up again. "Cook says she'll make a wedding dinner or know the reason why."

"No!" Dakota suddenly found her voice. Both Devane and his daughter looked at her in surprise. No wonder. She probably sounded as horrified as she felt. "These are difficult times," she explained swiftly. "Certainly a big party would not be proper in light of the hardships we are all facing from the enemy."

Abigail's braids bobbed as she shook her head vigorously. "Cook says all the best houses have parties." She lowered her voice to a mock whisper. "Cook says it will be scand'lous if you do not."

"Maybe Cook should mind her own business," Dakota muttered sourly. "This place is worse than 'Knots Landing.'"

Patrick's attention was snared by her words. Knots Landing. He wondered if that was near to Philadelphia. It was the first true nugget of information Dakota had provided for him, although he was certain she did not realize he had heard her words. He would peruse his maps of the colonies later on and see if he could find the town.

"Go downstairs, Abigail," he said, dismissing the child.

"No." Her lower lip protruded much as Susannah's had when she didn't get her way.

"You will do as I say."

"I want to stay here." A dangerous glint flickered in her eyes, as if a storm were gathering in the gray depths.

"Abigail, you will—"

Dakota reached for the child's hand. "Why don't you go downstairs and ask Cook for needle and thread," she suggested in an even tone of voice. "I have figured out the perfect way to repair Lucy and I can't find your mama's sewing basket anywhere."

"But I told you where it is," Abigail protested. "In Papa's cabinet."

Dakota shot him a fierce look of triumph. "I looked where you told me to look, Abby, but it wasn't there."

"It is!" Abigail started toward the chest of drawers, but Patrick placed a hand on the child's fragile shoulder.

"Go downstairs," he said, aware of Dakota's steady gaze upon him. "I will find the bloody sewing basket myself."

Still the child stood there, tiny feet planted like the roots of an oak tree. *I was stubborn like that once, as well,* he mused, then banished the thought for the foolishness it was.

Dakota turned from him and spoke to the child. Abigail nodded, then, with nary a look in his direction, ran from the room.

"Children respond to kindness," Dakota said. "It's probably an alien concept to you, but you might want to try it some time."

"Refrain from giving advice on child-rearing, madam," he said, "until you have attempted such yourself."

Her cheeks reddened at his words. "I don't need to be a parent to know what a child needs to be happy."

"And where did you acquire such profound knowledge?"

"I have a brain." Her implication was quite clear.

"Speak your mind, madam," he invited dryly. "Do you mean to say I lack the same?"

"No," she said, "you have a brain. What you don't have is a heart."

"And upon what do you base your observations," he asked, "when you have known me less than one full day?"

"Have you looked at your daughter's face?" she asked, her anger a third presence in the room. "She adores you and you cannot give her the time of day."

"She is well cared for," he said, wondering why he found it necessary to explain himself to a stranger. "When the storm ends, she will leave for Boston—"

"Where she will be somebody else's problem."

"Where she will receive an education."

"You can lie to me all you want, Mr. Devane—I really don't give a damn—but don't lie to yourself. You're too smart for that and she's too important."

He grabbed her by the shoulders and pulled her up until she was kneeling on the soft feather mattress. She used the language of a man to make her point, with little regard either for his sensibilities or her own. It should not have excited him—but it did.

"What business is it of yours, madam?" he demanded, his fingers pressing deep into the soft flesh of her shoulders. "What care you if I love the child or curse her existence, so long as she is not ill-used?"

Tears pooled in her dark eyes, then spilled down her smooth cheeks. "She loves you so. Doesn't that matter to you?"

"No," he said, remembering how it had been in the days before he'd learned the truth of the child's paternity. "It no longer matters at all."

13

"What a terrible—" Dakota stopped in midsentence as the vision rose up before her, clear as the view outside the window.

The room was in shadows. Muslin curtains had been drawn across the wide, leaded-glass windows, but the faintest rays of dawn were beginning to seep through the loosely woven material. From the kitchen came the spicy, sweet smell of apples cooking for breakfast. The pine cradle rested next to the big feather bed, piled high with quilts and knitted coverlets in soft whites and blues.

Inside the cradle the baby slept, her eyes pressed tightly closed against the coming of morn. She had a thick head of silky light brown hair and fingers that were surprisingly long and graceful for someone less than one month old.

But it was the man who drew Dakota's eye. He was bent over the cradle, his tall, strong form looking absurdly masculine in the gentle room as he looked down upon the sleeping child.

How he loved her!

Emotion flooded the darkest corners of his heart with golden light. He would fight lions with his bare hands to keep her safe from harm. Lasso the stars and hang them from the ceiling to make her laugh.

She was every good thing he'd ever done, every dream he'd ever dreamed but didn't believe would come true. She was his miracle.

She was his daughter....

Dakota opened her eyes and found herself cradled against Devane's strong chest. He was looking down at her, an expression of concern on his normally unreadable face.

She felt disoriented and strangely sad, as if she'd awakened from a dream she couldn't quite remember. "Wh-what happened?" she asked, pushing away from him as she struggled to regain her composure.

"I hoped you would tell me, madam."

"I didn't faint, did I?" She'd fainted all the time around Andrew McVie; his force field had been that strong.

"You swooned," he said in a careful voice. "Is that a common occurrence?"

She snapped her fingers in a nonchalant gesture that was at odds with the turbulent emotions raging inside her chest. "I do it all the time."

"There is no cause for alarm?"

"Not the slightest."

"You are not with child?"

She almost choked on her own saliva. "Absolutely not!"

He arched a brow. "You are a married woman," he noted.

"I'm a widow," she corrected him.

"Mayhap your stays are too tightly laced."

"Mayhap you should mind your own business." She glared at him. "Are you implying that I'm fat?" she asked, paranoid to the end.

"I did not say those words."

"Maybe not, but you thought them."

A damnable twinkle appeared in his deep blue eyes. "And you are privy to my innermost thoughts, madam?"

"Wouldn't you love to know," she muttered darkly.

"Is it so unusual for a lady to overzealously tighten her stays in the interest of vanity?"

She hesitated, once again reminded how different this world was from the one where she belonged. Back home they did it with Lycra spandex and step aerobics.

"Strange, madam." He moved closer to her. "There are times it seems as if you see the world for the first time."

"It's part of my charm."

"I had not thought of it thusly."

She gathered the tatters of her dignity around her and stood. "This interlude has been charming, Mr. Devane, but I'm afraid it's time I went back downstairs to help Abigail repair her doll."

"You are a kind and generous woman."

"Yes," she said, favoring him with a quick smile. "I'm glad you noticed."

His dark-eyed gaze swept over her body, igniting small fires everywhere it lingered...and a few places where it didn't. "There are other things I have noticed, as well."

"Your daughter isn't one of them." The words were out before she could stop them.

"Confine yourself to mending, madam. I will care for the child."

"Did you hear what Abby said?" Dakota demanded, meeting his eyes. She hadn't intended to broach the topic, but now that she had there was no stopping her. "The whole town is talking about us and I haven't even been here a full day."

"Amazing," he said dryly. "I would have ventured it had been much longer."

"Insult me all you want," she said, stung by his words, "but that doesn't change things. You've put your daughter in the middle of a mess and I want to know what you're going to do about it."

She didn't give a damn for herself—as soon as she found Andrew and Shannon and the hot-air balloon she would be on her way home again—but for some reason she cared greatly for Abigail. There were few enough ways in which a girl could make her mark in the eighteenth century. She didn't want scandal to be the way that was thrust upon Abby.

"'Tis of little consequence," Devane said in a voice that betrayed nothing of what he was feeling. "I have seen most of the Commandments broken by the good people of Franklin Ridge. Their opinions carry no weight in this house."

"Apparently they carry a great deal of weight with some people in this house."

"Cook has a marked affinity for the grape," Devane said, dismissing her concerns. "She speaks when she should be tending her fires."

"And she speaks to your daughter," Dakota snapped. "This ridiculous charade has gone entirely too far. If you don't tell her we're really not married, so help me, I'll do it myself."

"Do so, madam, and I will see to it you spend this night in jail."

"For telling the truth?"

"For being a spy."

Her breath left her body in a sibilant whoosh. "You're joking, aren't you?" she demanded when she could breathe again. "Me? A *spy?*" A bark of hysterical laughter echoed in the high-ceilinged room. "I'm the one who didn't even know what town she was in."

"A clever ruse," he said. "Like the sorrowful story of your widowhood."

"You're a cruel man," she observed, "delighting in the misfortunes of others."

"And you, madam, are a liar."

Patrick watched as she swept from the room as quickly as her full skirts would allow. It was obvious she wished to put

as much distance as possible between them, and he was relieved.

The wench was willful, argumentative and ungrateful,
and still she had managed to awaken inside his breast emotions he had thought long dead. He had believed himself
long past tenderness and compassion but when she had lain
unconscious in his arms he had experienced a surge of fear
that lingered with him still.

Why he should care about the well-being of a woman he
had known for less than twenty-four hours was a question
for which he had no answer, and he vowed to waste no time
pondering such things. He was a man and it had been a long
time since he had held a woman close. That was reason
enough.

The child, however, was another matter. Dakota Wylie
was right to be concerned for Abigail's standing in the town.
He did not love her for she was not his own and never could
be, but he understood the ways in which scandal could mark
her future, and he wished better for the chit.

She was the only true innocent in the whole unfortunate
matter of his marriage to Susannah. Even if he could not
find it in his heart to love her, he owed Abigail a future of
promise as befitted a man of his position, which was all the
more reason to see to it she reached the Girls' School of the
Sacred Heart as soon as possible.

He had little respect for the convenient morals of the good
people of Franklin Ridge.

How they loved to cluck their tongues in righteous disapproval over an eight months' baby . . . or the affairs of a
wayward wife. He had suffered the smug glances dripping
with amusement and pity and vowed that the opinion of
others would never matter to him again.

But her opinion matters, a voice inside his head mocked.
You desire her approval more than is wise.

The thought was laughable. Patrick Devane didn't give a
damn about anyone's approval. Certainly not the approval

of a woman whose lies were as blatant and poorly conceived as Dakota Wylie's. Each time he pressed her for the details of her situation, she grew flustered, then angry, and the centerpiece of her story shifted position like a willow tree in a windstorm.

Why that should endear her to him was a question Patrick did not wish to pursue. He had no patience with liars and no faith in women and she was both. Yet each time he looked into her onyx black eyes he felt something deep inside his soul stir with recognition, as if he had been searching for her his whole life long.

Damn nonsense, he thought as he caught the faintest scent of her perfume in the air. He wanted naught from her save answers to his questions. The mythical dead husband. The friends she longed to find. Where in bloody hell Knots Landing was situated and why the women of that town had strange names like Dakota and Shannon—

Andrew.

His gut tightened. She had said one of her companions' names was Andrew and that she did not know his surname.

Some say 'twas Andrew McVie dangling from the basket of the bright red ball in the sky....

And all of this had happened on the day he found Dakota Wylie under a pile of leaves.

"Damn nonsense," he said again as his heartbeat accelerated. McVie was dead. Why else would the risk-taking patriot have vanished so completely? Besides, the notion of a basket propelled through the air by a huge red ball was too laughable to countenance. There had been rumors of such monstrosities being constructed by the French, but all such attempts had ended in disaster.

Still, the coincidence of events made him uneasy and he vowed to keep a sharp eye upon Dakota Wylie while she was under his roof.

Which should be an easy task, since she was living there as his wife.

* * *

As the afternoon wore on, Dakota had the distinct feeling that time as she knew it had slowed and she was living many lifetimes in the space of a day. It was an odd feeling, as if time were trying to help her grow accustomed to her new way of life. She found herself acutely aware of her surroundings, senses heightened to the point of pain, as she drank in the details of eighteenth-century daily living.

And the fact that Abby thought she was her new mother.

They sat together near the fireplace in the front room while Dakota struggled with needle and floss. It had taken her a full five minutes to thread the damn needle. She wondered if they had a colonial Lenscrafter nearby. At the moment poor Lucy's chances for a full recovery were looking as grim as any guest-wife for the Cartwright boys on "Bonanza" reruns.

Great analogy, she thought, stabbing the doll's innards with the needle. Too bad there wasn't anyone around who'd know what she was talking about.

"Do you love Papa?" Abigail asked out of the blue.

Dakota stabbed her finger with the needle. A tiny drop of blood pooled on the tip and she popped it into her mouth. "What a question!" she said, forcing a small chuckle.

"Yesterday in the woods you didn't like him at all."

"Well," said Dakota slowly, "things have a way of changing, don't they?"

"I thought Papa lied when he told the soldiers we were a family."

Dakota swallowed hard. "I—I do not think he meant to share that fact with them, but the circumstances were such that—"

"Did you know I was your daughter when you first saw me?" the child interrupted, eager to move on to a more important topic.

Her heart lurched. She blamed it on major jet lag. "No, Abby, I didn't."

"You didn't like me."

"I didn't know you."

"I didn't like you."

Dakota grinned. She couldn't help it. The kid was so damned honest it was either grin or throttle her. "I didn't much like you, either," she admitted.

Abby nodded solemnly. "I know. You thought I was plain."

"I never said—" She stopped, cheeks turning red with embarrassment. "You heard it in here, didn't you?" she asked, placing her hand over her heart.

"Yes," said Abby. "And you thought Papa was going to kill you."

"He was very angry."

"Why would you be afraid of Papa if he was your husband?"

The kid would be a whiz at Twenty Questions. "Because even married people have arguments."

Abby considered her statement with all the gravity it deserved. "Papa doesn't like you."

"We had a disagreement," Dakota went on, stung by the innocent words. "It will end soon." *Like the moment I walk out the door.*

"You can't walk out the door," Abby said in a prim and singsong voice. "'Tis snowing harder even than before. Papa won't be able to send me to Boston for a very long time."

The child looked smug and proud of herself, as if she had called down the storm to suit her own needs. Who knows? Dakota thought. Maybe she had. Anything seemed possible.

She carefully placed two stitches along Lucy's right underarm seam. She couldn't control her thoughts, but she could control what came out of her mouth. It occurred to her that this was as good a time as any to begin laying the groundwork for the dissolution of her faux marriage.

"You know, Abby," she began as she tied off the end of the floss, "sometimes a marriage does not last forever."

"Mama and Papa were going to get a divorce," the child said sagely, "but Mama died."

Dakota couldn't hide her surprise. She was sorry the little girl knew so much. "Sometimes men and women believe they can live together but find it to be much harder than they thought."

"Reverend Wilcox says marriages are made in heaven and that God says they are forever."

Dakota thought of a number of things to say but they were all too blasphemous for the child's ears. She settled for a simple, "Nothing is forever, honey."

"You are," said the child. "You and Papa will be together forever and ever."

She's right, Dakota. Her mother Ginny's voice seemed to fill her chest with sound. *You finally met Mr. Right.*

Dakota almost laughed out loud. They had nothing in common, not even the century in which they lived. This place, this man's house wasn't where she was meant to be. It was no more than the paranormal equivalent of changing planes at O'Hare: complicated, a little dangerous and forgotten as soon as you got home.

But you'll never forget this, her heart whispered. Not that sad-eyed little girl with a head full of dreams she couldn't quite understand. And not the angry man who had held Dakota in his arms and kissed her the way no man had ever kissed her before or ever would again.

The farm

The sun rose and still Zane and Josiah did not return.

Neither Emilie nor Rebekah said anything about that fact as they fed their children steaming bowls of oatmeal and tended to the hearth fire and did the thousand other chores necessary to keep a home in proper running order.

They are safe, Emilie, Rebekah's look said across the bustling kitchen. *Put your trust in the Almighty and you will not be disappointed.*

But Emilie didn't have Rebekah's faith. All she had was a dark sense of foreboding that settled across her shoulders like a mantle of lead. There was so much Rebekah didn't know, so much Emilie had never told her.

So many times she had wanted to tell her friend the truth, but the words always died in her throat. How could she expect Rebekah to believe that the couple she had taken under her wing in the summer of 1776 had traveled across the centuries to be there?

Besides, the twentieth century was nothing but a distant dream to Emilie now. There was nothing there she wanted, nothing there she missed. Everything she valued in the world existed in this time and place.

But what if there was a way to go back? a small voice asked as she cleaned oatmeal from her daughter's chubby hands. *Think of how much more you could give them in the twentieth century.*

"No," she whispered fiercely. "Never!"

Sara Jane looked up at her, bright blue eyes wide with question. Emilie kissed the child's fingers as her heart thundered inside her chest.

She wouldn't go back, not even if the balloon landed right there on the front porch and promised she could pick up her life exactly where she'd left off, but this time with her husband and family by her side. She was part of something important here. Not only did she contribute to the cause of freedom with her work for the spy ring, she was part of a real community of people who understood the importance of liberty in a way her world of the twentieth century had long forgotten. She wanted this world for her children. She wanted them to grow up without drive-by shootings and crack dealers and the bone-deep pessimism that permeated every corner of life in the 1990s.

But what about Zane? that small voice continued. *Are you sure he'd feel the same way?*

It was one thing to make the best of an odd situation. It was another thing to embrace it, knowing there was a means of escape. He'd wanted to leave from the very beginning. She remembered the morning the balloon had appeared by the lighthouse, how she'd believed that he would leave her and return to the world they'd left behind. Did he ever regret his decision? she wondered. What would he do if he had a second chance?

The cloud formation was fainter than yesterday, but it was still there. She thanked God there was no sign of the hot-air balloon, but she knew in her heart that it was only a matter of time before it appeared. She had to find Zane before it was too late, before fate made the choice for both of them.

"Papa!" Andy pointed toward the hallway. "Papa home."

"Listen," said Rebekah, a bright smile wreathing her tired face. "Footsteps! They're back."

Emilie leapt to her feet and ran into the hallway.

"G'mornin', Emilie." Timothy Crosse, Rebekah's son-in-law, stood in the hallway knocking snow from the soles of his boots. "Got that flour you ladies been askin' for, and at a fair price, too. Hope that means you'll be makin' some of your biscuits."

"Zane and Josiah," she said, grabbing him by the lapels of his jacket. "They went out last night and haven't come back yet. Have you seen them?" She didn't care if Timothy thought they'd gone out whoring. She just wanted an answer.

"Ain't seen either one," Timothy said, "not since t'other day near the church. Lots of snow out there, Em. Reckon they're findin' it real hard to get home." His cheeks reddened as he obviously thought of another reason that two men wouldn't make it home at night. "Wouldn't be any real cause t' worry."

She drew in a deep breath and brushed snow from the young man's hair. "You must be freezing," she said. "Why don't you have some hot cider? Rebekah made corn bread this morning and it was grand."

"Don't mind if I do," Timothy said, obviously glad the topic of conversation had shifted to corn bread. "Big commotion north of Franklin Ridge," he said as he followed her into the kitchen. "Say the Redcoats caught themselves a big red ball that floated over the trees."

The blood pounded so hard in Emilie's ears that she could barely make out Timothy's words. *No! Please, God, no!*

"A big red ball floating over the treetops?" Rebekah laughed as she poured a cup of cider for her son-in-law. "Sounds to me like the stores of rum are fast being depleted in Franklin Ridge."

"They swear up and down 'tis true," Timothy went on, taking the cider from Rebekah with a nod of acknowledgment. "Even went so far as to say there were people floating with it."

"People?" Emilie couldn't keep the sharp note of fear from her voice. "Who?"

Timothy eyed her curiously. So did Rebekah. Emilie refused to meet her friend's eyes.

"Some say a man and a woman," Timothy ventured, obviously uncomfortable. "Some say two women."

Rebekah threw back her head and laughed. "The day we fly like birds over the trees is the day you can bury me six feet deep. Such nonsense!"

Timothy laughed as well, but Emilie didn't. It wasn't nonsense, not even close, but how could she expect her eighteenth-century counterparts to understand that? The advent of hot-air ballooning wouldn't dawn for another few years, and then it would be in France.

Not New Jersey.

Not today.

"Would you excuse me?" Emilie said, struggling to sound matter-of-fact. "I have to fetch my knitting."

"Emilie?" Rebekah forced Emilie to meet her eyes. "Is something wrong?"

"Just tired, 'Bekah. I don't sleep well when Zane isn't home."

Rebekah nodded, but Emilie knew her friend suspected something. *I'd tell you if I could, 'Bekah,* she thought as she hurried from the kitchen, *but you'd never believe me.*

Emilie grabbed her cloak and gloves from the peg near the front door. Her boots waited on the front porch. Quietly she slid open the drawer to the secretary she shared with Rebekah and removed a sheet of parchment. She dipped the quill into the inkwell and penned a note to her dearest friend.

Rebekah was the finest woman Emilie had ever known. If something happened to her and Zane, the children would be left in kind and loving hands.

She rested the note on top of Rebekah's sewing basket, then retrieved the small felt pouch of gold coins from her own basket, beneath her embroidery tools. Her heart ached with longing to kiss her children, but that would feel too much like goodbye.

And this *wasn't* goodbye. She refused to even consider that possibility.

She slipped from the house and, minutes later, guided Timothy's horse-drawn cart down the snowy lane toward Franklin Ridge.

14

It seemed to Patrick as he rode toward the meeting place near Jockey Hollow that the Almighty had conspired to test him to the very limits of his endurance.

Snow fell with unceasing fury, blinding his vision and making it difficult for his horse to gain purchase on the slippery ground. His heavy woolen coat did little to shield him from the bitter winds or from the harsh bite of his conscience. He told himself that it was for the greater good that he stayed safe and well-fed while others fought the enemy, but on days like this he found it difficult to live within his own skin.

Rutledge and Blakelee had been taken prisoner by the British, and it was Patrick who bore the blame in the eyes of the world.

Word of Patrick's treachery had already reached Franklin Ridge, and the chilly smiles of the townspeople he passed had frozen solid as the icy ponds. The Continental army teetered on the verge of collapse, and he sensed deep in the black emptiness of his soul that the worst was yet to come.

The thought was horrific enough to almost make him laugh. Indeed, how much worse could matters get? Already a new pair of boots commanded more than many farmers earned in a year. The cost of a new horse would support ten families. Did no one else see the excess that threatened the framework of the Revolution? Did no one else care?

He found the righteous anger of the townspeople amusing. How many of them were willing to risk their own comfort to aid the patriots about whom they wept? Quick to weep false tears and condemn all and sundry for imagined misdeeds, nary a citizen of Franklin Ridge saw fit to step forward and offer assistance.

His anger increased with each mile he traveled. The thick woods north of town were being chopped down, the logs dragged to the encampments to be used to build huts that would house the enlisted men. He wondered how it was that General Washington had managed to keep them from breaking rank and fleeing back to their farms and families in the face of almost certain annihilation at the hands of the Redcoats. And he wondered if it would ultimately be worth the sacrifice.

Death was everywhere. He saw it every day in the tear-stained faces of the men and women left behind. He smelled it in the air, heard it in the crack of rifle shots echoing through the dark night.

And all for a cause that might already be lost.

"What are we going to do?" Cook demanded of Dakota as General McDowell's men set up cots in the parlor and the dining room.

"I don't know," Dakota said. "Do they have the right to take over like this?" Of course, she knew the answer to that. They had every right in the world. This was war and the normal rules of society didn't matter.

"The mister is going to be mad as a hatter." Cook poked the rising lump of bread dough with an angry forefinger. "Joseph heard one of them say the general wants the library for a meeting room."

"Not the library!" Dakota exclaimed. How could she get her hands on that list of names if the place was knee-deep in soldiers?

"That's what I told him," Cook said, high color staining her cheeks, "but he wouldn't listen to the likes of me." She tilted her head in the direction of the library. "But he'd listen to you."

"Me?" Dakota made a face. "Why on earth would the general listen to me?"

"You're the lady of the house," Cook said, eyebrows raised all the way up to her mobcap.

"I'm the lady of the house?" Dakota muttered as she strode toward the library. She didn't feel like the lady of the house. She felt like exactly what she was: a woman looking for a way out.

She prayed General McDowell was a trusting sort, because she wasn't sure she could pull it off.

The general turned out to be charming, attentive and understanding—all the things Devane was not—but, unfortunately, he also had a will of iron.

"I understand your concerns, madam," he said in a lazy voice that had more than a touch of London nibbling around the edges, "and I would like to address them with your husband, if I may. Patrick and I are friends of long standing." He made a show of glancing about the room. "And where might the good fellow be?"

Beats me, she thought, offering him a demure, poor-little-me smile. The last time she'd seen Devane, he'd been stomping his way down the hall, looking ready to do battle with the world. "Cook informed me that my husband has gone for a ride."

"Madam, there is a full foot of snow in the hills and more coming. Now, I know Patrick is a most physical fellow—I can remember him riding to hounds on the most ungodly day—but you must admit that, even for so hale a fellow as your dear new husband, this is hardly riding weather."

Look, bozo, what do you want from me? All I know is that he's gone. She deepened her dimple, praying she wouldn't burst out laughing at the absurdity of the whole situation. "My husband cares not about the weather."

"And what pressing engagement tears him from the side of his new bride?" It was said with a wink, but Dakota sensed more than passing curiosity behind the question. Who could blame him? Few grooms would prefer a blizzard to their bride.

She lowered her eyes, the demure and blushing new wife plotting her next lie. "My husband has his concerns," she said sweetly, "as I have mine—to make him happy."

McDowell nodded, a benevolent smile on his face. "The way it should be, madam. The issue of the library will wait awhile longer."

Unbelievable, she thought in amazement. Either men had gotten a lot smarter by the twentieth century or she'd missed out on something big time. Were they all this easy to manipulate, or had she stumbled across a particularly malleable bunch?

She realized he was still talking.

". . . to celebrate your marriage."

Her smile widened. "How wonderful!" She hadn't the foggiest idea what he was talking about but unless someone had just suggested a trip to the guillotine, "how wonderful" usually did the trick. Maybe a career in diplomacy wasn't that farfetched after all.

She floated back to the kitchen on a wave of self-congratulations.

"Praise be!" Cook turned away from the hearth and beamed at Dakota. "He'll let the mister keep his library."

"He didn't actually promise anything," she said, peering into the soup pot, then back at Cook, "but he did say he'll postpone moving his gear into it. At least until he talks to Dev—I mean, to my husband."

"And a fine mood the mister will be in when he comes home," Cook said with a shake of her head. "We'll be thinkin' the war is being fought right here in the house."

"Yes," Dakota said, recognizing an opening when she heard one. "My husband is certainly very...particular about his home, isn't he?"

Cook tossed some cubes of turnip into the soup pot, then wiped her hands on the rough fabric of her apron. "Won't let a body into that library unless he's standin' there like St. Peter at the gates of heaven, watchin' everything that goes on."

"He does love his books." Dakota snatched a piece of warm bread from the pine table where it had been cooling.

"Books!" Cook pursed her lips as if she'd been sucking on a lemon. "If you ask me, it's not the books he's worryin' about."

"Hmm," said Dakota, feigning uninterest as she chewed her bread.

"Rosie said she thought he had gold hidden away in there, but I don't think it's gold. I think he's a sp—" The woman stopped midword.

Spy, Dakota thought. *You think he's a spy, too!*

"Beggin' your pardon, ma'am." Cook's ruddy cheeks burned hotter. "Joseph always says I talk before I think."

"You need not apologize to me," Dakota said. Of all times for the woman to have a crisis of conscience. "You have a right to your own opinion." *And I wish you'd share it with me.*

"You won't tell Mr. Devane what I said, will you?"

"Not a word," she promised as she left the kitchen.

McDowell and his men were closeted in the library, probably exchanging wallpaper samples and planning how to redecorate. She had to admit she understood what Devane must be feeling. She was enough of a loner herself to shudder at the thought of a platoon of strangers barging into her home and getting intimate with her things.

But it was more than empathy that had her lingering near the closed door, ear pressed up against the well-polished wood. She hadn't imagined the names Rutledge and Blakelee scrawled across that piece of paper and she wasn't going to rest until she figured out what it was all about.

A buzz began in her fingertips, gentle at first then growing stronger, more insistent as it moved its way up through her hands, wrapped itself around her wrists, slid up her arms until it vibrated behind her rib cage.

Let down your defenses, honey... soften that sharp tongue... this is what you've been looking for... this is the place.

The voice drifted away and, with it, the buzzing sensation inside her chest.

"Mom?" she whispered, leaning against the closed door for support. She waited, but there was nothing except the low rumble of male voices coming from Devane's library and the sudden, inexplicable sense that she was running out of time.

The meeting place was two miles southwest of the jail where Rutledge and Blakelee had been taken, a clearing behind a farmhouse owned by a member of their spy ring.

The man who had watched Rutledge and Blakelee taken away waited for him there.

"Son of a bitch!" Patrick's fist crashed into the man's chin with a resounding crack. "What in bloody hell have you done?"

"'Twasn't my fault," the man whimpered, spitting blood onto the snow. "The Lobsterbacks come and took 'em away and there weren't a thing I could do to stop 'em, not and live to tell the tale."

"Is there more?" he demanded, shaking the man by his shoulders. "Did the soldiers say anything that might help us find Rutledge and Blakelee?"

"They said—" The man gulped as if struggling to draw air into his lungs. "They laughed when they took them, said now it be too late."

"Too late?" Patrick snapped. "Too late for what?"

"I don't know nothin'," the man wailed like a frightened child. "They wouldn't be tellin' the likes of me about a hanging."

"A hanging? Sweet Jesus, man, tell me what you know or, mark me well, you will have breathed your last."

"There's a hanging in the wind and ain't nothing going to stop it now. Not even you."

He threw the man aside, as angry with himself as with the fool.

"Surprised you care," the man went on, rubbing his elbow where it had struck the ground. "Seems like you're the one everyone be talkin' about, you and your new wife what come to town with Andrew McVie."

McVie! Once again the man's name was mentioned after years of silence. How quickly news spread in times of war. What strange events were conspiring to bring his name to everyone's lips?

"Need I remind you that McVie is dead?" he asked in a voice of deadly calm. "Or that my wife never knew the man."

"Don't know what she been tellin' you, but a score of folk near to King's Crossing say they saw two women with McVie in a flying basket and one of those women sounded like she be your new wife."

"You're daft, man," Patrick said despite the doubts that suddenly plagued him. "You partake too much of the grape."

"Ask her," the man said, meeting Patrick's eyes. "Ask her where she be t'other afternoon." The man's expression shifted from anger to pity. "Maybe you went and picked yourself the wrong gal again."

* * *

By the time Cook served supper to Dakota and Abigail in the kitchen, General McDowell and his men had taken over most of the house from cellar to attic.

"An outrage!" Cook complained as she placed a bowl of soup in front of Dakota. "You'd think they were the king's men, and not our very own soldiers, the way they've taken over. After the last time, I swore I'd be finding a new place to work rather than serve the likes of them again."

"I like the soldiers," Abigail said as she chewed a piece of buttered bread.

Dakota glanced across the table at the child. "You do?"

Abigail nodded her head vigorously. "The house doesn't seem so big with them here."

Cook snorted. "Fine for you to say, missy. It don't fall to you to keep them all fed."

In truth, it didn't fall to Cook, either. General McDowell's private chef was en route from Philadelphia and was expected to arrive by midafternoon the next day. The general had already set into motion his plans to construct the additional kitchen off the west side of the house, one that would be off-limits to Cook.

"If the mister was here, he'd tell that general a thing or two."

Dakota swallowed a sigh. "He can tell them anything he wants, but it won't change a thing. They're here and they're not going to leave." They might be fighting a war for independence but that independence didn't preclude the Continental army's right to take what it needed . . . and what it liked.

Still, it annoyed her that Devane had removed himself from the situation. He had known that General McDowell's arrival would throw the entire household into an uproar and that Cook would be unable to cope. And, to make matters worse, Cook had adopted the annoying habit of deferring all decisions to the "mistress of the house," as the woman now referred to Dakota.

They ate the rest of their meal in silence, listening to the laughter of General McDowell and his cronies as they played cards in the front room. Outside the snow continued to fall, light and relentless, and Dakota found herself wondering if Devane was out there somewhere, stranded in the storm, or if he'd decided to bail out on the lot of them and head for Tahiti.

Abigail finished the last of her apple betty, then yawned. Her eyes were heavy, and Dakota's heart did one of those funny little lurches with which she was rapidly becoming familiar. The kid was crawling under her skin and she didn't like it one bit.

"To bed," Cook said in a stern but maternal tone of voice, "and no fancy talk."

Abigail's expression shifted instantly from sleepy innocence to hot-headed anger. She tipped over the rest of her apple cider and was about to lob Dakota's leftover piece of bread at the back of Cook's head when Dakota pushed back her chair and stood. Cook was frazzled to the point of mayhem. The house was in utter chaos. The last thing any of them needed was a full-fledged temper tantrum from a six-year-old expert.

She took one of the candles that rested on the sideboard and made sure it was securely placed in its holder.

"Come on," she said, extending a hand to the child. "Let's go upstairs together."

"No!" Abigail's lower lip protruded dangerously.

"Bring Lucy with you."

Abby threw Lucy to the ground and kicked her with the toe of her leather slipper.

Cook muttered something dark and threatening, but Dakota ignored her. She bent and picked up Lucy, then placed the doll on a ledge near the door.

She held out her hand to Abigail and waited.

The little girl hesitated for a long moment, then tossed the bread down onto her plate and put her hand in Dakota's. A lump the size of eight of the thirteen colonies formed in her throat.

"What about Lucy?" Abigail asked, casting a glance toward her companion.

"Tomorrow morning," Dakota said. "You can play with her again at breakfast but tonight she stays down here." Maybe when she returned home she could do a prime-time special on alternative child care.

"Cook doesn't like me," Abigail observed as they climbed the stairs to the second floor.

"No, she doesn't today," Dakota admitted, making sure she held the candle away from her voluminous skirts, "but you didn't give her much reason to like you, did you?"

Abigail's soft brows knit together in a scowl. "What does that mean?"

They reached the landing and turned right toward Abigail's room.

"It means that you can't treat people badly and expect them to treat you with kindness."

"Like Lucy?"

Dakota suppressed a smile. "Exactly like Lucy."

Abigail was quiet until they stepped inside her room and Dakota closed the door behind them. She touched the flame from her candle to the candle resting atop Abigail's small dresser. The soft light spilled across the yellow pine.

"Cook is unkind to people," Abigail said.

Dakota sat down on the edge of the child's small bed. "Why do you say that?"

Abigail shifted her weight from one foot to the other. "She's mean to Joseph. She yells at him and makes him sleep on the floor when he has too much rum and stays out real late."

"Married people often fight." *Not that I have any personal experience, but . . .*

"She hit Will with her cooking spoon when he did something bad."

"Why are you telling me this?" she asked the child gently. "Is there something you want me to know?"

Abigail shrugged her narrow shoulders, so fragile beneath her cotton dress. "My head hurts," she said suddenly. "I want to go to sleep."

Dakota stood and smoothed the front of her skirt with a surprisingly natural gesture. It frightened her how natural it was *all* starting to seem.

"Sleep well," Dakota said, moving toward the door. "Don't let the bedbugs bite."

A funny little giggle broke through Abigail's solemn demeanor. "I don't have bedbugs."

"I'm very glad to hear that," Dakota said with mock gravity. "I hope I'm just as fortunate."

The only thing she had to worry about in her bed was Devane.

Dakota couldn't sleep.

She'd tossed and turned for at least two hours, trying everything from counting sheep to counting calories, but no dice. She lay there, fully clothed, on top of the feather bed in the small room adjoining Devane's, waiting for the sound of his boots on the staircase. How could she possibly fall asleep when she knew he could turn up at any moment and climb in next to her? Not that she expected him to, but still . . .

Her pulse leapt into overdrive just thinking about it. She'd made a fool of herself this morning, going all feminine and vulnerable when he held her, and she was determined not to make that mistake again.

And it *was* a mistake. Not even a woman of limited experience like Dakota could possibly believe it was anything else. He was a gorgeous eighteenth-century misogynist and she was a chubby twentieth-century liberal. Opposites might attract, but sooner or later they'd end up trying to kill each other. Who needed the hassle?

That's what she told herself over and over as the minutes ticked by and then the hours with no sign of Devane.

Maybe he really has *gone over the wall,* she thought as the tall clock in the downstairs hall tolled midnight. He'd made no bones about wanting to get Abigail out of the house and up to school in Boston. His wife was dead and buried. His house had been taken over by the soldiers he hated. He had a fake wife he couldn't stand and, at least according to Cook, he was the most hated man in town.

He'd have to be crazy to hang around. He had enough money to go anywhere he wanted and no reason to stay in Franklin Ridge. Why was she wasting one moment of her precious time thinking about any of this when she should be worrying how she was going to get back home?

She climbed from the bed and went to light the candle on the nightstand, then quickly realized she had no idea how to go about it. No lighter. No matches. She considered rubbing her thighs together to make a fire but that would only encourage her cellulite and it wouldn't do a darn thing for the candle.

She thought for a moment then pulled open the drapes, and the room was flooded with moonlight bouncing off the snow. Just enough light to invade someone's privacy.

"So sue me," she muttered as she walked into Devane's room and headed for the massive armoire. She'd never claimed to be perfect. She'd been born with a slow metabolism and a hyperactive sense of curiosity about things that were absolutely none of her business.

But it is your business. How else are you going to find a way to get back home?

Not a great rationalization, but not half-bad, either.

His room was exactly the way she'd hoped it would be: vacant. The armoire was there and Devane wasn't. Maybe she'd finally get some answers.

If only Abigail hadn't chosen that moment to scream as if the hounds of hell had leapt onto her bed and were demanding kibble or her life. Dakota fought off the urge to run to the kid's side to see what was wrong.

She's not your problem, Wylie. Let someone else take care of it.

Surely Cook would come to the rescue, or one of the handful of parlormaids still in Devane's employ. She listened at the door for the sound of footsteps on the stairs, but heard nothing except Abigail's shrieks. Not even one of the soldiers peered out into the hallway to see if there was something amiss.

What was the matter with those people? Were they deaf? Couldn't they hear the terror in Abby's voice? Worse, didn't they give a damn?

Dakota glanced longingly at the armoire, then, with a sigh of resignation, ran straight to Abigail's side.

15

The White Horse Tavern

"Be happy to get you more stew if you have a mind for it, ma'am." The serving girl hovered by Emilie's seat, obviously intrigued to find a woman traveling alone.

"No, thank you," Emilie said in a quiet voice. "I would like some more cider."

"Pleased to oblige." The girl lingered, fiddling with the pewter knife that rested near Emilie's plate.

"Is there something else?" Emilie asked.

The girl started to say something but a burly man in the far corner of the room called out, "Molly! I ain't payin' you to talk, now, am I?"

Emilie's shoulders sagged as the girl hurried off. She forced herself to sit straight, then decided it wasn't worth the effort. She was exhausted to the point of lunacy and frozen straight through to the marrow. She'd been on the road for hours and she still didn't know where her husband was, and it didn't look as if she was going to find out any time soon. This was the tavern where Zane and Josiah were to have made the drop, and so far she hadn't seen or heard anything that would help her unravel the mystery.

She'd tried to find some of the members of the spy ring by visiting their usual haunts, but the storm had kept most people close to home. She'd stopped at churches and apothecaries and taverns in search of her husband and their friend, but had been met with nothing but blank looks and uninterest.

The townspeople had more fascinating things to think about. Everywhere she went, she'd heard about the bright red ball that had floated over the trees yesterday afternoon, and with each telling, Emilie lost another piece of her heart to fear.

"Who was in the basket?" she'd asked a farmer she'd spoken to a little while ago, right outside the inn. "Two men? Three? Men? Women?" She'd heard every combination.

"Too much snow to see real clear," the man said, eyeing her with great suspicion. "Shouldn't you be home where you belong, missy?"

Of course I should be home, she thought as Molly deposited another tankard of cider beside her plate. She should be bundled under a pile of quilts with her husband, safe and well-loved in his arms, while their children slept soundly in the next room.

A wild laugh erupted and she covered her mouth with both hands to muffle the sound. Too bad Zane didn't have a beeper or a cellular phone, then all she'd have to do was dial him up and see if he was okay. Or maybe she could fax the farm and ask Rebekah if the guys had shown up in time for supper.

It was all so absurd that you had to laugh or go crazy.

That was when she started to cry.

Dakota found Abigail crouched at the foot of her bed, eyes wide open in terror, small hands clutching her throat.

"Honey?" Dakota knelt at her side, frightened by the look on the child's face. "Did you have a bad dream?"

Abigail clawed at her throat while she gasped frantically for breath. Tiny veins on her forehead and neck pulsed fiercely while her legs stuck straight out in front of her like legs on a cartoon character. Was she choking on something? Dakota was about to wrap her arms around the child's slender body and perform the Heimlich maneuver when she realized Abigail was speaking.

". . . rope . . . the big tree . . ."

She was dreaming, but dreaming with her eyes wide open. Dakota tried to remember what you were supposed to do in that situation, but the only thing she could think of was an old episode of "The Honeymooners" where Ed Norton became a sleepwalker and Ralph turned into a baby-sitter.

"You're okay, Abigail," she said softly, sitting down on the bed next to the child. Cautiously she rested an arm on the delicate shoulders. "You're only dreaming."

"No!" Abigail's cry rang out. "The hangman! The hangman is coming!"

"Wake up, honey," Dakota said gently, touching the child on the shoulder. "You're safe."

"The hangman!" Abigail cried out again. "He's coming! He's coming!"

Suddenly Dakota saw herself twenty years ago, sobbing in her father's arms because she was sure the bogeyman had her name and address in his hip pocket and was on his way.

She gathered the little girl to her and hugged her close, stroking the fine brown hair with gentle fingers, whispering words of comfort in her ear, words that Abigail probably wouldn't remember in the morning but words that made all the difference now.

* * *

Patrick watched from the shadows as the woman cradled the child. They did not know he stood there in the darkness, and he wished it to remain so.

He was not a man easily moved by displays of emotion or sentiment. He had been trained to hold such displays suspect, and his brief interlude with Susannah had proved the folly of revealing your heart to another.

But there was something about the scene in the darkened bedroom that moved him beyond words on a day in which he needed to be reminded that life was not always a thing of darkness.

The child was curled against Dakota's chest, her head resting beneath the woman's chin. The woman's arms were wrapped about Abigail, holding her close while she talked to her in a low, soft voice that evoked memories of dreams he'd spent a lifetime struggling to forget.

All is not as it seems. The warning sounded in his head, but he turned a deaf ear to it. The sight before him was so powerful, so deeply compelling that all else faded into nothingness before it.

But it wasn't for him. Not the warmth or the promise of something that went deeper even than blood. Those things belonged to other men.

Two good men, men with faithful wives who loved them, with children who looked toward them for guidance—two brave men were marked to die, and all because Patrick Devane had failed as a patriot as he had failed as a husband . . . as he had failed as a father.

One hour ago he had learned the truth from the owner of the White Horse Tavern, a man known for being sympathetic to whoever held the purse strings. The British planned to hang Rutledge and Blakelee one week hence in Elizabethtown.

He looked at the child nestled in the arms of a stranger, a woman who had already provided more warmth and affection than he had given the child in years. For all he knew, Dakota Wylie was the one who had conspired to send Rutledge and Blakelee to the gallows.

Muttering a curse, he drew back into the shadows and turned away from the light.

The White Horse Tavern

Thanks to the storm, the inn was filled to overflowing with travelers. In the best of times, private rooms were the exception rather than the rule, and tonight it would be six to a room.

Emilie surveyed her possible roommates. She'd sleep in the stables with Timothy's horse before she shared a bed with any of them.

"Missus." The serving girl named Molly stopped her at the door. "You can have my bed upstairs, if you'd be of a mind."

"That's very kind of you." The girl was clean and neatly groomed, which was more than could be said for most people in the establishment. "There's a gold piece for your trouble."

Molly's green eyes widened but she shook her head. "Nay, missus. I'm just looking to help."

"Why?" Emilie asked, too tired to be polite.

Molly lowered her voice to a whisper. "I heard you askin' about your friends and I—"

"Molly!" the tavern owner bellowed over the noise of laughter and clinking glasses. "To work, lass, or out into the snow with you!"

She raised her voice. "Be there directly!"

"Wait," said Emilie, placing her hand on the girl's arm. "Do you know something? You must tell me—"

"The last room on the third floor," Molly said. "I'll find out what I can."

* * *

Dakota stayed with Abigail until the child fell back into a peaceful sleep.

She settled the quilts around Abby's shoulders, then smoothed a strand of silky hair from her cheek with a gesture that felt strangely familiar to her, as if she had done the same thing in just that way many times before.

Of course, that was impossible. Except for her volunteer work teaching children to read, she had little to do with kids. She'd never felt particularly comfortable with children, not even when she'd qualified as one of them. Even with her sister Janis's sons she'd felt that sense of not quite clicking—as if they spoke a language she'd never understand. Actually, it was pretty much the same way she'd felt around most of the men she'd dated.

Abigail was a hardheaded, hot-tempered brat and her father was about as dangerous as they came. A woman would have to have a few screws loose to even consider setting up housekeeping with a pair like that.

So why did this feel so right? Why did she feel as if the last puzzle piece of her life had settled into place?

Because you're a sucker for hard luck cases, she thought as Abby's breathing settled into a slow, even rhythm. *And because you know it's safe . . . that one day soon you're going to walk away from all of this and step back into your own life. . . .*

She was tired and lonely and far from home in every way she could imagine, but she'd have to be subhuman to not feel something for a terrified little girl who was crying her eyes out. It didn't mean she wanted to play a game of let's pretend and try on stepmotherhood for size. This whole thing was only temporary. If she knew nothing else, she knew that for a fact.

She closed the door quietly behind her and started down the hall. It was almost unnaturally quiet, as if the house were holding its collective breath, and she shook off an odd feeling of anticipation.

Halfway between Abby's room and Devane's suite she noticed small pools of water on the polished wooden floor, each one a man's stride away from the next. She bent and touched her finger to the liquid. It was cold and slushy, obviously melting snow.

Soldiers, maybe? She looked toward the top of the staircase but didn't see any footprints on the steps or the landing. "Weird," she muttered. How had they managed that trick? Did they carry their boots up the stairs then slip them back on, or walk on their hands like acrobats in Cirque du Soleil?

Even more unnerving, the trail of melting snow led straight to Devane's rooms. The door was closed. She was certain she hadn't left it that way. Cautiously she pushed it open and stepped inside.

The curtains were open. The candles were extinguished. Devane's bed was untouched. Everything was as she'd left it except for the trail of melting snow that led straight to the armoire.

Don't even think it, Wylie! This isn't the time to turn into Nancy Drew.

Hidden staircases and mysterious messages hidden in old clocks were fine in the pages of a book, but they had nothing whatsoever to do with reality.

Reality? Like time travel happens every day?

She had no answer for that. All she knew was that Devane had watched her comfort his daughter, probably even heard the child's cries, and chosen to do nothing about it. He had stood in the doorway to his daughter's room then turned and walked away.

He wasn't going to get away with it. Not if she could help it.

A towering sense of rage filled her and she swung open the door to the armoire, practically vibrating with the certainty that Devane's secrets were within her reach. She'd find him even if she had to track him through the centuries.

His treatment of Abigail was unconscionable. The thought that he could watch the child cry and do nothing, *feel* nothing, defied reason. He was the lowest type of slime crawling on the earth, and she intended to tell him so as soon as possible.

She peered inside empty drawers, felt around for secret compartments, would have settled for a pair of linsey-woolsey Jockey shorts with hearts embroidered on them, but no luck. The armoire was still as empty as her bank account back home, but the sense of certainty inside her didn't lessen.

She ran her fingers across the smooth wood of one of the inner drawers. The armoire was a strange piece of furniture. The drawers were flimsy and cheaply made, while the wardrobe itself was almost a work of art. Each piece of pine fit into the next piece seamlessly, as if the entire thing had been wrought from one enormous tree. The only board that didn't seem quite a part of the whole was the one in back, but that could be a trick of the dim light and not a blemish on the craftsmanship.

Or maybe it was something else. Her fingertips tingled as she ran them up the vertical grain and her pulse rate leapt exponentially. She'd experienced that kind of thing often enough in her life to know exactly what it meant, and she thanked God for it.

She slid the drawers out and stacked them on the floor by her feet. Her hands had a life of their own as she lifted out the runners and laid them next to the drawers. Then *bingo!*

Her palm found a slight depression near the seam on the right-hand side of the board and the metal latch she'd discovered earlier. She gave a tug and then a push, and as it swung open it was all she could do to hold back a whoop of exhilaration.

The passageway was dark and narrow, but she felt no fear. She was meant to be there. Every cell and neuron in her body told her so. Her extrasensory abilities were beginning to flex their muscles once again, and she felt more like her old self than she had since climbing into the hot-air balloon a thousand lifetimes ago.

She stumbled twice on the uneven stone floor but continued to move forward. Boards creaked overhead and she heard a scurrying noise that sounded awfully mouselike, but she tried not to think about it.

She'd read about secret passageways that snaked their way through old houses, and knew they invariably led outside. She didn't have a terrific sense of direction, but if her guess was right, she was heading toward the stables.

Why would Devane feel he needed to use a secret passageway when he owned the house in question and dominated everyone in it with his iron will and bad attitude? You'd think a man like that could come and go when he wanted without having to answer to another living soul.

A man who worried about his reputation would use a passageway like this to conduct a love affair away from prying eyes, but in Devane's case that didn't make sense because he was no longer a married man and could conduct a love affair in broad daylight in the center of town if that was what he wanted to do.

No, the only reason a man like Devane would go to such lengths to conceal his movements was if there was something greater at stake, something of such importance that it had to be kept secret at all costs.

Something like spying.

The explanation she'd been circling since she'd dropped out of the tree at Devane's feet was inescapable now. Everything he did, everything she'd seen and heard, all pointed toward the obvious conclusion. His hatred of the Continental army had been hot enough to blister paint. She'd sensed that he was a Tory sympathizer when they first met; now she was certain.

She consoled herself with the fact that when she found him she could berate him not just for being a lousy parent but for being a traitor, as well.

The passageway took a sharp left, narrowing until she wondered whether she'd be able to wedge her well-padded hips through. She could imagine some archaeologist finding her bones in the passageway a few hundred years from now and branding her demise as "death by cellulite."

She smothered a laugh. At least her sense of the absurd was still intact. Her courage, however, was another story. It seemed to be waning fast. Her ankle throbbed and she did her best to ignore it. A loud scratching noise sounded overhead and she cringed, convinced that one of Mickey Mouse's less affable cousins was going to make an unwelcome entrance.

Carefully she made her way down a steep staircase, navigated a series of sharp turns, then descended another set of steps that apparently led into the bowels of the earth.

Where on earth was she going to end up? The possibilities were not too pleasant. What if Devane had a guard posted, some bayonet-happy traitor who'd turn her into a human shish kebab? She hadn't thought to bring a weapon of any kind with her.

No matter. It was too late to turn back. That sense of destiny, of rightness, was gathering force with each step she took. Somehow it was all tied together—Patrick Devane and Abigail and this house and the sense that where she was at that moment was where she was meant to be, the path that would lead her home.

The White Horse Tavern

Molly Cutter's third-floor room boasted a thin feather mattress that rested atop a narrow iron bed. The ceiling angled sharply down to a waist-high window that overlooked the stables.

It reminded Emilie of her dorm room in art school, a sad little closet that was Dante's Inferno in the summer and a meat locker the rest of the year.

The girl's meager belongings were lined up neatly on the shelf that served as a dresser: a wooden comb, a length of black ribbon, a skein of indigo blue yarn and bone knitting needles.

That's all she has in the world, Emilie thought as tears stung her eyes. In the time she had left behind, even the poorest soul had more.

She turned away and looked out the window. Snow continued to fall. The wind had picked up some since she had arrived, and drifts were forming against the side of the stables. She thought about Timothy's horse and hoped that the stable boy had understood the coin she gave him came with the expectation of services rendered. If she wasn't so tired, she would go back downstairs and make sure, but a sickening lassitude had taken hold and it was all she could do to make it to the narrow iron bed and lie down.

She lay there for a long time, dozing fitfully, awakening herself each time a crimson hot-air balloon floated into her dreams.

At a little after midnight she heard Molly climbing the twisting staircase, and she sat up as the girl entered the room.

"What did you find out?" she asked as the door closed behind Molly. "Where is my—where are Rutledge and Blakelee?"

The expression in Molly's green eyes was serious. Too serious for Emilie's taste. Blood hammered in her ears, making it hard to hear the girl's words.

". . . or she'd take the strap to me."

"What was that?" Emilie stared at her. "Someone said she'd take a *strap* to you?"

"Yes'm," said Molly. "Said to stop asking questions that weren't my business or I'd be sorry."

"Did you ask about the red ball that everyone's talking about?"

"No'm, never got the chance. Soon as I mentioned your two friends it got quiet as church on Monday morning."

"So you didn't find out anything?" Emilie asked, on the verge of tears. "Nothing at all?"

There was a slight pause, so slight that under normal circumstances Emilie never would have noticed it.

"The Redcoats," said Molly sadly. "I'm sorry, missus, but the Redcoats are goin' to hang them."

16

Rum had never failed Patrick before, not even during the darkest days after Susannah left him. Rum had filled the coldness in the center of his soul where Abigail had been. Rum had warmed the bed where his wife had lain beside him.

But this time rum couldn't begin to soothe the ache inside his chest as he thought of the comrades he had condemned to death. There wasn't enough rum in the world to help him forget what he had done. To forget that two men would die because he had not recognized danger when she appeared before him.

He'd suspected it from the beginning, but something inside him, some weakness of the soul, had kept him from accepting the truth that he could no longer deny.

He heard the soft sound of her footsteps as she made her way through the dark and narrow passageway, and he felt a grudging admiration for her courage. He knew few men who would venture alone into that passageway and fewer still who would not turn back long before reaching their destination.

But still she came, moving closer to him with every beat of his heart. He found it hard to reconcile his suspicions with the inexplicable sense of joy he had felt as he watched her hold Abigail to her breast in the darkened bedroom.

"Bloody fool!" He gulped down more rum. The quickest road to disaster was to trust a woman. He would not make that mistake again.

"What has kept you so long, Dakota Wylie?"

She jumped at the sound of his voice. Squinting, she made out his shadowy figure near the end of the passageway.

"What are you doing here?" she demanded, as if she were Our Lady of the Passageway.

"Waiting for you, my dear wife. The night is long and cold without you."

"Stick a sock in it." Her aura was shooting sparks. She was surprised he couldn't see them arcing over her head, making her brave and powerful and impossible to deny.

"I am pleased you have decided to join me," he drawled. He was close enough for her to smell the faint scent of rum on his breath and she moved back, but she needn't have bothered. He made no move to touch her.

"You should be back in that house, taking care of your daughter."

"You served her well, madam. There was nothing more that I could do."

"Nothing more you could do?" She laughed out loud. "You did nothing at all."

"Nothing was required."

"She had a nightmare."

"All children have nightmares."

"And their parents comfort them until the bad dream passes."

"Who will comfort her in school, madam? It is time she learned the difference between dreams and life."

"You treat her like a stranger. Cook would be a better parent to her than you have been."

"You overstep your bounds." He loomed over her and she knew the only thing between herself and death was the extent of his self-control. "Even if it were your concern, this is not the place for serious discussion."

"The hell it isn't."

There was just enough light for her to see the surprise in his deep blue eyes. "Your language offends me, madam."

"Your treatment of Abigail offends *me*."

"She wants for nothing."

"Except for your attention."

"She is a child."

"She is your *daughter,* your own flesh and blood."

He turned and strode away, but she wasn't about to let him get off that easily.

"You don't want to hear it, do you?" she demanded as the passageway opened into a small room dominated by a large wooden table and a narrow bed. "Why do you hate Abigail so much? What on earth could she have done to deserve—"

"Be warned, madam."

"You owe it to her." She pressed on, the memory of the child's tears still fresh in her mind. "You're her father."

"Bloody hell, concern yourself with your own predicament, because it is considerable."

"My predicament?" She poked him in the chest with her forefinger. It was like poking Mount Rushmore. "You're the one with a predicament."

He pushed her down onto the bed. The mattress felt like a soggy matzo, but she didn't think this was a good time to lodge a complaint with the management.

"Mark my words well, madam, for they have great meaning for you. Today we lost two of our best men because I sheltered a traitor in my midst."

"Lost?" she asked. "What do you mean, *lost?*"

"Captured and condemned to death. Lost to all who care for them."

"Not to worry." She waved his words away like flies at a picnic. "I know all about that. They're in jail near Jockey Hollow."

"And how is it you know that, madam?"

"You just told me."

"I did not mention Jockey Hollow."

"I, um, I must've heard it somewhere else."

"Where?"

"I don't know . . . somewhere."

"That answer will not serve. Tell me the name of your spymaster or I will end your worthless life in this very room."

"Wait a minute!" she said, her face growing pale. "I can take a joke with the best of them, but this isn't funny anymore. I don't have a spymaster, Devane. I don't even know what a spymaster is."

"Two good men are sentenced to die, Dakota Wylie, and you are to blame. Why should you be spared?"

"Look," she said, "I know all about Rutledge and Blakelee. You don't have anything to worry about. Everything's going to be okay."

He grabbed her by the upper arms and lifted her off the bed. "Where are they?"

She neither blinked nor looked away, not discomfited in the slightest by the indignity of her position. Her courage was greater than the courage of a dozen men of his acquaintance. He would give all he had and more to have such a woman by his side.

"Put me down!" she ordered.

"Answer me first."

Her knee banged against his hip and he thanked the Almighty that her aim was left of center.

"Where are they?" he asked again as he lowered her to the ground.

"I don't know," she said honestly, "but I can make a guess."

"That is not good enough."

"Jockey Hollow," she said. "They're supposed to be in a jail near Jockey Hollow."

"A fine statement, madam, but I fear 'tis inaccurate. There is no jail near Jockey Hollow."

"There has to be."

"A law has not been passed to that effect," he said dryly. "I grow tired of this charade. Mayhap a night in the Franklin Ridge jail will bring out the truth."

She met his eyes. He wasn't kidding. *Go to jail. Go directly to jail. Do not pass Go. Forget about your two hundred dollars.* She'd read enough about those jails to know she'd never last twenty-four hours under such terrible conditions. *So what are you going to do, Wylie? Offer him your lily white body like Mata Hari would?*

Maybe she'd do something even more dangerous, like telling the truth. "You were right about Andrew McVie," she said. "He *is* a friend of mine."

The joy in his eyes was unmistakable and her heart soared. The lousy rat might be a spy, but at least he was on the right side.

Of course, he quickly masked his joy with a veneer of mild curiosity. "It is said he floated over the treetops in a basket suspended from a bright red ball."

"It's called a hot-air balloon."

"You floated over the treetops with him?" He tried, but he couldn't conceal his disbelief.

"Yes, I did."

"How came you to be separated from your friends?"

"The balloon was in trouble. We were falling from the sky and I—I guess you could say I bailed out."

"You abandoned your friends."

"We were going to crash."

"And so you chose to save your own life."

"No," she retorted angrily, "I chose to save your daughter's life instead."

"I fail to see how Abigail enters into this story."

"I heard her crying. I thought she was in danger."

"You leapt from the basket to save Abigail?"

"I didn't seem to have much choice in the matter."

"You would have me believe you risked your life for one you did not know."

She sighed. "I wouldn't have you believe anything, Devane. I'm just telling you what happened."

He considered her for a moment. "You say you are a friend of Andrew McVie. If that is so, where has he been these three years past?"

"I can't answer that."

"Cannot or will not?"

It was a little of each but she didn't dare tell him that. "I met Andrew only a few weeks ago. I have no idea what he was doing before then, but I *can* tell you that he's going to rescue Rutledge and Blakelee."

"That is naught but conjecture."

"No," she said carefully. "It's a fact."

"You would have me throw in my lot with a woman who claims to foretell the future?" If the look on his face was any indication, she'd better never tell him she could see auras, read tarot cards and chat with her mother long-distance.

"At least you know on which side my loyalties rest. Why don't you show me something to prove you're not a Tory? A letter of protection from George Washington, for starters." The man had written to everyone else in the thirteen colonies; he must have written at least a billet-doux to Devane.

"A letter of protection would render me useless," Devane said coolly. "The suspicion under which I am held is my most valuable tool."

"That leaves us in the same position we were before. I still don't know exactly where you stand."

"I am a patriot," he said after a moment. "I have no love for the officers of the Continental army, but a great deal of love for what this country can be."

"You can hate the army that fights for your independence and still call yourself a patriot?"

"The Colony of New Jersey has been cruelly used. Farms have been destroyed, houses confiscated by generals who ought to spend more time in battle. Women have been raped and murdered, all in the name of the Continental army. It is possible, madam, to support the cause but hate the way in which that cause is pursued."

"Would you feel that way if your wife hadn't run away with an officer from the army?"

A muscle in his left cheek twitched but he ignored the question. "I am perceived as sympathetic to the British and that allows me access to places and people closed tight to my brothers in the spy ring."

He was a smart man. He had to know he was handing her a sure way to betray him, but that still didn't mean he was telling her the truth. "Maybe you shouldn't be telling me this after all."

He met her eyes. "I have already done so."

She waited, but there was no flash of psychic energy, no buzzing vibrations along her nerve endings to tell her what to believe. In the end there was only her heart, and her heart could no longer be denied.

"I know," she whispered. "And I'm glad."

Reason told Patrick that only a madman who had taken leave of his senses would have done such a thing, but unfortunately his sense of reason had abandoned him the first moment she came into his life.

He had lost hope that she would find him. He had waited years for her, thought Susannah was the woman who would unlock his secrets, but it had been Dakota Wylie all the time. This uncommon woman with the strange name and unusual manner had performed a miracle he would have deemed impossible: she made him feel alive.

He hated her for the way she looked at him, as if she could see inside his soul, for the way she stood her ground, forcing him to see her as a person and not just a woman. He hated her for making him want things he knew could never be.

It was more than the soft dark curls that framed her face, more than the sweet scent of her skin, more even than the fact that her nearness roused in him a silken web of emotions that wrapped themselves about his heart and drew him closer to her. Not even Susannah with her great beauty had called to him in the same way as this uncommon woman with the uncommon name.

His entire world had been turned upside down since Dakota Wylie's arrival. His life seemed different with her in it, as if he had come to the end of a long journey to find that home lay at the end of the road. In truth, he feared for his sanity. Such changes in his heart and soul were not possible. He would not allow them to be thus.

Still, how else could he explain that even time itself no longer moved at the accustomed pace? Such intensity of feeling came with the passage of weeks and months. It was not possible in mere days. There was the sense that forces he knew nothing about controlled his destiny.

"I should not believe you," he said at last, "but I do. I should not trust you, yet I do. 'Tis a considerable problem, madam, one for which I see no solution."

"That's not surprising," she said. "We barely know each other."

"'Tis true, and yet I feel as if I have known you for a very long time indeed."

"Oh, God," she whispered. "You feel it, too."

"It is as if the nature of time has somehow changed."

"As if we're living an entire lifetime in the blink of an eye."

"I do not believe in magic, Dakota Wylie, but what I feel for you is unlike anything in my experience."

"I know." Her voice was low, almost inaudible. "It is the same for me."

"Why am I bedeviled as never before? Is it love, then, that we feel?"

Her eyes swam with tears. To hear those words from such a man. To be able to spend a lifetime as his partner, his lover. *His wife.* "I don't know. I'm not even certain that I like you very much."

"We are connected in some way that I do not understand."

Now's your chance, Dakota. Tell him the truth! Tell him how you really got here. "We share a friend in common."

"It is more than that, madam."

"We are both on the side of the patriots." How could she tell him she'd traveled two hundred years to be there? There was nothing in his frame of reference to help him believe something so bizarre. There were times when she wasn't sure that *she* believed it.

"This goes deeper, Dakota Wylie, to a place I have never been."

His words resonated deep inside her soul. Suddenly she wasn't longing for something she'd once had or dreaming of what she hoped to find somewhere else. The easy jokes, the layers of protective armor she'd built up around her heart had all been created to protect her from this moment, from the first wild stirrings of impossible love.

The room faded away and all she saw was the man standing before her.

"There was no husband," she said.

"No husband?" He cupped her chin in his hand. "No man to whom you have given your heart?"

"No one," she whispered, leaning into his touch. "No one in this world or any other."

A strange sensation filled his chest as he remembered the sweetness of her kisses. Was it possible he was the only man to have known them? The thought filled him with a towering sense of joy.

Her hair was soft against his hand, like fine silk. He found himself mesmerized by the gentle curls that entwined themselves about his fingers. He met her eyes.

"You are free to go if you choose." From this point forward they would meet on level ground.

Her eyes glittered with tears. She understood his meaning and she knew there was only one answer.

"I'm not going anywhere," she said, then stepped into his embrace.

For the longest time they stood together in the middle of the room, not kissing or speaking. Her head rested against his chest, the horn buttons of his jacket pressing into her cheek. She loved the smell of wool and soap, loved the sound of his heart beating beneath her ear, loved the fact that sometimes the unexpected happened and your life would never be the same again.

She ran her hands up his arms, relishing the way the wool tickled her palms as she felt the contours of his forearms, his biceps, his shoulders. She let her fingers trace the proud curve of his jaw, the straight nose, the swell of his sensual mouth. The lines that creased his eyes and cut into his cheek, lines so deep and sorrowful that she wondered how it was she hadn't seen them before. *A river of pain,* she thought. *An ocean.*

He said nothing as she touched him, but his pulse beat visibly at the base of his throat. That pleased her more than any words possibly could.

She trailed her hands back down over his shoulders, and he reached up and took her hands in his. Looking into her eyes, he raised her hands to his mouth and slowly, deliberately, kissed her wrists, her palms, each finger in turn, until she moaned deep in her throat.

He swept her up into his arms and carried her to the bed. Emotion filled every corner of her mind, it twisted through her rib cage and shot sparks of light from her eyelashes and fingertips and toes.

He laid her down on the mattress and somehow it seemed softer than before, more inviting. Candles flickered on the tabletop behind him, making it seem as if he were surrounded by a golden aura. It seemed like a lifetime since she'd been able to see anyone's aura, and the illusion somehow made her feel more sure of herself. More like the woman she had left behind.

"Is this your choice, Dakota?" His voice rolled over her like clover honey warmed by the sun. She'd never liked the sound of her name before, but the way he said it, it was a love song. "Yes," she said softly. "Oh, yes..."

He stripped off his coat and shirt with swift, sure motions, then sat on the edge of the bed to pull off his boots. His back was smoothly muscled, like the back of Michelangelo's *David*. A thing of unutterable beauty. Was this desire, then? she wondered. This sense of hunger and worship, this longing to both surrender and conquer?

He rose from the bed and looked down upon her. His breeches hugged his narrow hips and strong legs. Smiling, she glanced away, secretly delighted that she hadn't imagined his desire for her.

"Madam?" His voice was husky, urgent. He extended his hand toward her and she reached for it, then rose to her feet.

Puzzled, she frowned. "I thought—?"

"In due course, madam." His hands found the top buttons of her bodice. "First this." He kissed the base of her throat, then undid the first two buttons. "Then this." His lips moved down her breastbone. Two more buttons. "So sweet you are, madam. So finely made."

He trailed a line of fire between her breasts. Heat gathered low in her belly and it occurred to her that if she died right then, at that very moment, she would have known more than her share of pleasure.

"You tremble," he said as he unfastened the final button and eased the bodice over her shoulders. "You have nothing to fear."

She knew he spoke the truth, but the enormity of what she was about to do overwhelmed her. This was the man she'd dreamed about, the one who had captured her heart. She hadn't been looking for him. How could she, when she hadn't even believed he existed? He was hardheaded and difficult, complicated and more than likely dangerous, yet giving herself to him seemed the wisest decision she'd ever made.

Whatever happened, wherever the future led, she would always have this memory, and if it wasn't enough, it was more than she'd dreamed.

"I'm not afraid," she said, cupping his face with her hands. "I just don't know what's expected of me."

"Nothing is expected of you." He dipped his head toward her. "It is enough that you are here."

He nipped the side of her neck and she shivered with delight. His enormous workman's hands clasped her by the waist and she felt both fragile and powerful, exultantly, wildly female. Everything she'd thought possible for other women but never for her.

He kissed her collarbone, tracing his tongue across to her right shoulder. She was hallucinating. She had to be. Didn't he know she was just an out-of-work librarian from Princeton, New Jersey? The kind of woman men forgot the moment they met. The kind of woman name tags were invented for.

"Dakota Wylie." He kissed her shoulder, and the heat in her belly grew more demanding. "You are unlike anyone I have ever known."

She moaned low in her throat as his hands cupped her breasts. "You told me that once before," she murmured. "I didn't think it was a compliment."

He hooked a finger under the strap of her bra. "A strange device. A new invention, perhaps?"

"It's from Paris," she managed to say. "You'll be seeing a lot more of them in the future."

"And this?" he asked, his mouth against her tattoo. "'Tis a strange sight upon a woman's body."

She wanted to tell him it was a birthmark but couldn't manage the lie. "Are you offended?" she asked.

"Nay, madam." He worked the hooks on the bra easily. Apparently some men just had the knack. "I am intrigued."

"Not everyone likes tattoos," she went on, trying to pretend he wasn't unfastening her skirt. "Some people say they're—ohh." Her breath left her body in a sibilant rush of air. She was naked except for a pair of white cotton panties she'd washed and dried by the fire the night before.

He knelt before her and slid his hand beneath the waistband. "From Paris?" he asked, a devilish gleam in his dark blue eyes.

Actually, they were from the U.S. of A. via Macy's, but she didn't suppose he wanted that level of detail. He was on his knees before her, hands clasping her buttocks, his face dangerously close to where every degree of heat in the universe was gathering at the juncture of her thighs. His gaze never left hers as he slid her panties over her hips and down her thighs. She stepped out of them, thankful she didn't fall over. The way her legs were shaking anything was possible. Instinctively her hands went to cover herself, but he shook his head.

Tears of embarrassment welled up. "I'm too fat," she said, wishing they were lying on the bed. Or that she had a bathrobe. Or that the candle would extinguish itself. "I've been meaning to lose those last fifteen pounds but—"

" 'Tis something I do not understand, Dakota.'' He rose to his feet and gathered her against his chest. "Is it possible you do not know the effect you have upon my person?''

"If you want to stop, it's okay,'' she babbled on, feeling more gauche and uncertain by the second. "I've waited twenty-six years for this. It won't kill me to wait another twenty-six.''

He took her hand and placed it flat against his groin.

"For you,'' he said simply, "and for you alone.''

It was the greatest gift anyone had ever given her. With those words he erased the last of her fears and freed her to give in to the dazzling sway of sensuality that had lain dormant inside her for so long. Twentieth-century worries about cellulite and single-digit dress sizes didn't matter any longer. This was about reveling in the feel of someone's body against yours, about skin against skin, about the fact that he was laying her down on the bed and stripping off his breeches.

About the fact that she'd never guessed, never imagined, never dreamed that it could be like this, that two people could ignite sparks more beautiful than a Fourth of July fireworks display.

He found her mouth with his and she opened for him. Their tongues met and she tasted the faint sweetness of rum. He kissed her as if kissing was an end in itself, as if he wanted nothing more than this from her, but his heart-stopping erection told her otherwise. She'd seen enough *Playgirl* centerfolds in her day to know fate had dealt him a generous hand.

It didn't seem possible, what they were about to do, but she knew that it was. Still, the logistics of the whole thing boggled the mind. She wondered if it was like this for every woman, her body responding wildly to sensation while her mind offered color commentary like one of those guys on Monday Night Football.

And then he found the center of her being with his gentle fingers and she finally understood what heaven was all about.

Patrick had never seen a woman more lovely than Dakota Wylie as she lay with him on the narrow bed. The fire crackled in the grate and the play of light against her smooth white skin was more beautiful than the most wondrous sunset. Her skin was the purest marble, so exquisitely perfect that he could be content to feast his soul upon it for the rest of his life.

The soft dark curls that covered her mound beckoned to him, and he found her with his hand. She arched against his palm, whimpering softly low in her throat, and he knew a moment of exultation that not even paradise could match. No other man had heard that sound. No other man had separated her petaled lips. No other man had felt the honeyed walls of her sheath close around his fingers as he made her ready for him.

But it was more than the simple fact of her virginity that excited Patrick: it was her self. Whatever mysterious forces that had come together to create such an uncommon woman. Her strength. Her loyalty. The sweetness of her person, the graceful line of her limbs. Her sharp intelligence and the wit that she wielded as a shield for her vulnerable heart.

She had said there had been no other man, not in this world or any other, and it occurred to Patrick that he could say the same thing. There was but one Dakota Wylie on this earth and he held her in his arms.

Dakota felt as if she were riding wave after wave of sensation, climbing to the top of a swell then sailing down the other side only to be buoyed up again by the fierce power of the sea. He had the hands of a magician, amazing, wonderful hands that found beauty wherever they touched. Her breasts turned golden when he cupped them. Rainbows arced above her hips. The rapid sound of their breathing was a love song.

She gasped when he positioned himself between her thighs, then thought she would die when he bent forward and curled his tongue around her moist, pink bud of flesh. Pleasure and pain were indistinguishable as intense shafts of sensation tore away her last hold on sanity. She cried out, as much from longing as fear, as he sought entrance, his incredible erection sliding between the slick folds of her vagina.

He didn't move at first and she began to relax, feeling her body mold itself to his in a most amazing fashion. A restlessness began to grow deep inside in a place she'd never known existed, a yawning emptiness that cried out to be filled. It was so simple, so elemental, that tears spilled down her cheeks at the wonder of it all.

He saw her tears and felt as if a dagger had been plunged deep inside his soul. "I have no wish to hurt you," he managed to say, even as his own body cried out for release. She was so small, so tight, that he knew pain to be inevitable.

"You'll only hurt me if you stop."

Her words lifted him above the bed, above the house, above the clouds. Reining in his power, he angled his hips then swiftly broke the sweet band of flesh and felt the warmth of her blood on his member.

"No more pain," he whispered against the fullness of her lips. "Never again."

He began to move slowly at first, then faster, and nearly growled with pleasure when she moved with him. The thrust and parry of their bodies, locked in a primal rhythm, carried him closer and closer to the edge of madness, that place where life and death met and became one.

Dakota was sure she'd died because nothing else could explain the way she felt. Bright lights exploded behind her eyelids. Pinwheels of fire and sparks of heat danced across her skin. The ocean roared in her ears, while the smell of a forest after a rainstorm filled her head. Only death or madness could explain the barrage of sensations that rippled from her head to her feet then back again ... and always, always centering deep in the pit of her belly.

He filled her, filled every part of her until she cried out not from pain but from a hunger so fierce it knew no words. He looked different by the light of the fire, his naked body backlit by the glow. Stripped of clothing and the veneer of civilization, he was a powerful male animal in his prime. Sweat glistened on his shoulders like diamonds. It tasted salty and fine against her tongue. She wanted to know every part of him, to take him in her mouth and feel the surging power of desire, but that would have to wait.

This time it was about mating, the fierce, primitive urge to join together two separate beings and make them one. He moved above her in a seductive rhythm, urging her hips to lift up from the mattress to meet his thrusts. Her muscles clenched around him, drawing him more deeply inside her body. More deeply inside her heart.

An exquisite tension filled her limbs. She was waiting, striving, yearning toward something, some wonderful mysterious something that she'd only read about and never believed would happen for her. When it did, it was as if the power and beauty of the universe and everything in it belonged to her and her alone.

The world as they knew it disappeared and there was only that room, that bed, that moment in time.

17

They made love again, with greater urgency this time, as if they both were aware that what they'd shared was as fleeting and beautiful as moonlight on snow.

He was a tender, passionate lover who saw to it that she found one shuddering climax after another before he allowed himself to be pleasured by her. And pleasure him she did. With her hands and her mouth...with her heart and soul. There were no barriers between them, no inhibitions. In that secret room, with only the crackling fire for company, they discovered the secrets of each other's body, worshiping each other the way lovers had since the beginning of time.

He watched her as she slept, her lovely face in the crook of his arm. Her thick dark lashes cast a shadow on the smooth white skin of her cheek, and he was mesmerized by the sight. If he were an artist he would capture that shadow on canvas so that in some cold and distant future he could remind himself that once he had known how it felt to be truly happy, for somehow he knew it would not be forever.

Who are you, Dakota Wylie? he wondered as she slept. Nothing about her was as it should be. Her appearance, her actions, the freedom with which she expressed every thought that passed through her mind—was there another woman in that vast world like her? He could not imagine it to be so.

There was something so individual about her, so set apart from the rest of the world, as to make him wonder if she was flesh and blood at all but an apparition sent to ease the endless pain in his heart.

I do not wish to feel this way, madam, but you inspire in me something perilously close to love.

Dakota murmured in her sleep as she sank more deeply into a dream. The nursery... the hand-wrought cradle... the beautiful infant who slept peacefully beneath her lace-trimmed quilt... the man whose heart seemed too small to contain the boundless love he felt for the innocent babe—

She awoke with a start, surprised to find herself still nestled in his arms. How easy it was to get used to being happy. How dangerous when you know it could never last.

She opened her eyes slowly. His face was the first thing she saw. He was looking down at her with something approaching adoration. She closed her eyes again. *Anytime you want me, God.* It couldn't possibly get any better than this.

"You were dreaming," he said, smoothing a dark curl back from her temple.

She pressed a kiss to the warm skin of his shoulder. "How did you know?"

"You smiled," he said, drawing the quilt up over her shoulders and pulling her closer. "Mayhap the dream was of me?"

"I dreamed about you and Abigail," she said softly. She saw the nursery and the cradle, saw the sunlight streaming through the windows, felt the love filling his heart until it hurt him to breathe.

He pulled away from her as if she had slapped him. "I will not discuss this."

"Patrick, she's your little girl—"

"Do not pursue this line of inquiry, Dakota."

"She's your daughter—"

"I will not talk about this with you."

"Your flesh and blood—"

"The child is not mine."

It took a moment for his words to penetrate. She sat up straight, clutching the quilt to her breasts like a shield. "What did you say?"

He met her eyes. "I said I am not Abigail's father."

"Of course you're her father," she said automatically. "She's just like you. Anyone can see that."

"My wife took a lover in the same room in which you slept your first night in my house."

Dakota felt as if he had reached inside her chest and grabbed her heart with his bare hands. Cook had told her the same thing and she had urged the woman to share all the juicy details. How different those details sounded from his lips. And how ashamed she was of herself for wanting to know.

His tone was emotionless, but she knew it was only a front. "It was not the first time Susannah had broken her marriage vows."

"I don't care about your wife," Dakota said as a vision played out inside her head. "She doesn't matter. You were standing over Abigail's cradle, the one with the embroidered curtains that had belonged to your grandmother, and—"

He stared at her as if she'd sprouted horns and a tail.

Oh, my God, Dakota thought. *What have I done?* Abby wasn't an infant any longer, she was a little girl. The cradle had long since been replaced by a small bed.

And she was in big trouble.

"How do you know these things?" he demanded, placing his hands on her shoulders and forcing her to meet his eyes. "How is it you know of things that happened before you came to this house?"

"I don't think you really want an answer to that," she whispered. *And I certainly don't want to tell you.*

"Were you a friend of Susannah's?"

She had been right about the name and she knew she was right about this, as well. "I never met your wife."

"My family is dead. You cannot have learned this from them."

"Do us both a favor and don't try to figure it out. Just consider it a lucky guess."

"Tell me how you know these things."

"Would you believe I'm just very, very smart?"

His jaw grew noticeably tighter.

"I guess you wouldn't believe that." She regrouped. "Okay, here's the truth—I'm psychic."

"Say again."

When had the word *psychic* come into common use? "I have second sight."

"You see the future?" He sounded the way most people sounded when she told them.

She nodded. "Sometimes I get a glimpse of the past, too, but not very often."

Patrick had known from the start that Dakota Wylie was unlike most women, but he had not suspected anything of this most incredible nature. "And that is how you came to know about the cradle and the curtains."

"Yes." Her voice was soft, almost sorrowful. There was a new expression in her dark eyes, a tenderness he did not wish to see, for it would be his undoing. "You love Abby very much."

A great shaft of pain pierced his heart. "I loved her once." He paused. "When she was my child."

He had said those words to no man or woman who walked the earth. They tore into his gut and twisted hard. The pain burned deep into his heart and then, when he thought he could stand it no longer, she reached out and placed her hand on his forearm and he felt as if she had somehow laid a healing balm against his tortured soul.

"She *is* your child."

"No, madam, I assure you she is not."

"How can you know that?"

"That revelation was my wife's last gift to me." Again he had never spoken these words to anyone, but he felt compelled to speak them to the dark-haired woman who watched him so closely. Who seemed to know the contours of his heart. "Susannah had lain with two other men the month she conceived, either of whom could claim the child as his own."

His rage and sorrow permeated her skin and filled her lungs until she could scarcely draw a breath. Dear God, how much it had cost him to tell her. "I'm so sorry."

"You offer me pity?" he challenged, his gaze never leaving hers.

"I would never do that to you. I offer you truth. Abigail is your daughter. Six years of loving her is proof of that."

"I have made my peace with the situation and moved forward."

"You haven't moved. All you've done is turn away from your child."

"Have you not heard my words? She is not my child. Another man's blood flows through her veins."

"And what if it does?" she countered. "Does that change the love you had for her? Does that make her love you any less?"

"There are those who say I drove Susannah from our bed."

"You are a difficult man. Living with you wouldn't be easy."

"How quickly you have learned that."

"Don't punish your daughter for something your wife did." Dakota grabbed his hands in hers with a gesture so unexpected that another layer of his defenses shattered. "Abby needs you so much."

"I have no wish to hurt her, but I cannot change what is."

"Do you have any idea how lucky you are to have Abby? I'd give anything to—" She stopped, appalled by what she had been about to say.

"You cannot know how it is for me," Patrick said. "Such things are not in your experience."

"You're wrong," she whispered. "I cannot have children, Patrick, but I can tell you that I would love Abby as much as if she had grown beneath my heart."

The moments ticked by silently, then the minutes. They lay together on the narrow bed, not touching or talking, as the barriers between their separate lives once again fell into place and the empty chill of loneliness recaptured their hearts.

Dakota supposed she should be relieved. There was something terrifying about being that vulnerable before a stranger. Not even with him cradled inside her body had she felt so open and exposed as she had these past few minutes.

He isn't the man for you, Wylie. He can't even love his child. What chance would you have? The wounds Susannah Devane had dealt him had been fatal. Whatever capacity to love he'd possessed was gone now, destroyed by her treachery, and not even Dakota Wylie, girl librarian and psychic, could bring it back.

She and Devane had been brought together to help Andrew McVie take his place in history, and nothing more. Once that happened they would go back to their separate worlds and life would go on as if paradise hadn't been right there for the asking.

"It must be nearly daybreak," she said when she could stand the silence no longer. "We should be getting back."

"I will see you to the room, then set forth to find McVie," he said reaching for their clothes, which were scattered on the floor next to the bed.

"Not without me you're not." This was her destiny he was messing with. If anyone was going to find Andrew, it

had better be Dakota Wylie or she'd know the reason why.
"Where do *we* plan on searching?"

"*I* will begin with my neighbors. Mayhap he has sought
shelter with one of them."

"I'll come with you."

"Nay, madam. It is too dangerous for a woman."

"Too dangerous to visit the neighbors? I'll pretend I
didn't hear that."

"You will go back to the house and wait."

"*You* go back to the house. I've spent more than enough
time in your house." Didn't he realize the biggest danger she
faced was in pretending she belonged in his life?

"Your company will make my job more difficult."

"You're taking your beloved new wife out to meet the
neighbors. What better way to get into their houses so you
can snoop?"

"I am not known for my affability. Their suspicions
would be aroused if I came calling with my wife in tow."

"It's not like you have time to build secret passageways
to every house in Franklin Ridge."

A smile tugged at the right corner of his mouth and her
damnably vulnerable heart ached in response.

"You believe the good people of Franklin Ridge will take
you to their bosoms and reveal their secrets?" he asked.

"It's either that or I'll be forced to look in their medicine
cabinets."

"Madam?"

She sighed. *We couldn't have made it over the long haul
even if we wanted to, Devane. You'll never get my jokes and
I'll never be able to heal your broken heart.*

"You say nobody in town likes you, and from what I've
heard, you're probably right. If you start popping up on
their doorsteps for a cup of tea, they'll have you arrested."
She paused to let him consider the vastness of his unpopu-
larity. "If you take me along with you, they might give you
another chance."

"I am not that good an actor, Dakota."

"But *I* am. I'll make them believe we're the most wonderful couple since George and Martha."

He had cut himself off from the daily fabric of life in Franklin Ridge. Susannah's treachery had plunged him into solitude and it was that very solitude that had made it possible for him to move between the worlds of home and war. But now he needed the information he could glean from the townspeople, and to obtain that information he needed the woman next to him. Needed her in ways he dared not contemplate.

"They will watch us closely to see if we are indeed the happily wed couple we claim to be."

"And they won't be disappointed."

"You will do this for me?"

Her smile was quicksilver. It was gone before he could capture it in his soul. "No, but I will do it for me."

Dakota was silent as she followed him back through the dark passageway to the house. This was the stuff of a Victoria Holt novel and all she could think about was how many spiders were lurking overhead, ready to pounce. She hadn't given a thought to spiders when she was angry and her adrenalin was pumping, but now she was convinced there was a platoon of black widows waiting for her.

"Mmmph," she said as she walked headlong into his shoulder. "Why did you stop? I want to get out of here."

"The door is locked."

"That's ridiculous." She ducked under his arm and pushed hard. "The door is locked."

"Precisely, madam. Did you do so?"

"Of course I didn't. In fact, I meant to ask you how you managed to reassemble the armoire from inside the passageway. That was a pretty neat trick."

"It requires patience," he said, "and a degree of strength. Nothing more."

"So who closed it after me?"

"It would appear that someone knows of the secret passageway and is revealing that knowledge to me."

"Not very subtle, if you ask me. Why didn't they just leave a note? Everyone around here seems to be into writing letters. Maybe—"

"Madam, would you refrain from that constant chatter while I ponder the situation."

She couldn't believe her ears. They were locked out of the house, stranded in a secret passageway that probably bred spiders the way picnics bred ants. "Ponder? I can't believe I'm standing here in the dark with a man who'd use a word like *ponder*. How about a nice active verb like *escape* or—"

He clapped a hand over her mouth and silenced her.

"You will remain here," he said. "The hidden room exits beneath the stables. I will walk up to the main house and unlock the wardrobe to release you."

She removed his hand. "How do I know you won't forget about me?"

"It is a matter of trust between us."

"That's what I was afraid of," she said. "That's why we're going to do it my way...."

Dakota and Patrick entered through the front door just as Cook finished stirring the breakfast porridge. Standing in the hallway, they brushed snow from each other's hair and shoulders, laughing just loudly enough to draw Cook from the kitchen. The idea was to make the household believe the two lovers had gone out for an early-morning stroll in the snow.

"She's watching us from the hallway," Dakota murmured as Patrick pressed a kiss to the nape of her neck. "I think she is about to faint."

"'Twill reach Morristown by the noon hour," Patrick said dryly as Dakota straightened the collar of his jacket.

"News of the happy couple will be served with the midday meal.

The truth was it was frighteningly easy to play the happy couple. All Dakota had to do was think about how she had felt in his arms and she was awash with violent, spectacular emotions.

"G'morning, sir." A young soldier called out a greeting as he lugged a barrel of flour through the hallway. "And g'morning to you, too, ma'am."

Dakota favored him with a warm, wifely smile. "It's a wonderful morning, isn't it?" she asked, meaning every syllable. "The best morning ever!"

The soldier eyed her curiously, then shrugged his bony shoulders. "If you say so, ma'am, I s'pose it is."

"Do not overplay your hand," Patrick warned her as they strolled toward the kitchen for their morning meal. "Such exuberance might strain their ability to believe."

"Too bad," she retorted with a snap of her fingers. "We're newlyweds. Newlyweds are supposed to be exuberant."

He looked at her strangely but said nothing more.

"Good morning to you," said Cook as they took their seats at the table. "And a fine day it seems to be all around."

Patrick grunted a response, while Dakota beamed another megawatt smile in the woman's direction. "It's most definitely a fine day, Cook." She turned toward Abigail, who was seated across from her. "Morning, Abby."

"I waited and waited," Abigail said, looking from Dakota to Patrick then back again, "but Cook said I could eat my johnnycakes before you came down."

"Cook did exactly the right thing," Dakota said, leaning across the table to pat the child's tiny hand. "You're a growing girl. You need your food."

Cook served Dakota and Patrick each a plate of johnnycakes.

"And porridge afterward," said Cook, "if you have the appetite for it."

"These are wonderful, Cook," Dakota said with a smile as the woman served up some more of the pancakes. "Just what we needed to warm our bones."

Turning away from Patrick, Cook winked broadly at Dakota in a way that made Dakota want to giggle like a guilty teenager.

"Oh, I'm certain your bones are plenty warm, missus."

Patrick looked up from his steaming cup of chocolate. "Have you nothing better to do with your time, woman, save stand there simpering like a fool?"

"Begging your pardon, sir." Cook winked again at Dakota and turned back to stir the porridge.

Patrick muttered something dark about an unpardonable lack of privacy, but Dakota laughed and patted him on the hand in what she hoped seemed like a natural, wifely gesture. In truth, it was anything but. The simple touch of his hand beneath her fingertips sent ripples of sensation up her arm and straight to her heart. If this was what a wife felt every time she touched her husband, it was a miracle anyone made it to their first anniversary.

Abigail fidgeted with the bowl of porridge that followed the johnnycakes. Her eyes were heavily shadowed and she had none of her usual six-year-old sparkle.

"Abby?" Dakota asked. "You didn't sleep very well last night, did you?"

Abigail shook her head. Even her braids had lost their bounce. "My throat hurts," she said, placing her hand over her windpipe. "Like someone squeezed it real hard."

Dakota rose from her chair and rounded the table to the child's side. She placed the flat of her hand against Abby's forehead. "You feel cool enough. Are you sneezing?"

"No."

Something niggled at the back of Dakota's memory, like a forgotten phrase from an old song, but she couldn't quite grasp hold of it. "Maybe you should stay in today. It's just awful outside."

The room shook as another tree toppled in the woods behind the house. The solders were making short work of the thick woods as they raced to complete their huts before the next storm.

"Bloody fools," Patrick swore. "There will be naught but open fields remaining when they have done with it."

"You begrudge them their huts?" Dakota asked.

"I do, madame, and I begrudge the fact that my trees are used to construct a new kitchen for McDowell's chef."

Abby moved her spoon around in her bowl of porridge, then pushed the whole thing away from her.

"Why don't you go upstairs and get Lucy?" Dakota suggested. "I found a lovely piece of wool that would make a splendid dress for her."

Abby turned to her father. "May I, Papa?"

He nodded and the child ran from the room.

"What are they going to do about the foot soldiers?" Dakota asked, pouring herself some more hot chocolate. She was aware that Cook was hanging on every word. "Those poor men are sleeping in the snow."

"First the general's needs," Devane said, meeting her eyes across the table, "then the needs of his men. Neither of which are my concern nor should they be yours."

Behind her Cook sniffed, obviously distressed by Patrick's cavalier attitude toward the plight of the soldiers. Dakota had trouble suppressing the urge to defend him to all and sundry, but knew that would not help advance his cause. The suspicion under which he was held was his greatest asset.

He pushed back his chair and rose to his full height of over six feet. "We will ride out this afternoon to call on the Bradleys, the Vliets and the Atwaters. Be ready by two o'clock."

We're supposed to be newlyweds, her look admonished him. *If this is going to work, you'll have to play along.*

His glance held hers for a moment. A slow, lazy grin spread across his handsome face like daylight breaking after a stormy night. She could almost hear Cook swooning as she chopped vegetables for the soup pot.

"I will wait for you in the front hall."

He turned to leave, then apparently thought better of it. Dakota watched, mesmerized, as he closed the distance between them, then bent over her and kissed her.

Thoroughly.

If she'd been standing when he kissed her, she would have toppled over in a heap as bells, whistles and the Vienna Choir Boys exploded into full, exultant life inside her head the moment his mouth claimed hers.

"Two o'clock," he said, touching her chin with the tip of his forefinger.

"Two o'clock," she whispered.

18

After she recovered from Devane's unexpected kiss at the breakfast table, Dakota managed to compose herself long enough to ask Cook a few discreet questions. Within two minutes her worst fears had been confirmed. Probably the only thing between Patrick and the hangman's noose was the fact that he was not only the most disliked man in Franklin Ridge, he was also the wealthiest.

War had taken its toll on the small community, and without Devane's financial support they would be in even more trouble than they already were. Human nature being what it was, that made the good citizens hate him all the more. It wasn't going to be easy to get them to open their doors to Devane, but they would give it the old college try.

After the morning meal Abby ran off to watch the soldiers build their huts while Dakota went upstairs to tackle her main problem: What did a woman wear to visit neighbors who hated her husband's guts? She debated between the pale blue moiré she'd laid across the bed and the dark rose muslin with the flowered skirt that was draped over the back of the chaise longue. The blue moiré had a particularly low-cut neckline, which was terrific if you were built like one of the girls on "Baywatch," and not so terrific if you were actually human.

What about that nice yellow dress with the crocheted lace at the cuffs?

Ginny's voice was as clear and distinct as if she were standing in the room with her daughter. Dakota spun around and looked to make sure she wasn't.

"Ma!" she said out loud. "Is that you?"

Don't even think about that blue dress, not unless those falsies you made from the T-shirt will stay in place.

"Where are you?"

I'm at the kitchen table. Janis is coming over for a tarot reading in a little while and I thought I'd drop in and see how you were doing before things got too hectic.

"Drop in? You make it sound like I'm living in an apartment on the next block."

You're going to have to make a decision soon, honey. I hope you'll be ready for it.

"A decision? What kind of decision?"

I can't tell you that. But I can say that if you follow your heart, you won't be sorry.

"How are you, Ma? Is everyone all right?"

You've only been gone two days, honey. Everyone's just fine.

"I miss everyone so much," she said, blinking back tears.

You sound surprised.

"I am. Who would've thought I'd turn out to be such a wimp?"

He loves you, you know.

"Oh, my God!" Ginny Wylie, a Peeping Tom? "You didn't—?"

I'm insulted.

"Can't blame me for asking, Ma. You did read my diary when I was thirteen."

This is different.

Dakota laughed out loud. "You don't know the half of it...."

Listen with your heart, honey, as well as your head, and everything will be just fine.

Dakota shivered as if a cold wind had moved across her skin. "What do you mean, he loves me?"

Silence.

"Ma?" Her voice rose in alarm. "I'm coming home as soon as I find Andrew and Shannon and the balloon. This was all some kind of cosmic mistake. I really wasn't meant to be here. Say something, Ma!"

Wouldn't you know it? The first time in her life that Dakota actually wanted romantic advice from her mother and Ginny vanished without a trace.

She fondled the silky skirt of the blue moiré between her fingers and sighed. She'd look like a flat-chested female impersonator in it. The rose made her look like a new red potato. She hated it when her mother was right.

"Yellow it is," she said, struggling to ease the garment over her head and not suffocate beneath the weight of the skirts. Dozens of tiny pearl buttons ran down her back and for the life of her she couldn't think of a way to fasten them other than throwing herself on the mercy of a parlormaid.

She was considering changing into the blue dress with the buttons in the front when Abigail's scream split the air.

"What on earth—?" She'd seen the child not more than twenty minutes ago and, except for that sore throat, everything had been fine.

Gown still undone, she hurried down the hallway to the child's bedroom, where she found Abby huddled near the window in the fetal position.

"Abby!" She ran to her side. "What's wrong?"

The child lifted her eyes to Dakota, but it was clear Abby saw something—or someone—else standing before her. The child clutched her throat, pulling at the collar of her plain cotton dress as if it were choking the very life from her.

Dakota unfastened the top two buttons, but it didn't help. Abby pushed Dakota's hands away and struggled for breath.

She had the same look in her eyes she'd had last night when Dakota had comforted her after her bad dream.

"Abby, can you speak to me?" Dakota asked as she tried to hold the girl in her arms. "Can you say anything?"

A sheen of sweat broke out over the child's upper lip as she struggled to form a word.

"What was that?" Dakota leaned closer, straining to hear. "Say it again."

"An—Andrew."

The hairs on the back of her neck rose. "What about Andrew?"

"The hangman," she said, same as she had last night. "The tree by the gray house—"

"What house?" Her head was buzzing and the sound grew louder with each word Abby uttered. "Where is the tree, Abby?"

"The mountains," Abby said, erupting into noisy tears. "The big red ball can't save him!"

Abby's words seemed to be traveling toward her through a wind tunnel. "Abby, please, you have to tell me what you see! Where is the big red ball? Is anybody on it? What—"

"Papa!" Abby cried out, looking past Dakota. "Papa!"

Dakota turned toward the door in time to see Devane cross the threshold. Before he could say a word, the child hurled herself at him, crying as if her heart would break.

He pulled back, his spine stiffening noticeably, but Abby would not be denied. She hung on to him for dear life, her words lost amid the tears, but his hands remained resolutely at his sides.

His eyes met Dakota's. The world and everything in it seemed to come into sharp focus. His expression remained impassive but this time it was different. This time she could see beneath the surface, past his anger and his pain, to the part of his soul he hid from the world.

You have a heart, she thought, willing him to hear her plea. *Does it matter whose blood runs through her veins? She's only a little girl and she loves you so much.*

Devane looked down at Abby. The child's shoulders shook with her sobs. She was so tiny, so fragile despite the enormity of her spirit, and once upon a time she'd been the most important thing in the world to him.

Remember! Dakota pleaded silently. *Remember how much you loved her.*

Whether or not Susannah's parting words had been true, the fact remained that in all the ways that mattered Abby was Devane's daughter and always would be. He was the one who had held her when she cried. He was the one who had stood over her cradle and dreamed of her future. Nothing Susannah had done mattered compared to that.

Touch her, Patrick! Just reach out and touch her and it will all fall into place.

Dakota held her breath as he lifted his right hand, then slowly brought it to rest atop the child's head.

The child's hair was cool to the touch. The shiny brown strands were soft as the finest silk, and a powerful flood of memories, long buried, welled up deep inside Patrick's chest as he cupped her head with his hand.

Not that long ago he'd held her in his arms, terrified he might hurt her with his big clumsy hands. She'd been an infant then, a tiny slip of a thing, helpless as a baby bird fallen from the nest. He'd trembled when the nursemaid placed her in his arms, and had tried to hand the blanket-wrapped bundle back to the woman, but then the infant had looked up at him with her serious gray eyes and he'd felt the walls around his heart crumble and fall at his feet.

He cleared his throat, aware of the intensity of Dakota Wylie's gaze.

"What is the problem here?" His tone was gruff but he did not break the connection between himself and Abigail.

"The hangman!" Abigail cried out in a voice he'd never heard before. She sounded terrified, as if she'd witnessed something unspeakable.

"A bad dream?" he asked.

Dakota shook her head.

"I do not understand," he said cautiously, wondering what had become of the straight path his life had been. "What is this talk of the hangman?"

"The two men," Abby cried, tugging at his sleeve. He could see some of the terror giving way to a determination far beyond her years. "The tree by the gray house..." Her words drifted into soft sobs and he let his hand slip from her head to her shoulders and held her close.

"It's a premonition," Dakota said. "Your daughter also has second sight."

"I hardly think Abigail is a seer."

"Think again, Patrick. She has the gift."

It would explain so much about the child. How many times had Abigail surprised him with a bit of knowledge or information that seemed out of keeping with her tender years?

"You believe this to be the case?" he asked Dakota.

She nodded. "Absolutely."

He knelt in front of the child and, without thinking, brushed the tears from her cheeks with the tip of his forefinger. It was the first spontaneous gesture he had allowed himself toward her since Susannah had shattered his dreams.

Awkwardly he placed his arm about her fragile shoulders, and the child seemed to blossom before his eyes. A wave of guilt assailed him. It took so little to make her happy.

"The hangman is all ready," Abby said. "Now that the snow has stopped they can hang the rope from the big tree behind the house."

Patrick's eyes locked with Dakota's. Every house in the Colony of New Jersey had at least one big tree behind it.

Dakota crouched down in front of Abigail. "Honey, your papa and I are going to go for a carriage ride. Would you like to come with us?" And if she saw a gray house . . .

The elation on the child's face was painful to his eyes. "May I, Papa?"

He cleared his throat then said gruffly, "Yes, yes, of course you may. Two o'clock, Abigail. In the front parlor."

He turned toward the door but not before Dakota saw the glint of tears in his eyes.

Abby clutched Lucy to her chest as she sat on the edge of the top step and waited for the hall clock to toll two times. Her heart was beating so loudly inside her chest that it hurt her ears.

"Oh, Lucy!" she whispered. "Papa wants me to ride with him in the carriage." And even better than that, better than anything in the world, he had hugged her just like her friend Mary's papa hugged his children.

She leapt to her feet as the clock began to toll. Dakota had helped her put on her very best dress, a green-sprigged muslin that made her feel almost pretty. She smoothed the skirt and brushed a fleck of dust from her scuffed kid slippers, then flew down the stairs as if she had wings.

Papa stood near the door. He looked so handsome in his pale breeches and dark brown wool cape, and his hair scraped back and tied with a strip of leather.

"Abigail." His mouth quirked up at the sides as he turned toward her. "You look very pretty in that dress."

She buried her face against Lucy's yarn hair. "Thank you, Papa."

"Your hair," he said, looking at her carefully. "Is it different somehow?"

"Dakota combed it smooth then tied it with a piece of velvet ribbon."

"It becomes you," he said, nodding. "You should comb it that way all the time."

She would! She would comb her hair and tie it with a velvet ribbon every single day of her life if it meant Papa would smile at her like that, as if he loved her and was glad she was his little girl.

Jacob Wentworth, one of the good citizens of Franklin Ridge, watched their departure from his front door, his face taut with silent disapproval. If he had a shotgun, Dakota had no doubt the three of them—Patrick, Abigail and herself—would resemble Swiss cheese by now.

"You were right," Dakota said as she accompanied Patrick and Abigail back to their waiting carriage. "Everybody *does* hate you."

Patrick gave her a sidelong glance in the gathering dusk. "'Tis as I thought it would be."

"Ten houses and nobody would open their door to us," she continued. "They wouldn't even invite us in when Abby asked."

"Will you now allow me to obtain information in my own way?"

"I can't believe people would be so rude," Dakota went on, ignoring him. "Whatever happened to hospitality? It's freezing out here. Wouldn't you think someone would at least offer us a cup of hot cider?"

"Mayhap if the cider were laced with poison."

She couldn't argue with that. The withering hatred they'd encountered had put a new spin on everything. *So, you're not the heartless monster you pretend to be with Abby,* she thought. There could be no future for the little girl as long as Patrick was ostracized by the townspeople. The only hope for Abby was to send her to the Girls' School of the Sacred

Heart where she would be accepted into the fold in a way she could never be here in Franklin Ridge.

Abigail ran ahead through the snow to investigate a fallen bird's nest at the edge of the woods.

"Abigail!" Patrick's voice rang out as she disappeared into the shadows. "Do not venture too far."

He quickened his pace to keep up with the child. Dakota was about to quicken her own pace when something caught her eye. About ten feet to her left the pristine whiteness of the snow was marred by an odd, shadowy depression. Curious, she picked her way through the snow and bent to investigate.

She didn't know exactly what she'd expected to find, but she did know a loaded handgun wasn't on the short list of possibilities. She was no firearms expert, but she knew she'd seen this gun before and it hadn't been in a museum.

It was Shannon's, the one her friend had kept locked away in her desk drawer. A flood of possibilities rushed through her mind. Had the gun tumbled out of Shannon's bag or had she deliberately tossed it away, to keep the gun from falling into enemy hands? Instinct told Dakota it was the latter. While she'd come through time armed with jelly doughnuts, apparently Shannon had had the foresight to bring something equally lethal, albeit in a different way. She glanced toward the woods. Patrick's back was to her. She whispered a quick prayer of thanks. If he saw the gun, he'd ask questions and she'd be forced to tell him everything.

Quickly she reached under her skirts and tucked it into the top of her left cotton stocking, then continued on toward the carriage.

Approximately thirty minutes later Patrick guided the horses up the lane toward the house. To Dakota it seemed as if they'd been on the road for thirty days. The gun was wedged firmly between the carriage seat and her thigh and she'd shifted her position more often than a politician.

"'Tis the fifth time you have done so," Patrick observed. "What gives you such discomfort?"

She crossed her fingers beneath the lap robe. "My back hurts."

He nodded and she breathed a guilty sigh of relief.

Patrick brought the carriage to a stop at the front door. Abby, who had been napping beneath her lap robes, burrowed more closely against Dakota's side.

"It seems like a crime to wake her up," Dakota said innocently as Patrick climbed from the carriage and came around to help her. "She's sleeping like a log. Why don't you carry her upstairs to her room?"

He swung Dakota from the carriage, letting her slide slowly down his body until her feet touched the ground. As if they *could* touch the ground when she was this close to him.

"You try my patience, Dakota Wylie," he said as she met his eyes. "Can you not allow the future to proceed at its own pace?"

Oh, Devane, she thought wistfully as the gun slid down to the back of her knee. *If we only had the time....*

19

The house was in chaos when they returned. If possible, more soldiers than before were crowded into the front hallway and main rooms, and each one of them seemed to consider it his solemn duty to make as big a mess as possible.

"What in bloody hell is going on?" Patrick demanded as the door closed behind them.

Dakota glanced around at the confusion and noticed most of the furniture had been moved out. "Looks like Mc-Dowell meant what he said about throwing a party for us. I thought he was just talking to hear himself speak." She'd known lots of blowhards in her time and McDowell had seemed about as reliable as any of his kind. "He's probably moving the furniture to make room for dancing."

Devane's jaw tightened. "The house still belongs to me, whether or not McDowell wishes to acknowledge that fact. I will not have my possessions removed without my permission."

Abigail tugged on his sleeve. "Don't be angry, Papa. They'll be gone soon."

Dakota crouched down next to her and helped the child off with her cloak. "Not soon enough for your papa, honey. The soldiers will probably be here until spring."

Abigail's gray eyes took on the dreamy expression Dakota had come to recognize. "Not him," she said, tilting her head in the direction of the library where McDowell was sequestered. "He'll be far 'way by Christmas." Abby turned and ran toward the kitchen for a cup of cider.

Patrick stormed toward the library and Dakota seized the opportunity to flee upstairs with the gun.

There weren't a lot of hiding places to choose from, not with a child, an inquisitive male and a score of soldiers in the house. She slid it under the feather mattress in the anteroom, then smoothed the quilt and fluffed up the pillow. So what if it would be like sleeping on top of a hand grenade? The important thing was that nobody found it.

"Dakota! Where are you?"

"Be right there, Abby," she called out, thanking God the child hadn't popped up ten seconds earlier.

Abby stood near the armoire in Devane's room and, for a moment, Dakota was afraid the child had flashed on the hidden passageway, but Abby had something much more exciting on her mind.

"Papa found two more ladies!"

I'll bet he'd be dynamite on a treasure hunt. "Two more ladies?" she asked, tugging on one of Abby's braids. Probably new parlormaids to help Cook run the household. "Where did he find them?"

"They were standing right there at the kitchen door when I got there!" Abby's eyes were wide with excitement. "They're so pretty...."

Dakota's smile faltered. *I really don't want to hear this.*

"...And then she slapped Papa and called him a monster!"

She snapped to attention. "Somebody hit your father?"

Abby nodded vigorously. "The lady with the red hair. She said Papa had ruined her life."

A knot formed in the pit of Dakota's stomach. "Did she say how he'd managed to ruin her life?" *It's 1779, Wylie. Take a wild guess.*

Abby frowned as she thought. "She said her children would not have a father, and that's when Papa told me to leave."

"You stay here," she told Abby. "I'm going downstairs to see what's going on."

She went straight to the kitchen where she'd heard the commotion. Cook was kneading bread with large, angry motions. Will sat on a chair near the back door while a beautiful young blonde warmed her hands by the fire. Dakota winced. The girl was young enough to be Patrick's daughter, which meant she was probably exactly the right age to date him.

If that was the competition, she might as well fling herself into the stew pot and be done with it.

You're the mistress of the house, she told herself as they noticed her standing in the doorway. It might be a temporary role, but she was going to play it to the hilt while it lasted.

"My husband," she said to Cook, with a nod toward Will and the lovely young woman. "Where will I find him?"

"The front room, missus. But I don't think you want to be going in there, what with the commotion and all."

Let this one be homely, she prayed. *Thirty pounds overweight would be nice.* Just once in her life she'd love to nurse a healthy superiority complex about something other than the fact she could reshelve books faster than any librarian in the Western world.

Patrick sat in the wing chair near the window. He didn't look happy to see her. "Go back upstairs," he ordered. "Now!"

She resisted the urge to click her heels together and say, "Yes, *mein Führer.*"

The woman wasn't anywhere in sight. Obviously he hoped to keep it that way. "Abby told me we had company," she said sweetly. "I thought you might like to introduce us."

"I said leave *now!*"

She stepped into the room. "Don't bother trying to hide her, Devane, because I know what's going on."

"Do you?"

Dakota spun to her right at the sound of the female voice. A gorgeous redhead stepped from behind the door. She was a good six inches taller than Dakota and twenty pounds lighter, and she had a pistol pointed straight at Patrick's heart.

"Come in," said the woman with a brittle smile. "Sit down next to your husband. You might want to hear about the kind of man you married."

"No, thank you," Dakota said with an equally brittle smile. Damn the luck. If she still had Shannon's gun tucked inside her stocking, she could give the woman a run for her money.

"My wife knows naught about the situation," Patrick said. "Do not bring her into this."

The red-haired woman dismissed him with a contemptuous glance. "Then it's time she learned, isn't it?" She gestured toward a wing chair opposite Patrick's. "Sit down."

Dakota considered making a run for it, but it was obvious the woman was at the end of her rope. She sat down opposite Patrick.

The woman was still talking, but suddenly Dakota couldn't make out what she was saying. She could see the woman's lips moving, but the words were garbled. As if they were coming at her fast and loud but in a foreign language.

"What was that?" she asked, leaning forward in her seat.

The buzzing inside Dakota's head drowned out all other sounds. Patrick touched her arm. She knew he did because she saw his hand upon her forearm, but it felt as if he were touching her through layers of cotton wool.

What was going on? She had the same drifting, otherworldly feeling she'd had that last day when the balloon was about to sail off. But the balloon wasn't anywhere around.

A lighthouse...a sense of danger everywhere...a tall, red-haired woman—

"Emilie?" Dakota asked.

The woman looked down at her, gun still aimed at Patrick. "We know each other?"

"In a way," she said.

Emilie moved closer to Patrick. "Been talking about me, have you, Devane? I'm surprised. I thought you kept your secrets close to your vest."

"Let my wife go," he ordered, his voice cool as ice. "Grant her safety and I will tell you all."

"Tell me all," Emilie countered, "and then maybe I'll let your wife go."

"You're making a mistake," Dakota said, unable to keep silent. "Don't you realize you're both on the same side?"

"So he has you fooled, too," Emilie said, glancing toward Dakota with pity in her eyes. "The man's a spy."

"So are you."

Next to her Patrick started in surprise.

"You're right," Emilie said to Dakota, "but the trouble is he's passing our secrets on to the British and now my husband is going to pay the price."

Tell her the whole story, Wylie. Tell her you know how it's all going to end up.

"Where is Zane?" Emilie demanded in a tone of voice bordering on hysteria. "Where did they take him?"

"I do not know, madam," said Patrick. "I wish with my entire heart that I could find those two brave men, but thus far I cannot."

Emilie spat at his feet. "Liar!"

Dakota leapt to her feet. "Patrick is telling you the truth."

"If you believe that, you're an even bigger fool than Zane and Josiah were."

"He *is* on their side."

"Madam," said Patrick dryly, "I can fight my own battles."

"Apparently not," Dakota observed. "Otherwise she wouldn't have that gun pointed at your head."

"I never trusted you," Emilie said to Patrick. Her entire body was trembling. "Not from the first. But even I didn't believe you would do something this terrible."

Once again Patrick explained the situation, that someone from within the spy ring had betrayed Rutledge and Blakelee. But Emilie was having none of it.

"I realize love must be an alien concept to you, Devane, but my husband is everything to me. We have gone through a great deal to be together...we have two beautiful children and another—" She paused for a moment then shook her head as if to clear her thoughts. "Family is the most important thing on earth, Devane, but—"

Emilie swayed on her feet. Patrick leapt from his chair to catch her before she fell, while Dakota grabbed for the pistol.

"Damn you!" Emilie dropped to the floor and buried her face in her hands. "I have looked everywhere for them... asked everybody I met...but no one will—"

"Dakota?"

The room fell silent. In unison the three of them turned toward the door to find Abigail standing there.

She looked curiously at Emilie and then at Dakota. "You're both the same!"

"Go back to your room, Abigail." Dakota couldn't control the fear in her voice.

Emilie turned toward Dakota, eyes blazing with curiosity. *"Dakota?"*

The vibes between the two women were almost painful. Dakota felt as if she'd been hooked up to an IV drip and they were shooting straight adrenalin into her veins.

"'Tis a family name," Dakota managed to say.

Abby sidled up to Emilie and, to Dakota's horror, that dreamy expression was on her face again. "One day I'm going to—"

"Abby," Dakota said, fear rising. "Go upstairs!"

The child ignored her. "Sail away over the treetops in a bright red ball—"

"Don't, Abby," Dakota whispered. "Please don't. . . ."

"Just like you and Dakota did when you came here from the future."

"Oh, my God!" Emilie met Dakota's eyes as the child's words faded away. "You, too?"

Dakota nodded. She had a sudden, fleeting vision of a dinner table many years in the future and of families linked together through time. It vanished as quickly as it had come and she realized Patrick was staring at her. *I'm so sorry. I didn't want you to find out this way.*

"Explain, madam," he said, his voice tight. "I have heard much but understand little."

Abigail grabbed the sleeve of his jacket. "They rode in the big red ball, Papa. They came from very far away where people fly like birds with silver wings."

Emilie ruffled Abby's bangs with the easy grace of a woman comfortable with children. "ESP?"

Dakota nodded again. She couldn't find her voice.

"Beggin' your pardon, sir." Cook poked her head into the room. "Supper be ready in two shakes."

"Shepherd's pie?" Abigail asked, forgetting about silver birds for the moment.

"And a fine Indian pudding if you have the appetite, missy." If Cook was curious about what was going on in there, she gave no sign.

"I have to find Lucy!" Abigail cried and raced from the room with Cook close behind.

The tension in the room made Dakota's nerves jangle like bad jazz. There was so much she wanted to ask Emilie, so much Emilie probably wanted to ask her, but all she cared about was Patrick.

"We have to talk," she said to him.

He inclined his head but did not speak.

Emilie looked from one to the other, then rose to her feet and smoothed her skirts. "That shepherd's pie sounded wonderful. Would you mind if I supped with Abigail? I have not eaten since last night at the inn."

Patrick turned away from her, while Dakota managed a weak smile.

"We'll talk later," Emilie whispered, then left the room.

Patrick waited until the woman's footsteps faded away.

"What is it you wish to talk about?" he asked Dakota, although he knew the answer. Last night he had given her his heart. Today she would give it back to him, torn asunder.

"I think you'd better sit down for this."

"I will stand."

"Trust me, Patrick." She pulled one of the chairs closer. "You'll be glad you listened to me."

He was the kind of man who gave orders, not obeyed them. Still, there was something about her tone of voice that made him bow to her wishes. She paced back and forth in front of the fire. Her cheeks were flushed with color.

Do not leave me, madam, he thought, *for I cannot live this life without you in it.*

Dakota stopped dead in her tracks. "What did you say?"

"I did not say a word, madam." Had she managed to hear the thoughts inside his heart? "'Tis obvious you wish to deliver news of an unpleasant nature. It would benefit us both if you did so with no further delay."

"What's happened to you?" she demanded. "Did I imagine last night? I must have, because I seem to be the only one in the room who remembers what happened between us."

"I remember, madam," he said, his voice deadly calm. "I am reminded of it each time you speak of returning home. What we shared was a thing apart."

Dakota waited for him to say more, to declare his undying love, his eternal devotion, his unbridled passion, but he refused to cooperate. She sighed loudly.

"You're not going to make this easy on me, are you?"

"Nay, madam, I am not."

She sighed again.

"Louder, madam," he said dryly. "They have not heard you yet in London."

"Do you remember asking me where I came from?"

"Many times." He leaned back in the chair and rested his left leg on his right knee. His boots gleamed in the candlelight. "And I remember that your answer varied according to the story you chose to tell."

"There was a reason for that. I didn't think you would believe the truth."

He said nothing.

"I *am* from New Jersey, but not the New Jersey you know."

"I have not traveled south of Trenton, but have been told it is not unlike Franklin Ridge and the environs."

"That's not exactly what I mean." *Just do it, Wylie! He's not going to believe you no matter how nicely you phrase things.* "Damn it, Patrick, I'm from the future."

His jaw didn't sag open. His eyes didn't pop. He didn't leap to his feet and shout "Hallelujah!" The louse didn't do anything at all except continue to look at her impassively.

"Did you hear me, Patrick?" she demanded. "I'm from the future."

"I heard you clearly, madam." He brushed a speck of dust from the fine leather of his boot. "And from what distant world is it you come?"

"From 1993."

"The dawn of the twenty-first century?"

"Actually, we call it the millennium."

"And how did you find your way to this time?"

"Remember that bright red ball that flew over the tree-tops?"

"The one in which you rode with Andrew McVie and his woman."

"Her name is Shannon and yes, that's the one."

"You are saying you rode through the clouds from the future."

"I guess that's exactly what I'm saying." Even if it did sound like the biggest whopper ever told.

"And you are saying that Andrew McVie sailed with you from the future?"

"Exactly!" Finally they were getting somewhere. "You were wondering where he's been all this time and that's the answer."

Patrick leapt to his feet, toppling the chair with a crash. "You try my patience to the breaking point with these tales. Do you mark me for a fool who would believe such nonsense?"

"You're a smart man, Patrick. You know what I'm telling you is true."

"I know no such thing, madam, for what you tell me lies beyond the laws of nature and man."

But he was starting to believe her. She could see it in his eyes.

"Think about it. Andrew disappeared without a trace over three years ago. No one heard a word from him, no one saw him, no one buried him. And now here I am and suddenly everyone is talking about him. Doesn't it all make sense?"

"Such things are not possible. A man lives and dies within his own time. It can be no other way."

"That's what I thought, too, until it happened to me." She grabbed his sleeve and forced him to stop pacing and look at her. "You know I'm not like anybody else you've ever seen. My hair is too short." She lifted her skirts to the ankle, revealing her running shoes. "I *know* you wonder about those shoes." She let her skirts drop. "I don't think or speak or act like anyone you know."

"You are an individual with individual tastes."

"I'm weird."

"Your words, madam, not mine."

"Remember the shirt I was wearing when I arrived, the one with Jurassic Park written across my breasts? When did you ever see anything like that? Come on, Patrick, tell me!"

He was staring at her with eyes wide. "In truth, I have never heard a woman speak such words in my life."

"Jurassic Park?"

"Breasts."

She started to laugh. "There you go. Doesn't that tell you something?"

"You are plainspoken to a fault. That does not mean what you tell me is true."

She let out a shriek of frustration. "Wake up and smell the coffee, Devane! I'm from the future and that's all there is to it."

"Have you proof of your claim?"

"Shannon and Andrew could prove my claim."

"Shannon Whitney—she is from the future too?"

"She and Andrew met and fell in love in my time."

His brow furrowed. "And she chose to leave her own world to live in his?"

"She loves him, Patrick, and he was needed here."

"Do you love him as well, madam? Is that why you left your home?"

"I had no choice in it."

His eyes widened for the first time since she'd launched into the story. "They took you against your will?"

She described what had happened that last morning, the sensation of fading away into nothingness until the only thing anchoring her in the mortal world was the basket of the hot-air balloon. "You think I'm crazy, don't you? You don't believe one damn word I'm saying."

His silence told her she was right.

"Isn't this ridiculous? I've spent the past two days wondering how I was going to hide the truth from you and now that I'm baring my soul, you don't believe me." A wild laugh erupted. "Abby believes me! She knows it's true."

"Abigail also said she saw birds with silver wings."

Dakota grabbed him by the front of his waistcoat. His tension rippled through her skin. "She's right, Devane! Those birds with silver wings are called airplanes and they can fly hundreds of people anywhere in the world they want to go. China! Africa! Paris! And you can get there in just a few hours."

He pulled away from her. Anger and fear formed a shield around his heart that even she couldn't penetrate. "Madness! All of it. I will hear no more."

If only she had a newspaper or a photograph or a driver's license—anything to show him that what she said was true. She considered the gun, but in his frame of mind Patrick would probably chalk it up to one of Ben Franklin's inventions.

An idea popped into her head. It was ridiculous. Ludicrous. Embarrassing.

And it might work.

"Damn it, Devane, take a look at this!" She gathered up her outer skirt, her underskirts, her petticoat, then found the waistband of her panties. The manufacturer's label was still there. "Read this."

Patrick stared at the sight before him. Dakota Wylie's skirts frothed about her head in a profusion of yellow and lacy white. Her shapely, round legs were encased in pale stockings that, under other circumstances, would pique his curiosity. And covering her bottom and mound was that most intriguing bit of fabric that conformed to her lush body and left naught to the imagination.

"A tempting offer, madam, but one better extended in the privacy of my rooms."

She grasped a small tab of white fabric between her fingers and pulled. To his amazement the entire garment stretched like a lazy tabby after a long nap. "Just read it!"

"'One hundred percent cotton,'" he said slowly.

"Keep going."

"'Machine washable.'"

"There's more."

"'Made in the U.S.A.'" Blood pounded in his ears. He felt as if his heart would burst through his chest. "What is the meaning of this? What do these words represent?"

"U.S.A.," she said softly. "The United States of America."

20

"Sweet Jesus!" He leapt back as her skirts settled back into place.

"You're going to win the war, Patrick," she said. "It won't be easy and it won't happen tomorrow, but you're going to win." She told him that the thirteen colonies would one day become fifty states, that the nation they were fighting to create would still thrive and grow more than two hundred years into the future.

His chest heaved with the impact of her words. She could not know such things. No one could.

And yet, what wonderful words they were....

"Think about what you said last night," she urged, "that time itself has seemed different to you since we met, as if we're living a lifetime in a matter of days. You're not imagining it, Patrick, it's *real*, and I'm the reason why."

Patrick did not want to believe her, but he could no longer deny the truth. "Sweet Jesus," he said again. He saw her as if for the first time and wondered how it was he had been so blind. There was a glow about her person, a golden light that set her apart from the rest. "'Tis a fantastic story, madam, one that goes beyond the bounds of my understanding."

"I wish I could explain it to you, but all I know is that it has something to do with the balloon—they call those bright red things hot-air balloons—and some very strange cloud cover.''

Recognition hit him like a bolt of lightning. ''I had seen naught like those clouds in my lifetime. They towered upward like a great dark mountain yet had no effect upon the air.''

''Yes!'' came a voice from the doorway. ''That is how it was the morning I left. Those clouds are the key to it all.'' Emilie Crosse Rutledge glided into the room.

Patrick looked from Emilie to Dakota.

''I was just getting around to that part,'' Dakota said with an apologetic shrug. ''Emilie and Zane are from the future, too.''

Again his chest heaved as if struck a blow. Was there no end to this? He had worked with Zane for nearly three years and never noticed anything amiss.

Emilie considered him. ''You look as if you'd seen a ghost.''

''Nay, madam,'' said Patrick, slumping back into his chair. '''Twould be easier to understand if I had indeed seen an apparition.'' He gathered his thoughts into an untidy bundle. ''Were you brought here against your will?'' he asked Emilie.

''It was nothing I had looked for or expected,'' she said, meeting his eyes, ''but I thank the Almighty every day for giving me the chance to live this life.''

''And your husband,'' Patrick continued. ''Was it his choice?''

Emilie nodded. ''We had our chance to return a few summers ago but it was Andrew McVie who traveled through time in our stead.''

''But he's back now,'' Dakota reminded them. ''Andrew is the one who will rescue Zane and Josiah from the jail near Jockey Hollow.'' She groaned. ''That is, he'd rescue them from the jail near Jockey Hollow if there actually *was* a jail. We're going to have to work on that part of the equation.''

Emilie's eyes lit up with joy. "Andrew is back?"

Dakota nodded. "I traveled with him and Shannon."

"Please tell me he's happy. When he left he was so lonely...so alone."

"He's in love," said Dakota. "He and Shannon plan to be married."

Emilie's brows lifted. "This Shannon...is she a friend of yours?"

"A good friend."

"She'd better treat him right," said Emilie, "or she'll be hearing from me."

Dakota grinned. "I was thinking the same thing about Andrew."

"Still, that doesn't explain where Zane is being kept. You started to tell me something before," Emilie said, warming her hands near the fire. "That Abby had seen a vision or had a dream?"

Dakota met Patrick's eyes.

"It is not a pleasant vision, madam," said Patrick. "Mayhap you do not wish to—"

"I already know about the hanging, if that's what you mean. Molly told me what she knew last night." Her voice was steady but her hands trembled.

"Molly?" Patrick and Dakota asked simultaneously.

"A serving girl I met at the White Horse Tavern. Turns out she is your cook's niece. It was quite a coincidence, actually, that we met. Cook has been expecting Molly, but with the snow and all, Molly couldn't find a carriage heading this way." Emilie shot them a bemused smile. "And since I was already coming here to confront you, Patrick, I invited her along to keep me company."

"The hanging," Patrick said. "There was talk of it at the tavern?"

"They talk of everything at the taverns," Emilie said. "All I kept hearing about was the bright red ball and that it had fallen into British hands. I was so afraid it meant that Zane would—''

Patrick leapt to his feet, the future forgotten for the moment. ''That is what I was told the night Zane and Josiah were taken prisoner.''

''Yes,'' said Emilie, appraising him with her eyes. ''That's the night it happened. They said the Lobsterbacks brought down the balloon and took a man and woman captive.''

''Oh, my God!'' Dakota felt light-headed, as if she might faint. She bent forward, resting her forehead against her knees while she struggled to draw in a breath.

''Dakota?'' Patrick was at her side, his great strong hands holding her by the shoulders.

''I'm fine,'' she said, shaking her head to banish the buzzing sound building inside her brain. ''How did this Molly know about Zane and Josiah?''

''She said the tavern has been abuzz with talk these past few days. When I came asking questions, she put two and two together.''

Something wasn't right, Dakota thought as the buzzing grew louder. But what?

''She's a sweet thing,'' Emilie was saying, ''but she appears to be quite afraid of her aunt.''

Dakota shook her head to banish the cobwebs. ''Maybe it's Joseph and Will who should be afraid. Abby says that Cook makes her husband sleep on the floor when he's had too much rum.''

Emilie looked over at Patrick. ''How long has Cook worked for you?''

Patrick shrugged his shoulders. ''I cannot say with precision, but she has outlasted anyone else in my employ by some years.''

''I don't trust her,'' Emilie said. Her tone was apologetic; her words were anything but. ''I can't put my finger on it, but something just isn't right with her.''

Dakota disagreed. Except for her propensity for gossip, Cook seemed a harmless sort. "The only vibes I've picked up from Cook are curious ones. The woman's a born yenta."

"Yenta?" asked Patrick.

The two women laughed.

"That's a New Yorkism," said Dakota. "It means she's a real talker."

Emilie's expression turned wistful. "Somehow I never thought I'd hear the word *yenta* again as long as I lived. I miss our language."

"I miss raspberry-jelly doughnuts," said Dakota. "And toasted bagels with cream cheese."

"Pizza," said Emilie. "Pepperoni and onion."

"Big Mac, double cheese and large fries."

"You'll like it here," said Emilie. "They're big on cholesterol."

"Aren't you homesick?" Dakota asked, leaning toward the red-haired woman. "Look at all you left behind—electricity, indoor plumbing...Häagen-Dazs."

Emilie smiled the way she was supposed to but Dakota could see she didn't quite mean it.

"Häagen-Dazs?" she repeated. "The mantra of single women from coast to coast." Fat. Calories. Instant gratification.

"I miss all that," Emilie said, "but somehow none of it seems very important to me anymore." Both women were silent for a few moments. "I was meant to be here, Dakota. I never fit in that other world."

"That's what I thought, too," Dakota said, "until I landed here."

"The moment I got here I knew I'd finally come home."

"The moment I got here I started looking for a way to get out."

"Maybe the difference was Zane. When I realized I was pregnant with the twins, I knew this was where I was going to stay. I couldn't risk their lives, not even to go back with him."

Dakota's jaw dropped open. "He was going to leave you?"

"He came close. I'll admit I had a few bad moments when the balloon came back again. This has been a tough transition for him but I think we've managed to make it work."

"What made him stay?"

Color flooded Emilie's cheeks as she met Dakota's eyes. "Love."

"That's what I was afraid of," Dakota said. "That means I'm definitely on the next balloon out of here." The words were no sooner out of her mouth than she remembered Patrick was there, listening.

"Don't worry," said Emilie. "He left when we started talking Häagen-Dazs." Her tone made it clear how little she still thought of Patrick.

"He really *is* on our side," Dakota said. "He was distraught about Zane and Josiah."

"He should be. This was his fault. If anything happens to them, I'll—"

"But it wasn't his fault, Emilie, don't you see? This is history. Everything is unfolding the way it's meant to. This is Andrew's destiny. He's the one who saves your husband and Josiah, and it's going to happen very soon." The buzzing inside her head returned and she closed her eyes for a moment against a rising wave of dizziness. For a moment she imagined she could see the fabric of her skirt through the back of her hand, but then the image vanished. *Maybe even sooner than I thought.*

She told Emilie everything she knew, right down to the nonexistent jail in Jockey Hollow.

"I don't like the sound of this," said Emilie. Her eyes brimmed with tears. "How can Andrew save Zane and Josiah if there is no jail? How will he find them?"

"I don't know," Dakota admitted, "but I know it's going to happen." She took Emilie's hand in hers. "How else can you and Zane end up with five children and beachfront property?"

Emilie started to laugh through her tears. "Five?"

"Five kids, a mansion in Philadelphia, a summer place in Crosse Harbor and a mention in the history books."

Emilie squeezed her hand. "From your mouth to God's ear."

"Don't worry," Dakota said. "It's going to happen. I can feel it in my bones."

Now if only she could figure out how.

"Where did Papa go to?" Abigail asked as Dakota tucked her into bed a few hours later. "I looked for him right after supper but he was gone."

Dakota fluffed up the child's pillow and made sure Lucy was tucked in, too. "I don't know where your papa went to, Abby, but I intend to find out."

"Are you angry at Papa?"

"I'm not happy."

"Is it because of the lady with the red hair?"

I wish it was that simple. "Not exactly."

"Why do you want to go back in the big red ball?" Abigail asked.

No wonder she'd never been comfortable with kids. They asked the tough questions adults made sure to avoid. "Because that's where my home is."

Abby shook her head. "No," she said emphatically. "Your home is here with us."

"Coming here was a mistake, Abby. I'm meant to be back in the world where I came from."

"Your mama doesn't think so."

"How do you know what my mother thinks, honey?"

"She told me."

Ma, so help me . . . "She *told* you?"

"While I was eating Cook's shepherd's pie."

"What exactly did she say?"

Abby's face grew soft and dreamy. "Life's an adventure! Follow your heart!" She parroted Ginny's tone so exactly that Dakota could only stare at her in utter disbelief. "She says Papa loves you and that we can be a family."

Something inside Dakota's heart shifted like tectonic plates. "I wish that was true," she said softly.

"It is!"

She couldn't speak over the lump in her throat.

"Are you sorry you came here?"

Dakota shook her head. "I wouldn't have missed knowing you for the world."

"Then why do you want to go home again? Is it because you don't like me?"

"Oh, honey!" Dakota smoothed the girl's hair from her cheek. "I like you very much."

"You didn't like me when you first saw me."

"That's true," Dakota admitted. "And you didn't like me very much, either."

Abby buried her face against Lucy's yarn head. "I like you now."

"I know that. And I—" She cleared her throat. The words wouldn't kill her. She could say them and still walk out that door. "And I love you."

Abby lifted her head cautiously, then met Dakota's eyes. "You love me?"

Dakota nodded. When had it happened? Suddenly she couldn't remember when the sad-eyed little girl hadn't owned part of her heart. Dakota chucked her under the chin. "As it turns out, you're quite easy to love."

Abby's cheeks turned rosy with pleasure and her eyes once again got the dreamy expression Dakota knew meant the kid's ESP was kicking in. "You and Papa will be together for always."

To her horror, Dakota's eyes flooded with tears. "You said that once before, honey, but I don't think you're right this time."

"I am," said Abby, nodding her head. "I know it is true."

"I have to go home some day, Abby, and I don't think your father will want to go with me." Abby just gave her a Mona Lisa smile and said nothing, which undid what was left of Dakota's equilibrium. "There are things you don't understand, honey...things even I don't understand."

"I don't care," said Abby without missing a beat, "because I know you and Papa will be together always."

Dakota was overcome with a wave of maternal love and longing that was enough to send her racing toward the twentieth century without benefit of hot-air balloon. She could take just about anything life dished out, but she couldn't take this.

She ran from the room as fast as her shaky legs would carry her, then leaned against the closed bedroom door and let her tears fall. She didn't cry at sad movies or weddings, so why was she crying because a little girl with psychic abilities thought she saw a happy ending in her future?

You're wrong, Abby, she thought, wiping away her tears and straightening her shoulders. There could never be a future for her and Devane, not in a million years. She wasn't meant for the eighteenth century and she was damn sure Patrick wasn't cut out for the twentieth.

Quietly she walked down the hallway to the room she was sharing with Patrick and closed the door behind her. Emilie Rutledge was asleep in the room where Dakota had spent her first night, while Cook's niece Molly slept downstairs in the kitchen with the help.

A candle burned brightly in the window and she sat down on the bed, tired to her bones. Patrick had been gone for hours. He'd disappeared during her conversation with Emilie and he hadn't returned for supper. When she'd asked

Joseph where Patrick had gone, Joseph had shrugged his shoulders. "He told me to saddle his horse and he left," Joseph said. "'Tain't my place to be askin' questions."

"'Tain't my place, either," Dakota said to the silent room. Whatever magic she and Patrick had shared was over. Finished. Vanished as if it had never happened. You couldn't drop a bombshell like the one she'd dropped on him and expect to escape the aftershocks.

Patrick lived in a world without electricity or flush toilets, and there she was telling him about time travel and jet planes. She must have been crazy to believe for one second they had a chance. Talk about being geographically undesirable: she and Patrick were off the scale.

She lay back on the feather mattress and pulled a quilt up over her shivering body. She was cold from the inside out. Ever since dinner she'd found it impossible to get warm and, even more frightening, twice more her hands had seemed to grow transparent.

She buried her face in his pillow. The scent of his skin still lingered in the silky cotton.

She could feel the forces of destiny at work, moving the players around on some cosmic game board until they were all in position for the final play.

Andrew would meet his destiny. Zane and Josiah would be saved, and Andrew would achieve the recognition he deserved. All three men would be reunited with the women who loved them and their families would be together down through the years.

But what about Patrick and Abby? What will happen to them?

She tried to see into their future but all she saw was darkness.

Patrick returned to the house in the hour after midnight. He had ridden far in search of answers and had not been disappointed. The simplicity of it all astounded him and he wondered how they had not realized it sooner. But therein lay the beauty of the enemy's plan.

As he crossed the yard between the stable and the main house he looked up at the night sky. Clouds were moving in from the east, an unusual occurrence in itself, but these were clouds unlike any of his experience. He had seen the dark, jagged tower but one other time, on the day Dakota had come into his life.

Those clouds were a precursor to the events Dakota spoke of, events that would happen on the morrow. He now knew where Josiah and Zane were being held prisoner. He knew that Andrew McVie and Shannon Whitney lived. Tomorrow he would throw in his lot with fate and pray that when it was over, Dakota Wylie would still be at his side.

The only sound inside the house was the ticking of the tall clock in the hallway as he climbed the stairs to his second-floor room. He stripped off his clothes, washed, then climbed into the big bed next to Dakota. Her plain cotton nightdress was bunched up around her hips and she had tossed the pillow to the floor. He fit his body to hers spoon-fashion, then gathered her close.

She murmured something soft and infinitely appealing and pressed her rump against him. His arousal was violently sudden, springing to powerful life against her soft, firm cheeks. She moved again, a sinuous fluid motion, and he slid his hand between her thighs, then cupped her against his palm. She was wet for him already, her juices hot and sweet on his fingers as he stroked her lower lips, feeling them swell with her eagerness for him.

And it was for him. He would not think otherwise. No matter what else happened, he had been the first man to know her body. The first man to love her. The first man to take her with his mouth....

Dakota had never had a dream like this before. Voluptuous waves of pleasure washed over her, almost drowning her senses in sheer bliss. She felt graceful . . . infinitely desirable . . . moving perfectly with the ebb and flow of the tides.

Her back arched and she opened her legs wider. Wave after wave of sensation . . . wetness . . . heat . . . a throbbing pressure that was building . . . building—

Her eyes flew open and she realized what was happening.

"Patrick!"

He looked up from between her thighs. His mouth gleamed wet and hot by moonlight. "Your honey is sweet," he said, sliding up the length of her body. "Taste yourself on me."

"Oh, my God—" Not even in her most detailed fantasies had she even come close to this.

His mouth found hers, his lips slick. He ran his tongue along the place where her lips met, urging her to open, to taste. A shudder of delight rippled through her body as he deepened the kiss. Just the thought of his mouth pressed between her legs was enough to send her tumbling into madness.

His erection throbbed against her thigh and suddenly she wanted to do for him all that he had done for her.

"I want to taste you," she whispered, wild and hungry for him. "I want to feel you in my mouth."

"Yes," he said, his voice almost a growl of delight. "Take me in your mouth."

The bedclothes rustled as they sought a new way to love. She knelt between his powerful thighs and cupped him in her palms. "I won't be able to—" She stopped, not sure how to phrase it.

"Just suckle me," he said, placing his hand behind her head, guiding her forward. "As much as you can take."

His erection was smooth to her tongue and hot. She could feel the blood pulsing in the blue vein that ran along the underside.

"For you," he said, his voice floating toward her in the darkness. "All of it, everything."

Instinct took over. She drew him more deeply into her mouth, bringing him closer to ecstasy with her hands and mouth and tongue while he writhed beneath her. She felt more womanly at that moment than she ever had before, as if the secret of a woman's power were hers for the taking.

Suddenly, when she was sure he was near a climax, he grabbed her by the shoulders and pulled her up the hard, muscled length of his body. She straddled his hips and lowered herself onto him, feeling her body open for him, envelop him, draw him deeply into her secret self until she could no longer tell where she ended and he began. She didn't need to know. They were one being, one heart, one life.

She cried when it was over. Loud, messy tears of pleasure and sadness and he held her close and stroked her hair until the storm passed.

"There is so much to tell you," she whispered, rubbing her damp cheek against his chest. "So much I want to share with you—"

He silenced her with a kiss of such tenderness and love that tears again filled her eyes.

"There will be time for that later," he said, rolling her onto her back and moving between her willing thighs. "Tonight there is only us." He found her entrance. "Only this pleasure." He slid inside her welcoming sheath. "Only this moment."

21

"**Y**ou look beautiful," Emilie said as Dakota twirled in front of her. "Nobody would ever guess you grew up wearing jeans and T-shirts."

Dakota took one last look in the cheval mirror in the corner of the room. The dress she had chosen for McDowell's party was a deep gold satin with intricate embroidery on the bodice and sleeves. The bodice was cut low in front and, thanks to clever corseting, she actually had cleavage. She didn't dare tell Emilie that when she looked into the mirror she saw a beautiful dress but the woman inside the dress was fading away.

"You might try smiling," Emilie suggested. "If you go downstairs looking like that, they'll think there's trouble in paradise."

Dakota turned and met Emilie's eyes. "*Trouble* doesn't begin to cover it." She gestured toward the window. "Did you see?"

Emilie nodded. "I've been trying to ignore it."

"I can't ignore it," Dakota said. "It's like that damn cloud is screaming my name." She looked into the mirror again, and could barely make out her own image.

"Funny," said Emilie. "I'm afraid it's screaming 'Zane Grey Rutledge! Here's your second chance!'"

"No," Dakota said. "Trust me. This one has my name on it."

She'd awakened early to find Patrick already gone. If it weren't for the rumpled sheets and the delicious ache between her legs, she would have thought she'd imagined their wondrous lovemaking. Cook said he'd saddled up early and ridden off toward town, but as the hours wore on, Dakota began to worry.

"I don't think he's coming home," Dakota said, twisting the silver bracelets she wore on her left wrist. "He was furious with McDowell about this party. It wouldn't surprise me if he boycotted."

"Zane and I met General McDowell two years ago in Philadelphia." Emilie shuddered. "The man redefines the word *sleaze.*"

"Patrick seems to think McDowell's loyalties are suspect."

"I know," said Emilie. "McDowell and his wife introduced Benedict Arnold to his bride, Peggy Shippen, and we both know where that's going to lead. Besides, he—" She stopped and looked out the window.

"He what?" Dakota prodded. "What were you about to say?"

"Just that McDowell was instrumental in bringing Patrick and Susannah together *and* in tearing them apart." Apparently Patrick and Susannah had met at one of McDowell's parties and, a few years later, it was at another of McDowell's parties that she'd met the young—and very wealthy—officer with whom she'd run off, back home to Philadelphia. She'd abandoned both her husband and child, humiliating before an entire colony the man she'd once loved.

"No wonder Patrick hates the man," Dakota said.

"There's more to it than that," Emilie said. "Everyone in the colony knows McDowell is dealing with the British. The problem is getting proof."

"How did Susannah die?"

"A carriage accident near the Delaware. She and her officer friend drowned."

Dakota tried to muster some sympathy for the dead woman but came up empty. Patrick and Abigail continued to suffer from her selfish choices every day, in ways only they understood.

"Are you sure you won't join the festivities?" she asked Emilie.

The red-haired woman shook her head. "I'm too tall to wear Susannah's dresses. I'll sit in the kitchen with Cook and Molly and listen to the local gossip."

An odd sensation washed over Dakota as she looked at her reflection in the mirror. The dress glittered in the candlelight but the woman wearing it seemed as transparent as window glass. As quickly as the vision appeared, it vanished again.

"Tonight," Dakota said. "I can feel it in my bones."

Emilie glanced toward the window. If anything, the clouds seemed darker, angrier, the edges more jagged and threatening. "God help me, so can I."

Abigail was curled on the window seat in Papa and Dakota's bedroom. Lucy was propped up on the sill, looking quite pretty in the new dress that Dakota and the red-haired woman had sewn for her that afternoon.

Abby had wanted to put on a pretty dress of her own and go to the party, too, but Dakota had promised to save her a piece of sugar cake and tell her all about the music and dancing in the morning. Abby's temper had heated up really fast when she heard the word no, but when she'd thought about how much she wanted Dakota to stay with them and be her new mama, she'd decided to mind her manners.

Fancy coaches and carriages wound their way up the snowy lane to the house and Abby pressed her nose against

the windowpane as she watched the men and ladies step
down. Many of the men wore powdered wigs tied at the
napes of their necks with brightly colored ribbon. Abby
giggled as a fat gentleman tugged at his ponytail, only to
send his wig sliding down over one ear.

The ladies wore their hair in elaborate arrangements that
puzzled Abby. How did they make their hair stand up that
way? she wondered. Was it a secret you learned when you
grew up? She hoped so, because she would so love to look
beautiful.

It was great fun to sit there, so warm and cozy with Lucy
and watch the parade of guests as they arrived at the house,
but it was the big ugly cloud that fascinated Abby most of
all. She didn't know what it was, but the cloud made her feel
funny inside, the way she felt when a lightning storm was
coming, all jumpy and filled with excitement.

The bright red balloon was coming back and when it did,
Abby and Lucy would be ready.

Abby grabbed her cloak, tucked Lucy under her arm and
tiptoed toward the back stairs.

The blows came hard and fast but Patrick refused to sway.
They would have to kill him before he bent a knee before the
bloody traitors. The good people of Franklin Ridge, the
same good people who had ostracized him, had cradled a
viper to their bosoms. It should not surprise them when the
viper bared its fangs.

McDowell. The very name was a blight upon the cause.
May you rot in hell for eternity.

The crack of bone echoed inside his head. His bone? He
waited for the pain but it never came. He was beyond pain,
into another, more terrifying realm of sensation.

The butt of the musket slammed into his shoulder and he
staggered but did not drop. One week ago he had lacked a
reason to go on, but all had changed. His life had opened up
before him, filled with promise, and he would not, could
not, let it slip through his fingers.

Dakota. He saw her clearly in his mind's eye, saw the sweetness of her soul, the fire of her convictions. He saw her heart, the depth and breadth of everything she was... everything he could be.

He would not give up.

He would not die before he saw her face again.

General McDowell was outraged when he realized Patrick wasn't at the party.

"To leave you in such trying circumstances," he said, feigning sympathy for Dakota's plight. "A most ungentlemanly thing to do."

Dakota debated between defending her husband and siding with the enemy. She opted for the enemy. "Quite," she said, taking the arm the general offered. "I don't know what possessed him to do such a thing."

"Most thoughtless," McDowell went on. "I'm of a mind to have my men comb the area until they find the reprobate."

"Don't do that!" Dakota snapped, perhaps a shade too harshly. "I will not force my company upon anyone... especially not my husband."

"You have been ill-used, my dear," McDowell said as they entered the enormous front hall that tonight served as a ballroom. "Much as dear Susannah had been."

Dakota nearly choked on her own saliva.

"My plainspokenness surprises you," McDowell said, chuckling. "I do not mean to make you uncomfortable, my dear, only to remind you that you are not the first young woman Devane has mistreated nor, dare I say, will you be the last."

And thank you so much for sharing, you moron. If the situation had been different, if she hadn't learned what kind of man Patrick truly was, McDowell's comments might have been devastating. As it was, she regained her composure just in time to take her place in the receiving line to greet their guests.

Emilie was curled up by the hearth fire in the kitchen, pretending to doze. Neither Patrick nor Dakota put any stock in her suspicions about Cook, but the sense that all was not as it seemed had grown stronger as the day progressed.

One thing was certain: Cook was running poor Molly ragged. The young woman had kneaded a dozen loaves of bread, cut the vegetables for soup, plucked four chickens, then set out to lug an enormous bag of flour down to the basement.

"You can't do that," Emilie had said to the girl. "It's too heavy."

Molly wiped her forehead with the back of her hand. "Aunt says I must, ma'am, and she doesn't take kindly to slackers."

"Tell Will to come in here and do it."

"Will's off t' the stables, helping his father." Molly offered her a sunny smile. "'Tain't the worst thing I've done in my life."

"Still, it's too heavy for you. I would help you myself but I am two months with child and must be careful."

Molly's smile was maybe a shade too hearty and Emilie grew suspicious. "Like I said, 'tain't the worst thing I've done." With that, Molly set out to drag the sack out the back door then down the stone steps to the cellar.

All day long it had been that way in Cook's kitchen. Harsh voices. Even harsher tasks. Enough whispering to make the most trusting soul suspicious. Something was going on and Emilie was determined to get to the bottom of it. She didn't have Patrick's knowledge of the area or Dakota's extrasensory perception, but she did have the strong feeling that Cook was involved in something much bigger than what was in her stew pot.

"That's a lazy one," Emilie heard Cook say as she pretended to nap by the fire after supper.

"She's not a worker, Aunt," came Molly's sweet voice. "She's a guest."

"Hmmph," Cook snorted. "Guests sleep upstairs in a regular bed. They don't curl up by the fire like common folk."

You're a snob, Cook, thought Emilie. *But are you a traitor, too?*

Under different circumstances Dakota could imagine enjoying an eighteenth-century party in her honor. And there was certainly something to be said for men in uniform. Add to that the music and the rum punch and the laughter, and it made for a heady brew.

Too bad the *if onlys* made it impossible for her to enjoy.

If only she belonged.

If only the marriage they celebrated was a *real* marriage, not a sham.

If only Patrick had seen fit to be there with her.

What do you expect, Wylie? She thought as she twirled around the dance floor in the arms of a ruddy officer from Philadelphia. She'd turned Patrick's entire life upside down. She looked up at her dancing partner, who favored her with a huge smile. *What would you say if I told you I was born in 1967?*

She knew darn well what he'd say. He'd scream, "Witch!" and start a bonfire.

Patrick hadn't done that. He'd tried to understand and to believe, even when reason must have told him he was mad to consider it. Last night he'd made love to her, body and soul. It had been about so much more than sex, so much more than desire, that she'd felt as if their two hearts had become one.

He knew this wasn't her world. He knew she would be adrift in a sea of unfamiliar faces, unfamiliar ways. No matter how much he hated General McDowell, Patrick never would have left her alone at this party. Not unless—

"Madam?" The officer's brow creased with concern. "Are you unwell?"

"No—I mean, yes." She lowered her eyes and swayed. "I am feeling quite unwell. Will you excuse me?"

"Let me accompany you from the dance floor."

"No, no, you needn't do that. Please find another partner and continue dancing."

She hurried away before he had time to protest, and barely reached the back stairs before she ran into Emilie.

Emilie grabbed her by the arm and pulled her into the pantry.

"I was right!" Emilie's voice shook with triumph. "It's Cook!"

Dakota stared at her in the murky light. "What?"

"Cook is the missing link."

"That's crazy," Dakota said, even though the buzzing in her head and down her spine told her otherwise. "How could Cook possibly—"

"I don't have time to explain it all," Emilie said, "but Molly put the pieces together."

"You're talking too fast," Dakota protested. "Slow down. I don't know what you're—"

"Listen!" Emilie gripped Dakota's forearms and shook her hard. "Cook's sister Margaret works at the Ford house where General Washington is staying." Emilie paused for effect. "And Margaret is Molly's mother."

"So what? That doesn't make her a spy. My mother has a martyr complex but that doesn't make me Joan of Arc."

"Don't you understand? Cook and Margaret passed messages back and forth through poor Molly. The two women have had a rivalry going on since the cradle and finally Margaret had something to hold over Cook's head."

"General Washington?" Dakota breathed, suddenly beginning to understand.

"Exactly," said Emilie. "And the more detailed information Margaret passed on, the more jealous she believed Cook would get."

But Margaret didn't know her sister as well as she thought. Cook had bigger and better plans for the juicy information Margaret was relaying through poor Molly. No, Cook didn't get jealous; Cook was getting rich.

"... the White Horse Tavern where Molly worked..." Emilie's words penetrated the loud buzz inside her head.

She struggled to zero in on what the woman was saying, but she felt as if Emilie were a thousand light-years away.

"What about the White Horse Tavern?" she managed to say. "Isn't that where you met Molly?"

"And it's the place where Zane and Josiah were making the drop the night they were captured. The owner was a staunch patriot."

Dakota met her eyes. "Or so you thought?"

"Exactly," said Emilie. "The bastard betrayed us. Loyalists paid him in gold to alter his allegiance."

Dakota sagged against the cold stone wall of the pantry as dark images, shadows, danced at the outer reaches of her peripheral vision.

"Dakota?" Emilie kept her from falling. "Are you okay?"

"Patrick's in danger," she said, knowing the truth of her statement in every cell and fiber of her body. "I have to find him."

"It's dark out there. You don't know the area. You'll never be able to find him."

"I'll find him," Dakota said. It was her destiny, the reason she'd traveled through time.

"I'm coming with you," Emilie said.

"No!" Dakota was adamant. "You can do more here. Someone has to watch Abby and keep McDowell from getting suspicious." Her mouth curved in a quick smile. "Besides, you're pregnant. You can't take any chances."

Emilie sighed and placed her hands over her belly. "Godspeed," she said, hugging Dakota fiercely. "Come back safely."

Dakota hugged Emilie back but said nothing. It would be a miracle if she came back at all.

"Cook's coming!" Emilie said. "Give me two minutes to get her to the kitchen, then you can make a run for it."

It was the longest two minutes of Dakota's life. Finally she peered out from the pantry, saw nobody peering back in at her, then tore up the back stairs to the bedroom. She wasn't going anywhere without Shannon's gun. Abigail was sound asleep, sprawled across the enormous feather bed. Dakota resisted the urge to press a kiss to her forehead. Goodbyes were dangerous.

She slipped into the anteroom, slid her hand under the mattress and retrieved the gun. This time she didn't hide it in her stocking but tucked it in her bodice, fashion be damned, then grabbed her cloak and was off.

She bumped into Joseph near the top of the stairs.

"Don't go down there," he said, blocking her way. "Not if you're lookin' to get away."

Their eyes met. He was on her side.

"Use the passageway," Joseph said, glancing down toward the first floor. "I'll close up for you."

"Did you do that the other day?"

"Beggin' your pardon, ma'am, but I did. She snoops when she thinks no one's around," he said, meaning Cook. "If she'd be seein' that—"

"Don't apologize," she said with a gentle laugh. "Just don't lock it this time."

"'Twas that or you give the missus the surprise of her life."

Somehow Dakota didn't think there was much that could surprise Cook, but she let it pass. It was enough that Joseph was on their side.

"We'll have to be quiet," she said as he followed her into the bedroom. "Abby's asleep."

"Where?" Joseph asked as they stepped into the room.

Dakota turned around. The bed was empty.

"She was here a minute ago."

"Pardon me sayin' so, but you don't have time to be worryin' about the girl."

Joseph was right. Emilie would make sure Abby was safe. The time had come to leave and delaying it would only make it harder.

Joseph removed the last dresser drawer and Dakota swung open the doors to the armoire. With a whispered thank-you to the man, she vanished into the passageway. She was more surefooted this time. At least she knew what to expect at the other end.

Minutes later she reached the secret room. No candles or crackling fire awaited her. No Patrick with the raging heart she longed to soothe. She didn't linger but climbed the stone steps that led up to the stable, then quickly realized she had no idea how to attach the wagon to a horse.

She stepped outside into the cool night air. Maybe that wouldn't be a problem after all. The place was filled with wagons and carriages, all of which came with horses conveniently attached. No point getting too fancy, she thought as she surveyed some of the more elaborate rigs belonging to the party guests.

A small open wagon caught her eye. Especially the lumpy tangle of blankets in the back. For a second she thought she saw one of those blankets move, but it was her imagination playing tricks on her. Besides, who needed blankets when you had sheer adrenalin to keep you warm? The horse didn't seem too thrilled about being singled out but he didn't try to bite her. She took it as a good omen and climbed up onto the bench.

So far, so good. She had wheels. She had horsepower.

The horse gave her a snotty look over his shoulder, but she chalked it up to equine ego problems.

"You mind your business and I'll mind mine," she told him, grabbing the reins. "Now giddyap." To her amazement the horse did exactly that and the wagon bounced off down the snowy road.

Underneath the tangle of blankets in the back of the wagon, Abby clutched Lucy to her chest and smiled.

22

Rand McNally had nothing on Dakota. No wrong turns, no missed intersections, no false stops. Destiny held her in its arms and it wasn't about to let go.

A light snow was falling, just hard enough to lower visibility. She supposed she should be grateful for the snow. It illuminated the road almost as well as street lamps did in her time. Not that it mattered. Some other force was in charge here, guiding her to the place she needed to be.

Finally she crested a hill and the White Horse Tavern appeared, nestled snugly in a clearing. Her heart lurched. The place looked deserted. There wasn't a carriage or cart to be seen anywhere. A lone candle burned in an upstairs window.

Patrick's presence whispered in her ear. It reached into her heart and touched her soul. He was there and he was in trouble. She would do anything on earth to save him. Abigail needed him so much and—

And so do you.

"No," she said out loud. She refused to acknowledge the words. She had no business needing him. She wasn't part of his life and she never would be.

She urged the horse down the slope, then brought both horse and cart to a stop just inside the woods. She looped the reins around a low-hanging branch, made sure the gun was tucked securely in her bodice and set out to search for Patrick.

If she were an eighteenth-century man, where would she stash a prisoner? The cellar was an obvious choice. Maybe too obvious?

She crept toward the cellar door. Her heart was pounding so hard it hurt. *Please be in there,* she prayed. *Please be safe.* Carefully she eased back the latch and opened the door.

A guard slept at the bottom of the stairs. The man sat on a rolled-up blanket, his back resting against the wall. He cradled an ugly musket in his arms and, as far as Dakota could tell, he hadn't bathed in months. She peered inside. She saw a dark form in the middle of the room and she moved closer.

Oh, God. She stifled a cry. Patrick was chained to the floor in the middle of the room. His beautiful face was badly bruised. A cut slashed diagonally across his right cheek and one eye was partially closed. Her stomach heaved and she was afraid she would vomit. She willed herself to be strong, to remember why she was there. She hadn't traveled more than two hundred years through time to blow it now.

I'm here, Patrick. She concentrated every ounce of strength and power. *Open your eyes. I'm here and I'm going to make sure you get back to Abby before it's time for me to go.*

He shifted position, muttered something, then opened his eyes.

The look of joy on his face would be with her until the day she died...and beyond. She placed her fingers to her mouth. *Keep quiet, Patrick, or we're in big trouble.* Not that he could say anything around the gag jammed into his mouth.

The first step was to get the key from the guard so she could free Patrick and then—

A rough hand grabbed her from behind and threw her to the ground. *Wrong again, Wylie,* she thought as her bad ankle twisted beneath her. The first step should have been to knock the guard unconscious.

"What have we here, missy?" The foul-smelling guard slipped his hand beneath her skirts. "Someone be sending ol' Harry a present to warm his nights?"

I'll give you something to warm your nights.... She brought her knee up sharply right between his legs, then landed a palm-strike to his jaw.

I owe you one, Shannon, she thought as the guard doubled over. Karate really did work. The sound of Patrick's rage seared her brain as he struggled against the metal chains that held him fast.

"It's okay," she said, scrambling to her feet. "The keys are hanging around his neck. I'll—"

All things considered, she wouldn't have believed the guard could move so fast. He threw himself on his musket and before she could take in what was happening, he had the clumsy weapon aimed straight at Patrick's heart.

"You don't much care what happens to yourself, missy, but seems like you care a whole lot what happens to your friend." He jammed the musket into Patrick's chest.

Patrick's fury echoed inside Dakota's head, pushing aside her own terror.

"He's not my friend," she said, looking directly at the guard. She lifted her chin and prayed she was making the right choice. "He's my lover."

Her plain words had the effect she'd been hoping for. The guard licked his lips. His rheumy eyes traveled the length of her body. "You spread your legs for him, do you, missy?"

She nodded. "For him and any other man who pleases me."

He cupped his crotch with one hand and winced. "'Tain't kind the way you treated ol' Harry."

"I decide who lays between my thighs," she said, arrogant and powerful and totally in control. "You should have waited until you were asked, Harry."

She had his attention. Slowly she unhooked the frog closure of her cloak and let it drop to the floor. The guard's breath hissed as he devoured the sight of her in the shimmery gold dress. The dress cost more than he would earn in a lifetime.

It was obvious she wasn't a tavern wench trading her favors for a half crown, or one of the whores who followed soldiers from camp to camp. She knew exactly what the dress represented to the guard and she knew how to use it.

She moved a few steps closer to where the guard stood, his musket still aimed at Patrick, just close enough for the guard to catch the sweet scent of her perfume. She wasn't Dakota Wylie anymore. She was somebody else, a woman who would do whatever she had to do to save the life of the man she loved.

"Do you want me, Harry?"

He grunted. She'd take that as a yes.

She cupped her breasts. Shannon's gun had settled between the neckline and her midriff. Swallowing hard, she recalled every bad line of B-movie dialogue she'd ever heard.

"Do you want to do this to me?"

She slid the first two buttons from their loops, deepening the décolletage.

Harry groaned and lowered the musket to half mast.

She slid her hand inside the bodice.

"How much do you want me, Harry?"

Harry moved toward her, musket forgotten, and she pulled out the gun from between her breasts and pointed it straight at his head.

Patrick's anguished wail ripped through her, but she couldn't let his fear—or her own—stop her.

Harry stared at the gun, then coughed out a laugh. "Never seen a pistol that small before, but it don't matter much." He aimed his musket at the center of Patrick's chest again. "You want him so bad you'll be havin' to pay a high price for him, missy."

"The hell I will." She pulled the trigger. The bullet whizzed past Harry's right ear and pinged off the wall behind him.

"Now you done it, missy. May as well toss down your toy and play with ol' Harry."

He threw the musket down, confident she'd fired her only available bullet, and started toward her.

She aimed the gun.

Harry laughed. "Empty guns wouldn't be scarin' me, missy. Now why don't you—"

She pulled the trigger again and this time she didn't miss.

Harry fell backward with a thud. She forced herself not to notice the blood or the blank expression in his eyes as she lifted his head and removed the rope with the key attached to it.

You did what you had to do, she told herself as she ran to Patrick's side. *He would have killed the both of you.*

She unlocked the chains and he ripped the gag from his mouth.

"Oh, Patrick." She gently cradled his face in her hands. "What did he do to you?"

He took her hands in his and kissed them. "There is another cellar on the north side. The guards talked of the red balloon and the spies they had captured. With luck we will find McVie and your friend."

"Hurry!" Dakota urged, helping him to his feet. "It's all happening, Patrick. Everything...just the way I saw it...the way Abby knew it would be."

There was so much Patrick wanted to tell her, so many things he longed to say. He prayed there would be time.

They hurried around to the other side of the inn.

"It's locked," Dakota said, trying the door to the cellar.

He tried the key, but it didn't fit.

"We can kick it in," she said.

He looked at her, his magnificent warrior, and nodded. "On the third count ... one ... two ... three!"

The door broke open with a resounding crash. He could not remember a more welcome sound.

"Dakota!" A lovely, dark-haired woman flew across the room toward them. "My God, it's really you!"

The women embraced as if they had been separated for centuries, not days. Patrick looked over their heads and found himself eye-to-eye with Andrew McVie.

"Sweet Jesus!" he roared, clasping the man to his breast. "'Tis a wonder to lay eyes upon you again."

"And you are a welcome sight, Patrick Devane." McVie clapped him on the back, but the joy in his eyes was soon replaced by determination.

"Blakelee and Rutledge?" Devane asked.

"Aye," said McVie. "They took them not ten minutes ago to the hanging tree at the foot of Clover Hill."

"We can be there within the hour," Patrick said. "I will not lose two good men."

"No!" Dakota's voice rang out. "This is Andrew's destiny, Patrick, not yours. He must do this alone."

"'Tis too big an undertaking for one man. I will lend what assistance I can."

The dark-haired woman with the aqua eyes blocked his exit. "Let him go," she said, her tone pleasant but firm. "He *will* succeed." She lowered her voice so Patrick alone could hear. "You must let him do this alone or he will never believe in himself the way that I believe in him."

He could not argue in the face of so great a love.

McVie kissed Shannon Whitney and was gone.

"Was that your horse?" Dakota asked as they stood on the slope behind the house and watched Andrew gallop away.

"It was," said Patrick, "but he is welcome to it."

"I didn't even notice the stable."

"Mayhap you had other things to occupy your mind."

She started to say something but the words danced just beyond reach. She felt light-headed, as if she hadn't eaten

n weeks, and suddenly her knees gave out and she sagged
nto Patrick's arms.

"I do not understand," he said. "I see you before me, yet
. seem to see through you, as well."

"This is how it happened the other time, Patrick." Once
again she told him of her last morning in 1993.

"You tell me you had no choice in the matter?" Patrick
asked. "That your choice had been made for you by fate?"

Dakota's eyes glistened with tears. "Yes." *Say something, Patrick! Tell me you want me to stay. Tell me you
can't live without me, that life would have no meaning if I
left—*

"All that kept you from death was the touch of the bal-
oon?"

She nodded. *You don't understand. I had no reason to
stay there.... I didn't have Abby...I didn't have you.*

He said nothing more. She sensed that he was pulling
away from her, that sometimes not even a miracle was
enough to make a happy ending. *Like you expected anything else, Wylie? You came, you saw, you saved his life.
Now it's time to go back where you belong.*

"Who is he?" Shannon whispered to Dakota as Patrick
strode toward the wagon.

"Patrick Devane," Dakota whispered back.

"The traitor?"

"The patriot."

"I've heard nothing but terrible things about the guy."

"That'll teach you not to believe everything you hear."

"Looks like we have a lot to catch up on."

I know, thought Dakota, *but I'm afraid we're not going
to have time.*

They crossed the snowy field to the edge of the woods
where she'd left the wagon.

A familiar noise sounded in the distance, the deep hiss of
flame beneath a hot-air balloon as it drifted closer to the
clearing.

The ground seemed to lift and tilt beneath Dakota's fee
She breathed deeply and closed her eyes, willing herself
deny the inevitable. Patrick had given as much as it was
him to give, and it just wasn't enough. He'd been hurt to
deeply for her love to make him whole, and if he couldn
give her his heart, then she wanted nothing at all.

"Maybe it's not for you," Shannon said. "Maybe it
meant for someone else."

"It's for me," Dakota whispered. There was nothing f
her here. Not any longer.

She turned away from both Patrick and Shannon, h
tears blinding her to everything but the crimson balloon
it moved slowly, inexorably, toward her. The buzzing soun
filled her head, scraped against her nerve endings, scratche
against her spine. *It's over,* she thought as her heart cracke
in two. *All over.*

"Don't go." His voice pierced her heart.

She'd imagined the words. Conjured them up from
dreams and sorrow.

"Don't go," he repeated, more loudly this time. "Is
possible you do not know what it is I feel for you?"

"How would I know how you feel?" she countered. "Yo
haven't told me."

"Some things do not require words."

"This does," she said quietly. "I need some words righ
about now."

"Words are empty things. I have shown you what I fee
for you."

"Tell me," she said. "I need to hear it, Patrick."

The crimson balloon appeared grayish in the moonligh
a ghostly apparition.

"It is you I need, madam. It is you who makes my worl
complete."

The hiss of the balloon grew louder as it moved closer.

Her dark eyes searched his face and in that moment h
saw the future without her, saw the days of his life stretche

out before him, as cold and lonely as the snowy ground on which they stood. How could he embrace the bleak and endless night when he had finally learned to love the sun?

"This isn't my world, Patrick." Her voice was filled with longing. "You are asking me to turn my back on everything and everybody I've ever known...a way of life that will not come again for two hundred years. Do you need me to warm your bed? Do you need me to be a mother to Abby?" Her tone grew fierce. "Tell me, Devane! Tell me now before it's too—"

"I love you!" Terrible words of power beyond measure. Words with the power to strike a man down or to give him wings. With Susannah he had believed a golden future was his for the taking. Now he knew it for the blessed miracle it was, knew that life without this uncommon woman wasn't a life at all. "Stay with me, Dakota Wylie." He laid his heart bare for her, offered her his soul. "Be my wife and my companion and my lover in this life and the next, for I want no other by my side."

The crimson balloon skimmed the tops of the trees.

"I love you, Dakota," he said again, in a voice rich with yearning. "Only you. For all time."

"Yes!" She threw back her head and shouted her joy to the stars. "I love you, Patrick Devane. I love you! I love Abigail! I don't care if that balloon lands at my feet...nothing will make me leave you, Patrick, not as long as I—"

"Papa! Dakota! I'm flying!"

Abigail?

The balloon dipped low, dropping the basket to eye level.

"Oh, my God!" Dakota screamed. "Abby! No!"

The child was in the basket of the hot-air balloon. She clutched Lucy in one hand and waved madly with the other. "Look at us!"

"Sweet Jesus!" It took Patrick a full second to comprehend the astonishing sight before him. Abby's eyes were wide with excitement as the balloon dipped and swayed before them. The child was filled with wonder, alive to magic and possibilities . . . she was *his*. It had taken him so long to realize the truth, so long to understand all that Dakota had tried to tell him about love. He prayed God it was not too late to make amends.

Dakota raced past him, heading straight for the basket but he stopped her.

"Nay, I will not risk your safety." He closed the distance between himself and his daughter.

"No!" Dakota screamed. "Don't touch that basket Patrick!"

It was too late. He gripped the railing, then was thrown through the air with a mysterious power the likes of which he had never experienced. He hit the ground hard but wasn't hurt. He tried to stand, but some unseen force kept him on his knees.

Dakota heard Shannon screaming behind her, but she didn't take her eyes from Abigail. She felt as if she were running through wet cement. It was so hard to move . . . so hard to breathe. Her mind was tangled in knots. Abigail was the only thing that was important. She had to save her . . . had to . . .

The basket trembled, then tipped toward the ground. Dakota threw herself into the basket and grabbed Abigail by the child's upper arms. The child tried to wriggle away but Dakota held her fast.

"No!" Abby cried. "Where's Lucy? I can't go without Lucy!"

The balloon began to rise again. As it lifted above his head Patrick broke free of the invisible force that had held him captive.

Dakota met his eyes as the balloon began to rise again, and he nodded.

Summoning up the rest of her strength, Dakota lifted Abby over the edge of the basket and dropped her into her

father's waiting arms. Dakota's legs buckled. She grabbed
for the lip of the basket for support, but slipped and fell to
the floor. Lucy lay in the far corner of the basket, just out
of reach. The rough wicker cut into her palms as she tried
to pull herself up again and again, falling back to the bottom of the basket each time, growing weaker...fading...
fading....

*Late afternoon sun spilled over the kitchen table as Ginny
sat there, shuffling her tarot cards. A cup of spearmint tea
rested at her right elbow, a lighted Marlboro at her left. She
wore bright red toreador pants, a Princeton T-shirt and a
pair of dangling silver earrings Dakota had long coveted.*

"So what took you so long, honey? I was wondering
when you'd come to your mother for help."

"You were right," Dakota said. "He loves me, Ma."

"I knew that all the time. So what are you going to do,
honey—let that idiot balloon make the decision for you?
Fight for what you want!"

"What choice do I have? Take a good look at me, Ma.
I'm unconscious."

"No, you're not."

"I dropped like a rock. I'm out cold."

Ginny sighed. "You're faking it, just like you used to do
when there was a Latin test at school."

"You knew about that?"

"Of course I knew, and this is the same thing. You were
always good at ducking the tough questions."

"What's that supposed to mean? I love Patrick. I love
Abby."

Ginny smiled. "And you love me and you're afraid to say
goodbye."

"Oh, Ma—" Dakota choked on a sob. "You knew that,
too?"

"I'm supposed to know, honey. I'm your mother."

"I love you and Dad and everyone. I can't imagine never seeing you again."

Ginny clucked her disapproval. *"Linear thinking, honey. Time is fluid. This isn't goodbye. This is only the beginning."*

"The beginning of what? I don't understand. My destiny's been decided. There's nothing I can do to change it. I'll probably be home in time for dinner."

"Take a stand! You've spent your whole life straddling the fence. Commit to your new family. Your old one will always be here for you any time you want us."

Always...always....

She was instantly, completely awake. Her hands were solid. Her aura was back where it belonged. She was trapped in the basket of a hot-air balloon and the ground was fifteen feet below.

"I don't suppose you have a ladder?" she called out to the three people waiting for her on the ground.

"Jump!" they yelled in unison. *"Now!"*

She looked at her friend Shannon and thought of the new life she was about to start with Andrew McVie. *You're going to be happy, kid. You made the right choice.*

She looked at Abigail. *My child,* she thought as her heart filled with love. She grabbed Lucy and tucked the doll under her arm.

And finally she looked at Patrick Devane, at the man she loved and had almost lost, and knew she'd finally come home. He was proud and hot tempered, stubborn and opinionated—but then again, so was she. They were destiny's children and not even time could tear them apart.

"You sure you can catch me?" she called out. "I'm not exactly a feather."

"Madam, cease your infernal talk and *jump!"* His tone was fierce, but the smile on his glorious face was anything but.

He loved her and she loved him back.
Life just didn't get any better than that.
She climbed to the top of the basket and jumped headlong into their future.

Epilogue

Christmas Day, three weeks later

Patrick Devane and Dakota Wylie paused at the top of the main staircase before joining their guests.

"The whole town is here," Dakota said, amazed by the crowd milling about. "I can't believe it."

"The news has spread, madam. They all wish to meet you."

"Funny how quickly things change. A few weeks ago they wouldn't let us in their houses."

"'Tis different now," he said, drawing her close to his side. "Your magic has worked wonders."

"It wasn't magic," she said, wrapping her arms about his waist. "It's you." News of the spy ring and Patrick's bravery had spread throughout the countryside. His ability to move with secrecy was gone, but he had gained the respect and admiration of the townspeople.

He arched a brow. "I am the same man I was, madam."

"You're a hero to them, Patrick. The stuff of legends." *The stuff of my dreams.*

He kissed her soundly. "'Tis you who made it happen."

She leaned her head against his shoulder and thought about the past three weeks. Cook had been marked as the traitor she was and carted off to jail. Ironically, Joseph and

Will looked happier than ever, and their gratitude and loyalty to Patrick for keeping them in his employ knew no bounds. Dakota suspected that some of that gratitude had to do with the fact that Cook no longer ruled their lives with a wooden spoon.

Poor Molly had been so distraught over her part in her aunt's treachery that she had fled the area the night the balloon had returned for Dakota. Wherever she was, Dakota wished her Godspeed, for the young woman had been a pawn and not a willing participant.

His Excellency General Washington had personally arrested McDowell, and it was rumored McDowell would meet his Maker before a firing squad when the New Year dawned. The list Dakota had found her first night in Patrick's house had been a list Patrick had confiscated from the British. The names had represented men whose loyalty to the thirteen colonies was thought to be suspect. The Redcoats had planned to approach Patrick about winning the men over to the side of the king. Rutledge and Blakelee had been on that list; Benedict Arnold had not.

So much for the best-laid plans.

It warmed her heart to know Andrew McVie had indeed fulfilled his destiny as the history books had reported, especially since she had played a major part in revealing that destiny to him. Zane Rutledge and Josiah Blakelee had been seconds away from death at the end of a British rope when Andrew had managed to save them.

One week later Shannon and Andrew had been married at the First Presbyterian Church of Franklin Ridge. Dakota didn't need psychic abilities to know their future was as golden as their auras.

"Papa! Dakota!" Abigail appeared at the foot of the stairs. "Reverend Wilcox says it's time to start!"

Patrick lifted Dakota's chin with the tip of his index finger.

"You have sacrificed much to be with me, Dakota Wylie," he said, his eyes filled with love. "I will never give you reason to regret your decision."

"I know that," she whispered.

"Second sight?" he asked, kissing her mouth.

"No." She placed his hand over her heart. "Some things a woman just knows."

"Hurry!" Abby cried, rushing up the stairs to the landing. "Aunt Shannon and Aunt Emilie say they'll come up here and drag you, Mama, if you don't hurry."

Mama. Dakota's heart did a little tap dance.

"You're crying," Abby said, eyeing her.

Dakota bent and hugged her daughter. "Only because I'm happy."

"That's silly," Abby said, smoothing Lucy's yarn hair.

"Just you wait until you're grown up," Dakota said, chucking her under the chin. "I bet you'll cry on your wedding day, too."

And so it was time.

Harpsichord music drifted toward them from the front parlor. A line of Continental soldiers formed an honor guard in the hallway. People she didn't recognize swarmed about, eagerly vying for a glimpse of Patrick Devane and his bride-to-be. But there, at the foot of the stairs, were the friends who would share the adventure with her. Emilie and Zane. Shannon and Andrew. Rebekah and Josiah. The friends with whom she would share her life.

"Madam." Patrick sounded anxious, appealingly vulnerable. She had never loved him more than she did at that moment. " 'Tis time we were wed."

" 'Tis time," she said softly.

Abby stopped them. "These are for you." A pair of dangly silver earrings glittered in her small palm.

They were the earrings Ginny had been wearing the night Dakota made the decision to stay.

She slid the earring wires into her lobes and gave her head a shake. "Thanks, Ma," she whispered.

Next to her Patrick started with surprise and placed a hand against his left cheek.

"Patrick?"

"It is not possible," he said, eyes wide with surprise, "but I believe someone kissed my cheek."

Welcome to the family, Patrick.

"Did you hear that?" he asked Dakota.

Dakota and Abby looked at each other and laughed.

"That's Grandmama Ginny," Abby said.

"My mother," Dakota said. "You'll be hearing a lot from her."

Patrick nodded as if the explanation made perfect sense. "Whatever you say, madam." Life with Dakota Wylie would never be dull.

She had an eighteenth-century husband and daughter to love and cherish, and her twentieth century to make her crazy...and to keep her sane. And as if that weren't enough she had friends from both centuries to share the joys and sorrows that life sent her way. Somehow she'd stumbled into the best of both worlds and she wasn't about to let go.

Dakota slipped her left arm through Patrick's, then took Abby's hand in her right.

It was going to be a wonderful life.

She could feel it in her bones.

MIRA BOOKS

Proudly presents
the newest novel from

BARBARA BRETTON

Guilty Pleasures

For a sneak preview
please read on....

Look for *Guilty Pleasures*
in the fall of 1996

Prologue

Lili Spaulding had given up furs, cigarettes and red meat in the name of political correctness, but she'd be damned if she'd give up her Rolls.

"Admit it, darling," she said to the young woman seated next to her in the back seat of the sleek gray car. "Some things in life are meant to be savored."

"You know my take on this, Mrs. Spaulding." Corey Prescott's voice was low, her tone even. "Conspicuous consumption went the way of the eighties. If you have to ride around in something flashy, the least you can do is buy American. Better for the image."

Lili spread her slender arms in a gesture so inherently graceful it set Corey's teeth on edge. "Darling, this is my image. You've been with me how long...eight months? Certainly you know what I'm about by now."

Corey leaned back against the buttery leather seat and counted to ten. Twice. *You need this job,* she reminded herself. Without her position at Lili! International none of her plans had a chance to come true.

She and Lili Spaulding had spent the day at a department store opening in Center City, Philadelphia, where Lili! hosted a formal luncheon for four hundred matrons who had money to burn. As director of publicity, Corey had made sure the spotlight was focused on Lili's perfectly coiffed head while the older woman offered up newsy tidbits like hors d'oeuvres to eager local news crews.

I can help you, Lili had promised the women gathered in the glittering ballroom. *Watch me, and I'll show you the way.*

Revlon and Rubinstein had done it. Lauder had turned it into an art form. But only Lili had figured out how to bottle magic and package dreams. No matter what you thought of the woman, you had to admire the tycoon. She'd turned a dying company into a twenty-first-century corporation, and she'd done it with nothing more than charm and a pair of balls the size of Granny Smiths.

The Rolls purred to a stop in front of a low, rose-colored brick building. The structure was U-shaped; it curved around a stand of dogwood and red maple trees in full bloom. Beyond the building the Somerset Hills rose gently into the early evening sky. Corey peered out the window at the rolling lawns, the profusion of yellow freesia and forsythia framing the wide, double doors. Except for the discreet sign that read Lili!, it could have passed for a country home belonging to the hunt set. She'd seen pictures of the main plant but they hadn't come close to doing it justice.

She turned back to her boss. "What are we doing here?"

Lili flashed one of her lightning-quick smiles in Corey's direction and patted her hand. "It occurred to me you might enjoy a closer look at in-plant operations."

"It's after six," Corey said with a glance at Lili's vintage Cartier tank watch. "Why don't we come back another day when the first shift is on." Hadn't the woman ever heard of the concept nine to five?

"I have a surprise for you," Lili said, her smile widening to impossible dimensions. Her teeth were white and even, like the keyboard of a Steinway. They probably cost just as much. "The test run for Night-Way rolls off the assembly line in twenty minutes, and I'm here to sign the first bottle."

"Twenty minutes." A buzz of apprehension rippled through Corey. Had Lili lost her mind? "The test run wasn't scheduled for another six weeks."

"Change of plans, darling. We're going to launch in September, in time to capitalize on the Christmas trade."

"But that's less than three months from now. We don't have advertising in place, the campaign is only half-formed—we haven't even settled on a face."

"You'll manage," Lili said over her shoulder as she exited the Rolls.

"Manage?" Corey sputtered, climbing out after the woman. Her red silk skirt rode halfway up her thighs and Ed, the limo driver, winked as she tugged it back into place. "You're asking me to execute a full advertising campaign for a virgin product in time for the holidays?"

Lili spun around to meet her eyes. "Are you telling me you can't do it?"

"That's not what I said."

"That's what I heard."

"Then you heard wrong."

A perfectly groomed dark brow arched. Lili Spaulding could convey more with an eyebrow than most men could with a loaded rifle.

"You misunderstood," Corey amended, hating herself for letting the woman get to her the way she did. "I was clarifying my position."

"You don't have a position, darling." Lili slipped on a pair of sunglasses, but not before Corey caught the glint of fire in her dark green eyes. "I take a position. You implement it. If you understand that, then we won't have any more problems."

Lili started toward the front of the building. Her stride was long, her pace as quick as her temper.

"You got off easy," said Ed. "I've seen her leave high heel marks on a man's back."

Corey smoothed the lapels of her short, tight-fittin jacket and touched the strand of pearls at her throat. "Don worry about me, Ed," she said. "I can handle the boss."

"Right," said Ed. "That's what the last publicity direc tor said just before—" He drew his index finger across h throat. "If I were you, I'd keep that résumé up-to-date, M Prescott. That's the best insurance policy you can g around here."

He didn't know the half of it. Corey winked at the drive "I'm going to be around for a long, long time."

"Anything you say, Ms. Prescott," he said, grinning bac at her. "Nothing wrong with positive thinking."

It's more than positive thinking, Corey thought as sh followed Lili into the building. She'd spent her entire lif waiting for this opportunity and nothing was going to get i her way. She'd feed overblown egos, soothe ruffled feath ers, do whatever it was she had to do to carve out her right ful place in the corporate hierarchy. There was no job to menial, no challenge too great.

Corey's breath caught as she took in the splendor of th front lobby. It had been constructed in the grand traditio of public buildings of the thirties and forties, the kind o building designed to show human beings how insignifican they really were. Carrara marble floors, towering pillar reminiscent of Greek architecture, and the pièce de résis tance, a cathedral ceiling complete with a stained-glass sky light designed to display the Lili! logo in shades of rose an periwinkle and cobalt blue.

"Good afternoon, Mrs. Spaulding." A sixty-somethin man with a neatly trimmed white moustache greeted then near the security guard's station. He wore charcoal gray trousers and a plain, white shirt. There was something ap proachable and down-to-earth about the man and Corey found she liked him on sight.

"Ben." Lili leaned toward him for the obligatory continental kiss on either cheek. She patted his ruddy cheek with
a beringed hand. "You've been using Spaulding pour
homme," she said with an admiring nod of her head.
"Your skin looks marvelous."

Ben beamed, his ruddy cheeks growing ruddier. "Ruth
said the same thing last night, Mrs. Spaulding. I should have
started using it years ago."

"Is Ruth still teaching?" Lili asked, eyes wide with interest.

"She retires in June. We're looking forward to doing
some traveling this autumn."

"Call me before you make any plans," Lili said. "I have
a wonderful travel agent. She'd be happy to help you work
out a splendid itinerary."

I've got to hand it to you, Lili, Corey thought. *You've got
schmoozing down to an art form.* Lili didn't give a damn
about Ben or his wife or what they did on their vacation. She
was there to do business.

Poor Ben, however, hadn't a clue. The man positively
glowed under the spotlight of her attention. He launched
into a long, detailed story about his granddaughter's up-
coming fourth-grade dance recital. Lili's smile never wa-
vered. She asked the right questions, admired a photo of the
latest grandbaby and made Ben feel as if chatting about his
family were the sole reason for her visit to the factory.

It was all Corey could do to keep from bursting into ap-
plause. Meryl Streep couldn't have turned in a better per-
formance. She doubted if Lili had ever set foot inside a
grammar school, much less attended a fourth-grade dance
recital, but you'd never know it to listen to her.

Lili turned toward Corey and placed a hand beneath her
elbow. "Ben, this is Corey Prescott." Lili paused long
enough for Corey to realize the man hadn't the foggiest idea
who she was. "My new director of publicity."

"Ben Krementz." He extended his own hand in greeting. "Are you the one who pushed through the Amaryllis promotion?"

"Guilty."

"Great job." His eyes met hers and she saw nothing but sincerity. "We moved a lot of product and got some good press. Can't ask for more than that."

"Great product," she said, warmed by the praise. It was a rare commodity in the beauty business. "You make my job easy."

Lili was observing them with a deceptively bland expression on her flawless face. "How wonderful," she said, linking arms with both Corey and Ben. "My two favorite people have become friends."

Ben and Corey exchanged bemused grins over their employer's head. Both knew that was Lili's way of saying it was time to shut up and get down to business.

Ben explained some of the complexities surrounding the launch of a new skin care product as they walked through the winding corridors that led to the conference room.

"We've been having one hell of a time with the animal rights people," he said as they passed the life-size portrait of Lili's late husband, Grant Spaulding. "It's slowed the testing process down to a crawl."

"That's one of the bullet items we'll need to discuss for phase two," Corey said, making a mental note to follow up from the office tomorrow morning. "We can't afford to be anything but cutting edge on this issue."

"I refuse to be intimidated," Lili stated flatly. "Any decisions we make will be based on effectiveness and cost considerations, not on the terrorist tactics of a group of social misfits."

"An enlightened attitude," Corey returned. "There are alternatives to animal testing, Mrs. Spaulding."

"None of which are acceptable."

"Research shows that public opinion falls on the side of—" Corey stopped cold as Ben opened the door to the mahogany-paneled conference room and a score of expectant faces looked up at them from around an enormous marble-topped table. The best and brightest men and women in the field and their expressions were the same as those of the wealthy Philadelphia matrons at the luncheon that afternoon.

They were looking to Lili for magic and damned if she didn't provide it.

When it was over an hour later, Lili stood in the center of a crush of admirers, fielding more compliments and dinner invitations than Corey had received in a lifetime. Somehow Lili had turned the simple act of signing a bottle of night cream into a celebration and even Corey had to admit the woman had enough personal charisma to start her own religion.

Ben Krementz was leaning against the doorjamb, a bemused expression on his face.

"She's something, isn't she?" Corey asked, joining him in the doorway.

"That she is." He angled a glance in Corey's direction. "You don't like her very much, do you?"

Corey started in surprise. "I admire her," she said carefully. "She's a great businesswoman."

"Right," said Ben with a chuckle. "But you don't like her."

"It shows?"

"A little." He adjusted his glasses. Corey noted the angry red furrows left by the nosepiece. "Nothing time and experience won't take care of."

In her eight months with Lili! no one had suspected Corey was anything but a devoted disciple. "I'll have to work on my poker face." She managed a smile. "I don't suppose you can smoke in here."

The ends of Ben's moustache tilted upward with his answering smile. "That depends on how you feel about the death penalty."

She tilted her head in Lili's direction. "Tell Mrs. Spaulding I'll be waiting by the car."

"Mind if I join you?" Ben asked. "It isn't every day you find a kindred tobacco lover."

They started for the door.

"Ben!" Lili's voice rang out over the din of celebration. "We need your expertise." Her tone made it clear that saying no wasn't an option.

Ben met Corey's eyes and laughed. "Take a drag for me."

"With pleasure," Corey said. She considered asking him to keep her opinions about Lili Spaulding private but somehow she knew that wasn't necessary. Ben Krementz was one of the good guys.

She walked quickly through the quiet corridors, aware of the click of her high heels against the polished marble floor. The upkeep on these floors alone would probably fund a small nation for a year. The security guard looked up as she approached.

"Is it over?" he asked.

"Not yet," Corey replied. "Give them another week or two."

Her words lingered as the door closed behind her. What was the matter with her tonight? She'd spent the better part of her life hiding her feelings and now they were popping out everywhere, like stuffing from a rag doll.

Ed was dozing behind the wheel of the limo, the bill of his chauffeur's cap pulled low over his eyes. Corey hopped up onto the front fender. She reached into her briefcase for a pack of Virginia Slims, then stopped. The air was cool and sweet with the fragrance of lilac and freesia and the sharp tang of pine. Smoking suddenly lost its appeal and she leaned back on her elbows and drew in a deep breath.

So far not even the great and powerful Lili Spaulding had een able to duplicate the magic of a night in spring.

When she was a little girl she used to sit outside and look p at the stars and make a wish. The constellation varied. Ier wish never did. A home. A family. Someone to love. he might as well have asked for the moon.

Corey stifled a yawn as she thought about what she'd said Ben Krementz and the security guard. Maybe it was pring fever that had made her let down her defenses and isk everything she'd struggled to achieve. The years of earching, of planning, of working twice as hard as any-ody else because she'd had to travel twice as far to get here she wanted to be. But it was almost over. She was so lose to her goal, so close to grabbing the brass ring that she ould almost feel it, cold and shiny in the palm of her hand.

Voices floated toward her from the doorway. Lili's hroaty alto. Krementz's husky bass. An assortment of so-ranos and tenors, mingling like the dissonant sound track rom an obscure foreign movie.

"My schedule is so full..." she heard Lili say. "Let ne—"

The rest of Lili's words were lost as an explosion rocked he quiet night. The force of the blast threw Corey to the round. Her knee slammed against a rock and she was ware of hot blood pouring down her leg as she shielded erself from shards of broken glass and chunks of brick alling from the sky.

She looked up to find a wall of flame quickly devouring he south side of the building. The lobby had been reduced o a rubble of rose-colored brick and pink marble. The only ounds were the crackling roar of a fire and faint strains of irdsong drifting incongruously from beyond the hills.

"Holy shit!" The limo driver appeared at her side. 'What the hell happened?"

Corey grabbed Ed's arm and struggled to her feet. "Call or help," she ordered the man. "Police, fire, ambu-

lances—everything you can get. Do it now! There's no tim
to lose!''

Turning, she started to run toward the building.

"You can't go in there!" Ed screamed, tackling her abo
the waist and holding her fast.

She rammed her elbows into his rib cage, then broke fre
Waves of heat rippled toward her, thick with smoke and t
smell of fear. Her throat burned as she got closer and sl
was aware of how little air actually made it into her lung
She blinked rapidly, trying to maintain her focus. Ben Kre
mentz's body lay beneath a pile of brick and stone, restir
next to what was left of the security guard. A young, re
haired woman in a white lab coat had been thrown clear. Sh
lay facedown in the dirt in a splatter of glass and blood an
enormous chunks of marble. Corey saw it all, but she re
fused to let it register. If she let it register, she wouldn't stan
a chance.

"You can't help them!" Ed yelled from behind he
"Don't try to be a hero!"

She wasn't a hero. It wasn't courage propelling her fo
ward: it was thirty-three years of anger and pain and lon
liness. Thirty-three years of wondering why it had to be th
way.

"Lili!" Her voice rose up over the chaos. "Lili, where a
you?"

A faint moan sounded to Corey's right. She wheele
about, straining to see through the haze of smoke and th
gathering darkness. She made out the slender line of
woman's leg poking out from behind the heavy foliage tha
had once landscaped the building.

Moments later she pulled Lili Spaulding's body into
clearing. Blood streamed down her unlined forehead, seep
ing into the fine fabric of her designer suit. Corey crouche
down next to the woman and felt for a pulse at her wrist, he
elbow, the base of her throat.

"Come on...come on...don't die on me...don't—" Elation tore through Corey with the same powerful impact as the blast had only minutes before. "Help me, Ed!" she cried. "I've got a pulse."

Ed stopped ten feet away from where Corey knelt by Lili's side. "Ah, Jesus," he moaned, wringing his hands together. "Look at her, will you? Look at all that blood! She's gonna die!"

"She'll live," Corey whispered fiercely as she cleared Lili's air passages, then bent down to breathe life into the woman's lungs. "She'll live because I haven't finished with her yet."

Hold on, Mother. This is only the beginning....